P9-AQF-942

edge city

edge city

sin soracco

A DUTTON BOOK

DUTTON
Published by the Penguin Group
Penguin Books USA Inc., 375 Hudson Street,
New York, New York 10014, U.S.A.
Penguin Books Ltd, 27 Wrights Lane,
London W8 5TZ, England
Penguin Books Australia Ltd, Ringwood,
Victoria, Australia
Penguin Books Canada Ltd, 10 Alcorn Avenue,
Toronto, Ontario, Canada M4V 3B2
Penguin Books (N.Z.) Ltd, 182–190 Wairau Road,
Auckland 10, New Zealand

Penguin Books Ltd, Registered Offices:
Harmondsworth, Middlesex, England

First published by Dutton, an imprint of New American Library,
a division of Penguin Books USA Inc.
Distributed in Canada by McClelland & Stewart Inc.

First Printing, November, 1992
10 9 8 7 6 5 4 3 2 1

 REGISTERED TRADEMARK—MARCA REGISTRADA

LIBRARY OF CONGRESS CATALOGING IN PUBLICATION DATA:

Soracco, Sin, 1947–
    Edge City / Sin Soracco.
        p.   cm.
    ISBN 0-525-93520-7
    I. Title.
    PS3569.0667E34   1992
    813'.54—dc20   92-52885
                                                    CIP

Printed in the United States of America
Set in Simoncini Garamond
Designed by Leonard Telesca

PUBLISHER'S NOTE
This is a work of fiction. Names, characters, places, and incidents either are the product of the author's imagination or are used fictitiously, and any resemblance to actual persons, living or dead, events, or locales is entirely coincidental.

edge city

Mail call. A shiny strip of cheap paper with four photographs from an arcade machine fell out of the envelope, caught just before it hit the cement floor.

"Ooh girl, look here. Reno wrote me a letter. Sent me her picture too."

"No shit. Let me see those. Ain't she lookin' good, hey now."

"What you mean she lookin' good? Looks the same she ever did."

"Somethin' about the air out there, girl. Air on the streets just make a person look better."

chapter one

I n his luxurious flat above above the Club Istanbul, Mr.
Huntington dropped his gold pen and glared at his gold
watch. He rolled his elegant head trying to work out
the cricks, felt his scattered energies itching through his
clogged veins. He didn't approve of tension; he ought to be
beyond nervous anticipation.

He stepped across the thick carpet to the sideboard, poured
himself a tumbler of single-malt scotch, let it slide down his
throat, tasted it at the back of his tongue, along the sides of
his mouth, his lips pulled forward, slurping noisily to suck at
the drink again. He did as he pleased when he was alone. He
was a practical man, an obsessive angular art deco man.

His electronic pocket organizer plugged into the small
blinking computer, he began to arrange his latest column, cor-
recting as he typed. Conflicting information piled up: art gossip. Byzantine finances, labyrinths a less avaricious man would
never traverse. The autumn cold seeped into his bones, into
his mind. A jungle of things lived there, chilled into a kind of
stasis; most of these he managed to keep contained, properly
sorted.

Things sometimes shook loose, demanded his attention: the

3

silvery ghost of a slender wicked girl, long dead, rose up through the murk. He examined it, aiming for dispassion, but he was still unable to distance himself—he had been young, foolish, struck mad by events beyond his comprehension.

He drank more unblended; as he waited for that amber warmth to hit, he relived those hours: finding Aisha on his couch, her hands folded casually around a string of worry beads, her long eyelashes trembling with each thin breath but never quite lifting even when he touched her, spoke her name. She was turning blue so he rouged her cheeks, her nipples, he painted her lips a darker red—she'd already done her nails.

Memories are corrected printouts. He never allowed reality to interfere with anything. In his edited memory he left the gold scarab necklace around her neck—a sacred gift symbolizing their love/he never recognized his own platitudes/he'd actually taken it off her neck, slipping it in his pocket with hardly a thought: all Aisha's gold belonged to him.

He remembered taking her long gold earrings, wondered, irritated, what he had done with them—had he sold them or put them in the safety deposit box? An aggravating lapse.

He remembered, distantly, how he arranged her naked, still pliable corpse on his bathroom floor, told the doctor she must have been going to take a shower after rehearsal, then a sudden heart attack.

Gave meaning where there was none.

Nice girls, good wives didn't overdose on heroin back then anyway. Certainly not on his couch.

He shook his head. Coffins. Satin-cushion composting boxes. Coffins, he thought, were the worst. At his request her body was immediately cremated. No public autopsy report, no worms.

Refusing to justify his choices, he pushed keys to send away the dead silvery face leering at him from the computer. These exorcisms took time. Furious, he put his spoiled column aside, intending to get back to it later, modem it to the magazine in the small hours.

In his minuscule odorless kitchen—no smell of actual food or cooking in there, all his entertainments were catered—he washed the tumbler, put it upside down in the center of a paper towel, glanced at his reflection in the window, rinsed his mouth, splashed his face, patted it dry with a linen towel. Turning away from the window he flicked invisible specks off his cuff. A tidy gesture.

Frustrated, he sucked what pleasure he could from the way his every lovely possession was arranged in a precise relationship to everything else. Small comfort. It was time for him to put in an appearance downstairs at the club.

chapter two

The pudding-faced woman gave Reno the old fish eye. "Papers?"

Reno chewed on one denim-blue painted fingernail; shifting her weight, she scowled, her wide mouth set in a defiant pout. What the hell, nothing else she could do. Reno handed over her papers, didn't say anything, didn't trust herself to use the right words, just sat on the hard chair facing the metal desk. Waited.

Reno felt like an immigrant, a petitioner from a darker world.

Still caught by the slow limping dream of prison, alone with nothing but spiders as company for too long, Reno listened to the dried souls rattle in her mind, her ritual gourd—like a miser she counted memories for protection—not nearly enough to fill her need: bend them weave them wake them shake them; over and behind the rattle she heard the judicial voices murmuring, always the same: "She shows no remorse." "Lock her up." "Of course. Of course."

Reno knew that parole was just a shuffle-around to fool the citizens into thinking justice was served; a vicious plan designed to catch her up in hope, then throw her back in jail. "Lock her up, of course. Of course."

6

The officer scanned the sheet, her narrow eyebrows lifting in practiced disdain. She had no interest in Reno; her job was to spy on serious criminals, rapists, axe murderers, the important basher-slasher contingent that makes the news. There was no time in her busy schedule to follow a rowdy little burglar. She levered herself up from her padded chair. "Okay, give me a urine sample." She spoke as if her teeth hurt.

Reno was out of prison all of seven hours, most of that spent on a kidney-wrenching bus, yet the crazy bitch wanted to see if Reno had scored. Such confidence. "Hey. I'm a burglar not a dope fiend."

"Says here your closest associates have all been drug addicts." Tapping the folder. Smug.

"What you expect? I been in jail." Reno took the plastic cup, rolled her eyes.

The officer followed her to the bathroom.

"But, hey, now I'm out, I'll only consort with the righteous. I promise." Subtlety was lost on the parole agent. Reno finished, stood up. Pushed the cup at the officer. "You know, bankers. Priests? Members of Congress?"

Ignoring her, the officer fussed with the plastic lid, held the cup up to the light, frowned at the small amount of liquid. Reno wondered if the podgy woman liked her work as much as she seemed to. Maybe she was just compulsive. Back in the office the officer sat behind her desk, spread her hands out over Reno's open file like she was dowsing for evil. "You got a job yet?" She kept moving the cup.

"Sure. Oh yeah. While I was on the bus—" Reno stopped. What the hell. She pushed ahead. "Right. The guy across the aisle offered me a job as auctioneer at Butterfields." She didn't hide her disgust.

"Don't get smart with me."

"That's what he said." Bland, one shoulder lifted in a small shrug.

"You have a week to get a job." Mouth pulled tight across her painful teeth, the officer put the cup of piss in her drawer.

Snapped Reno's file closed. "Remember to notify this office if you move out of the hotel the Mercy Sisters found for you." Flapped a wet hand. "Don't let me find your name on the hot sheet." Thin smile. "Come back in twenty days for another UA. I expect a job report from your employer then."

A job report. Time to belly up to some responsibilities, arrange interviews for a real job, fade into law-abiding middle-class citizenship. Didn't hold much appeal. Not her fault the world was set up so her talents never seemed to get the kind of appreciation they deserved: Reno could take a complicated lock apart, put it back together so the original key couldn't work it anymore, wipe it clean, be gone in under a minute—seemed to her this gave her as much worth as any soldier field-stripping his gun on the battlefield. Correct action under pressure. Value.

The secret workings of alarms, computer-regulated security shields, trip wires, weight sound heat and motion sensitive devices were merely appetizers to the main entrée. Entry. This woman could get in and out of almost anyplace—of course anyone could do that, given the heart, the time, and privacy. Her trick was to do it fast.

She had an uncanny knack of spotting the one or two portable items worth stealing in nearly any room. An eye for real value. This alone ought to qualify her to work at an auction house. A dealer in fine antiquities. Of course if they took her prints to bond her she'd be up shit creek. Even her fake ID couldn't help her if people insisted on finger scrutiny. Their loss. Here she was, a skilled professional, thorough, competent. Honest up to a point. And unemployable.

Didn't want to make a wrong move, didn't know any right ones. Every day on the streets would be potentially fatal.

The first couple days out of jail it's hard to know what's normal, what's not: the sun comes up, it crosses the sky, falls off the edge of the earth; people pop in and out of their cells, filling up the street with noise—lots of activity on the bricks, swarms of people, a whirl of color. So many people. Dogs.

Buses. Cars. Busy busy busy. What the hell they up to all day, all night? All day. All night.

Reno paced her room, back and forth, peeking out the window, back and forth, went to the corner store for pints of tequila, Camel filters, French bread, back and forth. Watching the street. She didn't fall asleep until morning.

Fog slipped in from the east, a gray bandage, cold winds whipped the street trees, blood red gangrene yellow leaves flashed briefly on the branches, faces hovered in that darkness at the edge of vision, distorted. It was late afternoon when Reno woke to the howling beneath the fog.

Didn't know where she was.

Never had a nightmare about being locked up the whole time she was in prison. Never. If her first sleep on the streets was any indication it seemed her dreams would face constant intrusion: gray hands moved over her body with a fleshless contortionist click, bones rattling on damp cement—infinite, chest-tightening, airless—a dreamtime vacuum designed to suck out her heart.

Iron bed, change of sheets once a week, three-drawer dresser with half a mirror on a nail, brown wall-to-wall, one green painted door with a simple lock, one filthy window with a rattling yellow pull blind, sink on the opposite wall, couple clothes pegs, two sacks of stuff. Inside/outside: home.

Washing off the sleep sweat over the little sink Reno tried to arrange her thoughts. Ants in a hurricane. She ran a comb through her tangled hair, squeezed her ass into a pair of tight old Levis, pulled on her cellmate's black turtleneck, a precious thing, a talisman from another world, then a green sweater with only a small hole in the sleeve. Tilted her head at the mirror. Lipstick. Her wide mouth open in a seductive smile for an invisible lover, she gave a wink for the hidden camera. Ho. She tucked a pair of thin kidskin gloves into her hip pocket—might come in handy, never can tell. Ready. She stepped out the door. Bold. Ready.

The hall smelled of cheap tobacco stale underwear ammonia

piss old onions early evening nothing ever changes so much for high hopes. She slipped down the stairs close to the inner rail, listening for anyone moving above or below her. Careful.

At the foot of the stairs a dusty rubber tree strangled a glass cubicle containing the Royal Hotel's captive Hindu, a small brown man who never hurried, nothing to hurry for, nowhere to go, the world, all the creatures in it, infinite reflections of the Great I Am. He put his sloppy cigar down on the counter, repeated his sacred mantra. "No visitors, no food in the room, no drinking, no drugs allowed, women's showers on the second floor only." He spit greenish phlegm into a handkerchief.

"Sure thing, Kazam."

A popular rap tune pounded boom-chukka from a radio.

The man chanted some more at her. "Doors close at nine-thirty tonight, you got to be back by nine-thirty every night. No visitors, no food—" cigar fumes, sweat and grease, the incense of night clerk "—in the room. Remember no drugs or visitors allowed." He kept trying to zip his pants.

"Your mother fucked a camel." Reno thought the Mercy Sisters had to be an FBI front group, hiring a creep like that.

He didn't listen to her. He didn't listen to anyone. He didn't have to, he was Streetside Control, Key Keeper, gun in his pants, hand in his pocket, fondle fondle fondle. Another small time bully diddling cold rolled steel. He'd trained in Oakland to be an FBI agent; calling himself Rupert X he posed as a bigshot in a secret revolutionary force—but that was before he sold himself to the local Catholic charity, became Kazam from Calcutta.

Reno couldn't explain how she knew these things. She wasn't responsible for his identity crisis; she had trouble enough with just that thing on her own hook.

Behind the glass there were secret phone lines back to the prison, to the bounty hunters, to her fat preoccupied parole officer, to the local charity, to the Chinese mob; Kazam notified them all every time she went out. Every time she turned in her sleep.

She didn't know why this was so, but she could feel the surveillance, she could smell the hot desire to send her back to prison. Tried to convince herself she didn't give a shit. Reno was nearly out the front door when she heard the phony Hindu braying for his key. His key.

He tried to drill her with another mantra. "Must leave key with me. No coming back late tonight. No visitors. Showers on the third floor." He shook his cigar at her. "Remember. Doors close at nine-thirty."

Showers were on the second. The man never left the cubicle, what did he know. She held the key just beyond his reach, staring at the spot between his eyes, ferocious; Hindus were supposed to be sensitive about their third eye or something, but Kazam was unconcerned. There was no question in Reno's mind: he was FBI agent Rupert X from Oakland, assigned special duty to watch her. She let the key drop to the floor. "Narc. FBI agent. Hong Kong spy."

He slithered out of his glass cage all eager angular motion.

She turned her back on him, imaginary bullets spinning past her ears. "You're a moron with a face like a dildo, you know that?" She didn't care what time he locked the damn doors, she'd already copied the keys.

It was a sodden autumn evening, the final slide into winter. Below a sky as gray as old newspapers a frigid wind sliced through Reno's sweater; the tired neon signs flickered in frozen puddles of rain and piss; cigarette butts and half-empty bottles of beer testified to the passage of people huddled in on themselves, hurrying toward warmth, home, safety.

Reno sucked in the bracing smell of gas fumes, checked for enemy agents lurking in back alleys; she knew they were out there comparing mugshots, identification lists, waiting for the perfect astrological conjunction to pick her up. Ship her back on a technicality: out after dark looking for a good time. Fuckum.

Stepping on down the road to a personal speculative six-eight boogie beat, Reno examined the limits of her world. The evening sidewalk filled with brisk paunchy men in open sport coats, narrow-lapelled wool suits; they hunched their padded shoulders, exposed wallets bulging out of their pockets. Reebok-footed women scurried past, carrying half-locked leather briefcases, open canvas shoulder bags, replacement shoes, credit cards.

Reno groaned, her fingertips itched. She didn't understand how these people managed to have anything left when they got wherever they were going. Half the posers on the street were working undercover anyway. Had to be.

Gloomy, kicking the slippery street crap out of her way, Reno turned a corner and confronted a place she used to know, a long-time-ago-a-long-way-away-place: Club Istanbul. She didn't think the garish new paint job improved it. Behind the twisting green and red vines peppered with dumb-looking stars it was probably the same old dump.

A shaggy young man lounged in front of the Istanbul, a cigarette cupped into the palm of his dot-tattooed hand, his head filled with secrets, duties, brothers, empty infinite possibilities. He turned his collar up against the cold wind rippling the red velvet curtains at his back. With brash good cheer, his head tipped back, he bellowed at the sky: "Hey everybody! It's SHOW TIME!"

The smell of Chinese stir-fry drifted from the apartment building next door; fragments of plaintive music spilled out from the club, filling the street with promises as strangers pushed by, untempted.

Reno waited for the traffic, huge hungry vehicles, to thin out, then rushed across the street. She peered up at Eddie over her shades. Half smile, Camel filter slanted down in her mouth, every prison dream riding on her glance, she looked beyond him into the Club Istanbul's interior: hot red velvet star bangled spinning mirrored bojangled. Good. She stepped closer, inspected a tacky sign advertising DANCING GIRLS EVERY NIGHT! STARRING SU'AD THE FORTUNATE!

Girlsgirlsgirls! Girls! Just the ticket.

The doorman aimed his voice at her, a razor cuttin the cold air: "Listen up everybody! It's show t scuffed his worn boot on the pavement, looked side ing. "Wake myself up sometimes hollerin' that ˢⁿⁱ·· dead sleep."

Reno shook her rain-damp hair. Nodded at him. Show Time. She danced toward him, away, dithering. She needed to be careful but she wished she were more/something/decisive? She had nothing on which to base a decision. Parts missing.

He grinned at her. "Hard ta go back ta sleep after that, yunno." Hands palm up, waist high, held out toward her; he closed one pale eye. "But what canya do?"

She didn't know. "Wear ear plugs maybe." Shrugging, she pushed past him through the velvet curtains into the red showroom of the Club Istanbul. An oasis.

The smell inside the club was spicy, pungent, female; the music dripped down Reno's spine as if she were diving into a pool of warm scented water.

The dancer, a delicious fantasy, shimmered, untouchable, tantalizing, out of reach on the small stage; she flashed a warm impersonal smile into the dim footlights, lifted an elegant lazy hand. Rings sparkled. Something subtly disturbing about a curl of sweat-damp hair at the nape of her neck, a secret shadow, as if she were unaware of the seductive effect of her naked limbs. She floated across the stage, making certain to catch every eye. All curving grace and balance, she performed the classic moves, a slow ripple began with her fingertips slithering up her torso then back down to her hips, she wavered as if made of smoke—boneless, alluring, soothing, liquid. A genteel tremble, another fragile smile, a sweet perversity in the placement of her hand, palm back, on her hip, she dropped to the floor, writhing. A long hand beckoned again: forbidden snake pleasures.

Reno concentrated on the fantastic atmosphere of the place,

precisely calculated, perfect. Her lips curled up in a contented smile. The fresh comfort of illusion. Safety.

But when Reno turned her full attention to the dancer, a faint stirring of recognition made her uneasy; never can be too careful when memories pick up again, things aren't always how they seem. After a few more moments, Reno swallowed hard. She knew the woman on the small stage; long ago, Reno had adored her. One of those clever, cosmopolitan women, all long bones and curves, Susanna used to smile the money out of the same tight pockets Reno tried to pick.

She was into athletics then. Basketball. No shit. Susanna was the local star, determined to win, always to win. Reno, a few years younger, a million years less experienced, checked out the competition, bet the games, made a little money. Started doing good, running hard, ready to set both of them up, steady for life.

But Susanna always kept her eye on the main chance. One day that chance blew into town, took her with him on his way south, too far then for Reno to follow. Turned out she didn't need to. Susanna returned, silent, within the month.

Next time Reno saw that particular main chance man she tried to put his eye out with a broken bottle, leaving town just before they grabbed her on a mayhem-attempted murder beef. Caught up with Susanna some months later. They never discussed it.

It embarrassed Reno to think about it; she shoved that memory back into its ashy corner, another fragile paper soul for the ritual gourd. She was not a violent woman. In spite of the evidence. Any evidence. It's all bunk. Right. Reno turned her attention back to Susanna, trying to piece together the course they each followed to the Istanbul.

When Susanna, a professional chameleon, decided to capitalize on ethnic, she chose Lebanese; at that time Beirut was recognized as the New York of the Middle East. Susanna's own father was a proud Sioux Indian from the Dakotas; brought his family to the coast of California for a taste of the easy life, died when Susanna was tiny. Her mother followed him in a matter of months, leaving her child to be raised white.

By the time Reno met her, Susanna had perfected a new self, a brittle upper-class sophisticated one; she admitted no pleasure or pride in her Indian heritage: "They's no romance in poverty." She claimed nothing of her father's world except her strong bones, her bright skin. Her alcoholism. "Alls I remember about it is pain." She wouldn't talk about it. "What do I know about Indians? No more'n you do. Less maybe."

The last time Reno saw her, Susanna had switched her ethnic identity from Lebanon to Brazil, still following the main chance: even with the rain-forest disaster Brazil held onto that glamour that Lebanon lost. Apparently she hadn't liked samba as much as dancing Raks al Sharki—perhaps she missed the rhythms of the darbukka—because here she was, Club Istanbul's very own Su'ad the Fortunate. An ass-shakin' money-makin' dream come true. As advertised.

Reno's good fortune. Maybe. Never know what the night might bring, every time different intonation, same meaning. Reno slid up onto a stool at the back corner of the long mahogany bar, thought about identity, about camouflage. Pulled at the collar of her cellmate's turtleneck. Brightened. Tapped the drum riff on her knee. Some of us just born to boogie.

Su'ad bent backward, hands flat on the floor, lovely arch, she shifted her hips, fluttered her stomach in a tricky maneuver worthy of praise, but the men at the edge of the stage seemed most interested in the clear crotch shot. Subtle.

Majestic as a young sheik, the doorman ambled across the smoky showroom, a bored look on his face. He barely glanced at the glittering woman on stage, slid behind the bar, lifted a sad professional eyebrow. Working double duty as doorman, as bartender. "What'll it be, sugar?" His voice slow, all Southern caresses as if he still breathed magnolias.

Wondering what other jobs the fellow might perform, Reno

put one of her two fives on the bar. "Johnnie Walker Black. Water back. Please." Hoped he'd give her back lots of change. Shuu-ga'. Been a long time.

Su'ad, mesmerizing her audience, moved with a languid stroll to the front of the stage, her hips locked onto the drum beat dum-dum tekka tek dum tekka tek tekka. Swaying, nearly naked in the bright spotlight, a lazy flourish of her hand down her body reminded them they were fortunate to be in her presence. At that moment. In that place.

Glowing, she lifted her arms, twining them above her proud head, her smooth belly curved outward, rippling, rolling, sucking in and down, down, repeating the undulation, again, absolute control, merciless desire. The jewels at her pelvis began to shiver.

She seemed to dance for herself, a private performance as if the audience were peeking through a crack in the curtains. She slithered across the stage with a tremble designed to shake the money out of the most well-protected wallet, she melted into the music, she appeared suspended from the mirrored ball above her, her head rolled back, her neck exposed as if ready for the executioner's blade.

Su'ad might not have many illusions left, but she knew every corner of that dream, writhing ecstatic beauty tied to the pulse of primitive drums. Never hurts to be looking good. Rear view. Perhaps she wasn't so young anymore, but she had great long legs, her body firm, sensual, warm-toned, dusky. She liked the word, the beginning of the night. She lifted her dark curly hair, no gray at all, stretching her arms above her head, smiling at no one, content.

Su'ad bent her knees, dipping, turning, demure, eyes closed; the gentle pose mocked the dream as the music rose in waves of salary-specific frenzy; Su'ad came into the audience for tips, shivered delicately away from sweaty hands trying to run a finger across her nipple while putting a dollar in her bra.

Pausing at the far end of the bar for a moment she bent forward to settle the sequined straps higher on her shoulders, took a gulp of the soda water Eddie set up for her. The shiny fabric draping her hips gave her skin a rich tone; she shook her ass to the rhythm, looked at the youngsters lining the edge of the stage, hopeful: they'd get lucky or they wouldn't. It was up to her.

Reno paused in the middle of a swallow, holding the scotch in her throat so it burned, wondering if Susanna would recognize her, what they could say to each other. Behind her shades one bloodshot eye half closed against the smoke, the other eye opened, fearless, amazed, ready ready ready, setting herself for the inevitable encounter with her old dreams.

The previous afternoon Reno passed a man jumping and jerking from the cold, hand out for spare change. Every time anyone gave him a few coins he bowed and crossed himself. Bowed. Crossed. A bizarre ritual, intense and pointless. Economically irrelevant. He continued bobbing as if he could force the gods of street luck to bestow another few coins on him.

His actions weren't those of a beggar at all but rather of some wild terrible necromancer—Reno hadn't seen anything like that in years. Never maybe. Not even on TV. She swallowed some scotch, smacked the glass down on the bar. Snap. A wild necromancer.

Susanna/Su'ad didn't even glance her way.

Reno needed to put something together before she ended up jerking on the street with dung-covered camel's feet, elbowing for a corner out of the wind. Connections were everything, all potential flowed from that central premise. But she had none, been gone too long. Even her fake driver's license was useless without supporting plastic. Credit cards were the ticket. No one gave a shit if she seemed street legal, she needed a line of credit. That was identity. Prosperity. Survival.

She searched the faces in the bar, fighting paranoia. What could she say to Susanna: Thug anger, I got thug anger.

Reno heard the dusty voices: Say you're sorry Reno. Repeat

it out loud a thousand times. Admit you're wrong Reno. Say it. Say it.

Thug anger. Reno lifted the glass again, knocked back the little that was left, promising herself she'd only stay at the Royal Hotel/rooms by the day by the week by the month pay up front/a few more days. Sure.

Hey. Hey everybody. All of you. It's show time.

Looook out—the artichoke woman's back in town. She lurk on the corner, she just hang around. She come out her burrow in the dead of the night, raving and slashing, eager to fight— robbery perjury larceny dope, she be the dancer who just missed the rope.

Her scotch gone, Reno sat at the bar of the Istanbul telling herself something come together soon, she disappear into better quarters. Life would start in earnest and all the rest of that. Good times. Never end.

chapter three

The change off the scotch wasn't all Reno hoped—only enough for one more. She turned her glass, smudging the rings on the bar top. Never can tell. Might get lucky.

Or not. Reno knew the end of every life: bones in a hole.

Reno knew many things that turn out not to be true, but she never let that stop her from knowing. The night before she got out of prison she threw up again and again—knew she was gonna puke herself to death before morning.

When the sun finally came up, she was still among the living. Slick as owl shit the high prison gates creaked open for her. She never looked back. Caught a bus up the coast; her hands were sweating, she had trouble swallowing because her mouth was so dry. Surprised, uncomfortable, needing to take a piss the whole ride long, trapped inside a grunting bus with a bunch of strangers, she eyeballed the other passengers for signs of aggression, mayhem, cannibalism—whatever people do on buses. They behaved themselves so she behaved herself.

Reno knew she'd forgotten a lot, worked hard trying to remember, but things slipped away.

In prison whole concepts simply disappeared. Ideas didn't

19

stick, common words didn't work, no pulse in them—blood rushing through the sentences on sound alone, rhythm, breath, lifting pounding everything held in: a verbal gesture. Failure was acknowledged in the quietly shifting tides of women's voices. There's more to prison, more to language, more to failure than that.

A wild hunger, beyond need, beyond curiosity, possessed her. She would eat the city, eat the world, swallow it whole with her eyes, her skin, her mouth, suck it dry not even chewing, simply open up, ingest it.

Now. She thought, I want everything. I want it all.

I want those years back.

Reno sipped her scotch. She had no plans, no place no future no failures. No nothing. Hiding in baroque visions, opium ease for her deepest fears, she wasn't interested in a simple rebirth back into street reality: stark staring never going to change same old same old "Girls Girls Girls Talk to a Completely Naked Girl for One Dollar." Reno lifted her glass, drank it empty. Got to be something else out there for her.

"Well, little girl, been a while. Lovely to see you again." Su'ad the Fortunate held back a smile, soft and cool.

Reno was surprised, so deep into her own head she didn't hear the other woman approach. Typical. Still, she hardly missed a beat. "The pleasure is mine, there's more of you to see." Eyes up and down.

While Su'ad simpered Reno fished in her shoulder bag, came up with a six-dollar Lotto ticket. "I always was good with numbers, Suuuu-ad." Sarcasm below the surface. "Whattaya think, Miss Fortunate? Perhaps this your lucky night?" Reno held the folded ticket out. "Didn't know as you'd recognize me."

Su'ad smoothed the ticket, the hopes of the week, tucked it in her belt. "No one could forget that thirsty mouth of yours." Su'ad dimpled. "Think this ticket will go six for six?"

"Guy on the corner practically guaranteed it." Reno wondered how much if anything Susanna remembered about her arrest, her years in prison—wondering if she'd care. Wondering, finally, what good all this wondering could possibly do.

The bartender-doorman passed another Johnnie Walker over. Pushed away Reno's last fiver. "Hey, you a friend of Su'ad's, you don't pay." Reno didn't argue. He crossed his arms on the bar. "Whole Lotto thing's rigged, man. They be better things to do with your money." He flipped his hair back out of his eyes, solemn. "You ever know anyone who won? No. Those people on TV are movie extras. Get fifty bucks to do the spot, pretend they won big. It's a shuck. Believe me."

Su'ad leaned toward him, purring. "Take good care of my friend, Eddie. Sometimes she gets lucky." An afterthought. " 'Course, other times she's a damn fool. Listen. I'll give you fifty bucks to do the spot for me when I win, Eddie."

Eddie nodded. "Sure. Okay." Flicked a smile on, off. Cool. He tensed his skinny body, muscled a beer keg onto its rack. "You ain't gonna win." Thinking: there's another fifty dollars he'd never see. A lot of that going around.

The Club Istanbul's newest manager, Sinclair, crowded up behind Su'ad. He wore a white linen shirt, tight black trousers with no back pockets, a silky black beard edged his jaw, his ivory skin stretched to a ruddy shine on his cheekbones below brooding, wicked black eyes. His head was shaved clean. Good bones. When he spoke his voice was deep, temporarily pitched in the key of sorrow.

Reno, observing with greater interest than she would admit, discovered his voice caught her somewhere around her navel.

"Mmm. Hate to tellya, Su'ad, but you ain't dancing this weekend." He rocked on his toes.

Su'ad compressed her full lips.

He sighed. The weight of the world. Like the secretary general at the UN. "Sorry, baby."

"Sorry, baby?" Su'ad's hips no longer bounced to the rhythm. She saw money, suddenly winged, slipping beyond her grasp. "Those my nights."

"Aw, listen. Our weekend meal ticket put it in his contract that he picks the opening performers."

"Asshole's afraid of being blown off the stage."

"Blown off the stage? Fabulous Farouk? You're feverish."

"I can't believe you would do this to me." As if the man didn't know better. "Ruin my weekend. Fuck up my night. Every time a male dancer hits the city the place goes nuts. As if any of these fancy-ass guys could dance better than a woman." She fumbled along the bar for her soda. "This business is lousy with guys who want to be Tommy Tune—but they can't dance for shit." Muttering. "Dickheads. Why they always want to take my place?"

"Hey, baby, it's a tough world. Men hafta make a living too." He shook his large head, shrugged his large shoulders. "Eva's not dancing either."

Su'ad's steamy glare poached him. "That doesn't concern me one way or the other."

"Oh hell." He changed his voice to maple syrup. "You gonna cocktail for us this weekend or what?"

"Or what. Listen, if the place fills up with a bunch of stiffs like the time you booked that blues band in here, you in real trouble, Sinclair."

He looked pained.

Relentless. "I don't make any money, you owe me big."

"Okay, Su'ad, I'll owe you big."

The drummer, rubbing the head of his drum with one hand, motioned for Su'ad to come back on stage; when she didn't respond he tapped the microphone, lit a Camel, blew the smoke into the colored lights, looked superior. The santur player glared out at the audience from huge sad eyes, his picks vibrating the strings like hungry mice in a piano. The loud player was drooping over his bulbous instrument. He seemed comatose, his melody a distant whisper of fingers on the strings. None of the men smiled. Another long night just beginning; they didn't have to work too hard for Su'ad; she was a pro, could carry the show by herself. At least she could if she'd ever get back on the stage. Wasn't until Eva's set they'd have to put out—arrogant blond bitch never shared her tips with them. The damn flute player still hadn't shown up; sometimes he didn't get to the club until late in the night. A quiet sexy wife, many loud children. The musicians sighed. Life in the fast lane. America. The drummer tapped his drum, not impatient, just bored.

Su'ad waved the drummer in-a-minute, spoke without turning around. "Sinclair, you owe me big now."

Sinclair's eyes went misty, sorrowful, the heavy lids closed halfway.

Su'ad flexed her back at him, a dancer's move; she spoke over her shoulder putting the sound of summer in her voice. "Oh hell, don't worry about this weekend, dear." She cooed. "I'll just go out there among the great hairy unwashed, be one terrific waitress for you." Graceful curling hand arched through the air dispensing alcohol to beatific drunks.

Sinclair started to relax, a little smug. Things were easy for a man who knew how.

Su'ad stretched forward to put her mouth right to his ear, hissing, "Coat the damn stage with KY jelly and broken glass."

Sinclair contemplated this in silence. He could've been working any number of other jobs, he reminded himself, he was a very versatile fellow. Yet here he was at the Istanbul, involved in tawdry flesh peddling. Fish piddling. Commerce of the dreariest. He sighed. He seldom managed to draw a good crowd into the bar—when he did, the dancers got snotty. Grateful? Not these ego-driven hags. Ugleee. He never did see such uglee old broads. Hah.

He wished he didn't like to gamble; losing always limited his options.

The gloomy santur player started picking out a tune, his head working left and right; the drummer diddled diligently, giving Su'ad the eye; a few old customers looked half asleep, amber worry beads drooping soundlessly through listless fingers, cigarette smoke curling in a thick arabesque above their heads. An odd sort of contentment. Timeless.

A dark smoky voice melted over the silence: "Give a warm welcome to our flute player, finally here after serving his time in the trenches."

The flute player, a small weary man, climbed on stage. He nodded to his fellow musicians, bowed, a brief bend, to his customers, settled himself at the side of the stage with his flute clutched to his chest. He waited.

"Su'ad the Fortunate will join our eminent musicians, all of whom are just panting to feed your favorite fantasy in just one moment." Slowmotion paused. No one was listening to her. They never did. A good thing.

The flute player tried a tentative trill, calling.

Su'ad ignored him, turned to face Sinclair, too casual. "So. Who's opening for The Fabulous, anyway?" Rubbing the back of his neck with her left hand.

"Ah." Sinclair touched his shiny head, pulled at the ruby stud in his left ear, ran a finger along the trim lines of his beard; settling at last on the coins in his pocket he stared at them as if the answer lay in these decorative effects. "Ah. Who indeed. Perhaps I don't know?" He risked a glance at her, was not reassured.

"Give it up, Sinclair."

After some thought he replied, "The Surfing Sufis." He tried to move away.

She grabbed his neck, starting a small but vicious tug-of-war over ultimate possession of his head. "Say what?"

Silence. He pulled away by millimeters.

She increased the pressure. "You want to repeat that, you bald-headed freak?"

"No."

"Surfing Sufis." She rolled the words around her mouth like little turds. "Surfing Sufis. That what you said." Her grip didn't relax. "Who the hell are they?"

He spoke fast, his voice thin. "Some Los Angeles punkers

went to North Africa, got stoned, tranced out with a bunch of musicians in the Rif mountains, put on those long blue djellabas. That's all she wrote."

Su'ad let go. "God."

"Yep. God. Allah in the original tongue." Touching his throat with a tentative hand Sinclair took a small step away from her.

Su'ad followed. "I've got an original tongue for you."

Warding gestures. "The female version of god was once called Al Uzza or Allat. Allah's name was taken from hers." He paused. "Does that make you feel any better?" Su'ad didn't answer. He slid farther away. "She was worshipped as a block of stone." Like all the women he knew. So there.

Slowmotion's golden voice, thick with just enough scotch and Virginia tobacco, interrupted their gentle exchange. "Returning to us now from the magical lands of the Mystical East! The fabulous Su'ad!" Sarcastic. She glared down the bar at the two of them. "All the way from the tents of the Great Khan. Let's have a round of applause for our lovely dancer."

Su'ad stepped with a lot of force on Sinclair's foot. "Get out of my way."

Slowmotion's voice got brighter: "All right! Put your han's together for Su'ad the Fortunate!"

The rapid chirring of Su'ad's finger cymbals drowned Sinclair's swallowed yelp as she twirled onto the stage.

On a signal from Sinclair, the drummer moved his stool out of the way, tossed his cigarette aside. Standing up close to Su'ad he held his black dumbek under his arm, rattled his fingers on the head for a moment then built an authoritative rhythm with light rapid strokes. Su'ad answered his every volley with her hips, her arms, a toss of her long thick hair; she slanted heavy looks over at him, responding almost carelessly to his rhythmic prodding. Precise movements, trills raging from her finger cymbals, she turned her back on him, snapped her hips, challenging. "Match this, sucker." Fastest ass in the West.

He knelt on the stage, watching the glass-beaded fringe of her hip belt as if hypnotized, his knife-sharp face only inches away from her belly. He seemed both the snake and the charmer, the drumbeat, his heartbeat.

He involved Su'ad in a private discussion, call and response, on topics Reno could only dream about. They didn't take their eyes off each other, each one glaring in triumph.

A single amber spot came up, pulsing. Red. The drummer pushed Slowmotion's light rhythm on his drum, playing with it. Su'ad began to shake, slowly as if the motion were something she could not control, as if invisible fingers stroked her; she seemed enmeshed in an irresistible net. Faster. Rainbows shot from her hips, her hands; she turned her back to the audience as if she couldn't be bothered with people that didn't understand. Didn't respond. It looked to Reno like the best orgasm anyone ever had. A string of glass beads from the fringe of Su'ad's belt whipped across the drummer's face, a red line appeared by his lip, he didn't even blink. His tongue flicked out, his hands never paused, seeming to work directly on her body.

The drummer's hands fell at last with a crash, his head bent forward as he curled over his drum. A bow, or total surrender, Reno didn't know.

Su'ad faced her audience, stretching her arms out as if in an embrace.

The regulars, the connoisseurs of fine single-malt scotch, the sailors the businessmen the bikers all whistled—stamping their feet, sweating—they followed her every twisting gesture, moaning: she-loves-me; suddenly they were aware of the strain their universal erection put on their pants. Slowmotion chanted. "Su'ad! Su'ad the Fortunate. The Mistress of the Mystic East!" They reached for their wallets, hoping to take off some of the pressure.

chapter four

M r. Huntington posed by the bar planning his next politically correct facial expression; he spoke to Su'ad as she swished by him, his words round and smooth as pearls: "Ah, my dear, you were fabulous again. Can we talk a moment?" Seductive little bastard.

"Hunt, I'm pushed tonight. Haven't much time." But Su'ad remained by him, her mouth in a sweet pout. Taunting him, one hip jutting to the side. If you got it, flaunt it.

"I wanted to continue our earlier conversation." He stepped away from the bar, closer to her; the man believed in not letting a good thing out of his grasp, not for a moment. "You look lovely." His chin was pointed at her cleavage.

He waited the proper length of time for her to speak, but she merely stood there, doing the sphinx routine. Annoyed— the years spent filling his small bloated belly with imported delicacies should set him above the ordinary petitioner—his voice was sharp as silk. "Surrender is the central premise of the dance." He concentrated on her glossy immobile red-brown lips. "An art not much practiced in these times." The self-assurance of a viper. "You do it so well." The s was hissed.

She lifted the corners of her lips—apparent amiability couldn't hurt her career. "Surrender?" Her eyebrows arched. She made her smile larger, a sensual fullness.

He ran a strand of her dark slightly curling hair through his manicured fingers. "Belly dance is sheer emotion—the way you do it is like an arrow in the gut. Female power, inescapable, unforgettable. Eternal."

She pulled away from him with small gestures, as much of an enticement as an escape. "I don't suppose you'd care to put that in print?"

He answered her question with a gentleman's sigh, looking up at her with false modesty. "You know I'd love to do it. But I never"—his suave hand floated in a graceful arc toward the bar—"never write about my own backyard."

"Oh Hunt." She shrugged. A small precise gesture. "You never write about anything but your backyard."

Long-fingered like all elegant villains, the man placed his hand over hers, gazing at her with repressed heat. "Belly dance is hot. Visceral. Primitive." He purred. "I know how you feel, nonetheless what you do is not art—it's something, certainly . . ."

"But it's not art?" Su'ad shifted her shoulders back a little, lifted her head, laughed at him. Her throat was lovely. "Art isn't concerned only with the marketplace, it's the foundation, the source of the finest endeavors—"

His voice was tentative. "What you do could be called a vital luxury."

"That's a contradiction."

"Perhaps." Eyes partially closed, a cat in cream, Hunt's hand moved over the smooth curve of her rump and up her spine. One finger at a time. "Not art. Religion maybe. Or economics." He pushed her hair back from her cheek with his other hand. Possessive. Words within words, seduction proceeding under and over any sense. Or lack.

At the other end of the bar Reno's eyes narrowed in dislike as she lit a cigarette; the old pervert was a government agent. Men like that—Reno stopped the thought, didn't need to complete it. She glanced at Sinclair; he looked much more interesting than Su'ad's creepy suitor.

Sinclair stood by the side of the stage tapping his fingers on his thigh, counting the house, impatient. The clean lines of his face were arrogant, disdainful of the company he seemed forced to keep. He smiled when he caught Reno looking at him.

Su'ad, tender as a butterfly, teased Hunt with her smile. "Economics is preferable to religion, Hunt." She did that thing with her eyes. "But what I do is art." She touched his cheek, left him standing there.

Hunt's gaze shifted, focused on Reno. Thought she lacked aesthetic grace. People like that should stay home. He looked back at Su'ad. That one might be able to give him what he needed, but he was still unsure of her rates—the cost of supporting her would need to be balanced against her nature, her long legs, her hair, her skin, her body, her smell. Commodity Aesthetics. His art.

Su'ad pushed the red curtain aside, stepped out into the dim street. Took a couple gulps of thin neon air. She stood for a moment suspended, spangled in reflections, didn't turn around when Hunt slipped a twenty into her belt. She was playing this one for keeps. Winner take all. Loser take a dive? She thought about Reno. Maybe she would collect on the side.

Make the bet, play the hand, get on with things. Unless you win, then you get on with other things.

Hunt stepped up to the bar, smooth as a greasy dance-hall john, he motioned for Eddie to pour him a scotch. Eddie was in no hurry. Hunt murmured, "Leave it up to Eddie to get the drinks, we'll die of thirst."

Eddie smacked a shot glass on the bar in front of him with an icy thud. "Be polite, Hunt, I'd be just as happy t'shove this glass up your unlovely ass."

Hunt slid a sawbuck on the counter. "Don't bother trying to keep up your end of this conversation, Eddie, just keep them coming." He lifted his glass, a condescension to Reno on the stool next to him. Gave her what he thought was a debonair smile. Expensive dental work.

Eddie filled her glass too.

"Thanks."

Eddie's pale eyes gleamed silver in the bar light. "Don't thank me, thank Mr. Huntington. He's paying."

Reno moved her glass at Hunt, a small lift; she didn't thank him. Turning back to Eddie, she spoke to fill an awkward silence. "How about you?"

"Oh." Eddie looked glum. "I only drink when they's nothing better around." He sighed, looked with great intensity at the frayed cuff of his shirt, unbuttoned and rebuttoned it, stared off at the other end of the bar. "Usually nothin' better around. Stupid world."

The sentiment fit.

Out in the back alley a lonely cat raised its overheated voice in a yowl.

There was an odd urgency in Hunt's voice. "Gimme a bottle of cheap champagne. Quick. One with a plastic cork."

Eddie scowled. "What you want to go be doin' that for?"

"Just gimme it." Under his breath he muttered, "Stupid faggot."

The cat yowled again. Plaintive. Abrasive. All of that.

Eddie, stubborn. "I'm not a faggot. Besides, the cat got a right to cry."

Hunt went around the end of the bar, grabbed a bottle of André, peeled off the tinfoil, loosened the wire cage. Gave the bottle a vigorous shake, headed for the alley door. His big flat thumb released the cork—an explosion of champagne, a cat's scream, then absolute silence in the alley.

"Got the bastard."

Eddie went down to the tiny sound booth built above the far end of the bar. Reno followed, happy to leave the vicinity of the viperous Mr. Huntington.

"Hey, Slowmotion. Get some blue gels, it's all blue this weekend. They want a lotta blue."

Slowmotion was a dark, big, round blur; impossible to make her out in the murk of the back bar lights, but a sense of wicked power, restrained delirium, seemed to surround her. She turned the lights up so she could see Reno a little better. It was her job to know who was who and doing what, or who. Whom. Language wasn't her strong point.

In the stronger light Slowmotion appeared to be a large black mountain wearing headphones over an A's baseball cap; a snaky-haired mountain with flexible lips snapping a piece of gum, snapping eyes that didn't miss a trick, and fat clever fingers sliding switches up and down, four sometimes five different directions: a masterful audio massage on the soundboard.

Slowmotion worked in the club before the belly dancers arrived; before that she'd watched as the hard-rock strippers faded from the street; she'd still be there, huge and immovable, when the belly dancers were replaced by flamenco, Brazilian sambistas, or House. No one knew how she was paid, or where she lived. She didn't encourage intimacy.

Slowmotion lifted one earphone away from her ear, didn't look at Eddie; she kept her eyes on Reno, scrutinizing. "What you say, Eddie?" Her voice rumbled way down low, her hands never stopped moving, the stage lights dazzled, bounced with the music. A show all to themselves. "Blue. What a bore. How in hell you know?"

Eddie spoke to the ceiling. "Fabulous Farouk's manager just called Sinclair. I listened on the extension, thought it might be his connect, or one of the people from the bank, you know. But the bitch just rattled on about how great Fabulous Farouk was, said something about people don't need bright lights when the dancing's really terrific."

"Fabulous don't want people to see how fat he's got. He wants them just to grooooove." She flashed a toothy grin.

Something familiar. Reno thought maybe she knew Slowmotion from one of her innumerable trips through the local county jail—she stopped the thought, angry with the need to identify everyone, a narc on every corner, a bunco artist behind every desk. A snitch in any nightclub.

Eddie swayed closer. "You suppose Farouk will bring in any real money?"

"Not likely." Slowmotion winked at Reno. "Maybe."

Eddie groaned. "Fuckheads."

Slowmotion shook her head, snaky braids bouncing, she smiled, slow and mean. "You wanta work in this circus you gotta shovel a lotta camel shit."

Eddie stepped closer, with a Southern gentleman's courtesy, he addressed his remarks to Reno. "Fat men shouldn't dance. At least not for money." That said, he turned back to Slowmotion. "You got a quarter for me or what?" He kept the whine out of his voice but left a strong impression that he was hurting.

Club Istanbul was a rolling fantasy for Reno. Everyone in the place was drenched in drama, not a simple unembellished thought among the lot of them. People played out their chosen roles just to amuse themselves, or just to confuse everyone else. Reno didn't know if what she felt was necessary paranoia or some abstract fear dry-humping out of habit in the rubble-filled corners of her brain. She looked into her scotch glass, suddenly dubious about the success of the rest of her life.

"Or what." Slowmotion spoke with a professional's crooning intonation. An honest woman. A woman with fast hands and a well-padded bottom who might have a quarter for Eddie. Couldn't be a snitch.

"Aw, Slowmotion. Come on." Eddie forced himself to take a few deep breaths, watch the stage begin to glow again as Slowmotion faded out the elevator music. "Hey, Slowmotion, whyn't you ever play any Sinatra? Sinatra is God. He so powerful he doesn't let it out, you know what I'm saying, Slow?"

"Nah. Could he have been mayor? No. You hear what I'm sayin'?"

"Mayor? Shit. We're talking about a man who could take

over Bolivia with a phone call. What's he wanta be mayor for?"

"Bolivia?"

"I mean, think of all the money he has, billions. He doesn't do fuckall for it. Screw women sing a couple songs get drunk on the best champagne, make a couple deals, decide the fate of nations. Man."

"Started out a slimy little punk. Still is."

"After Sinatra's sixth or seventh million he left all that petty shit behind him. Way behind."

The moody tune coming over the footlights was the flute slithering up the scale; it faded out as the other musicians woke up. Slowmotion addressed the audience. "Well, okay now! Put yer lazy han's together. Come on. A round of applause please for our next lovely dancer, all the way from the harems of the caliph of Baghdad! The Enviable Eva! Exotic Ectoplasmic Eeeeeva!"

The woman moved onto the stage like a coy teenager with a secret between her legs, purposeful, sexy but not graceful; she smiled, evil and arrogant, as she jiggled Kewpie doll breasts barely contained by the even smaller bra; she had a tiny waist, big thighs, an ass like two cantaloupes.

Something about the Exotic Eva's heart-shaped face, the way her feral smile contrasted with her practiced, perfected gestures, maybe just the way the woman wriggled inside her smooth skin, was disturbing. The sight of her made Reno itch.

"Weasels rip my flesh." Reno couldn't watch the woman; turning back to Eddie and Slowmotion, she mumbled, "How did they let that one outta her cage?"

Eddie nodded. "But what ya gonna do? This is all the choices people like us get." He sniffled, rubbing his nose with his sleeve. "Sinatra don't care about money. He said alls he ever really wanted was just enough money to warp his perspective." He stared with a pale eager gaze at Slowmotion.

She favored him with a small sarcastic smile. "Now, who ever said that Sinatra never had an abstract thought?"

"Hey. I bet if Sinatra lived around here things would be entirely different." He squinted at her, waiting.

"Sure, Eddie." Slowmotion growled low in her throat, bitter as absinthe. "Sure, Eddie. Then people like us could get terrific jobs as bartenders dancers disc jockeys dope dealers and whores."

"Mmm." Eddie gave it some time. Started to walk back to the end of the bar where the thirsty hordes congregated. "You probably right. That part always be the same." He pulled out some cash. Planning to warp his own perspective. Slowmotion eyed it with disdain. He muttered, "Ah shit. Be back in a minute. I can do better than this."

"Fifteen minutes all I wait on you for." Slowmotion seemed to only half listen to him, her basilisk gaze never left Eva's mechanically posturing form. With a nasty smile she changed the follow spot to a bilious green; Eva looked over at her, sharp.

"Don't worry. Somethin' will come up." Eddie eyed the thirsty crowd. "Somethin' always come up."

Reno's throat was dry, she took a long swallow of the scotch. Tapped a cigarette out of her pack.

Slowmotion, shifting her large bulk, leaned out of the sound booth, flipped her lighter open. A narrow flame, couple inches tall, floated in the dim light before Reno. A gritty voice. "Say. Do I know you? Who are you and what you do?"

Reno leaned toward the flame and sucked. Leaned back into the shadows. Exhaled. "Nobody and nothin'." Sincere. "Hope to keep it like that for as long as I can."

chapter five

"You can watch this lovely dancer another time." Su'ad materialized by Reno's side, squeezed her hand, pulling her toward the stairwell behind the bar. "The 'Lovely Eva' has Eva Braun's mind and Eva Perón's arms."

"And Eva Gabor's vocabulary?" Reno didn't get up from the bar stool; she didn't want to go downstairs, didn't need to see the machinery behind the mirage, the guts and grease of enchantment; on the other hand she thought it might be wise to move out from under Slowmotion's scrutiny. The woman was unnerving.

Grumpy, confused, all Reno wanted to do, really, was drink.

Su'ad waited, not letting go of Reno's hand. "Eva has the vocabulary of a fishwife. Come on."

"What's a fishwife?" Reno waved at Eddie as she was dragged to the landing of the stairwell behind the bar. "Hey. What's upstairs?" She pointed to the carpeted stairs leading upward. "Who's Slowmotion anyway? And what brothel did that dancer escape from?"

Su'ad shrugged. She led Reno downward.

Reno admired Su'ad's back, musing. "Hey. That drummer. Pretty fancy. He a real Arab or what?"

"They're all real Arabs. Arabs or Eye-talians from New Jersey. Same thing." She stopped, her voice a few tones deeper. "Stay away from them." She continued on down. "That particular one's a toady to the bald-headed bastard what runs this place, that's what he is." Flat voice. "Do anything Sinclair says. Hell, I don't get paid enough to dance that hard."

"You got at least one twenty."

Su'ad turned around, their faces about level with each other. "I earned that one, believe me."

"Oh, I believe you."

"Oooh little girl, you ain't changed a bit." Su'ad continued down the narrow metal stairs, her voice bouncing off the bare walls. "I don't have to sit with the customers here, don't even have to pay them no mind. Of course tips are better if I hang out in the showroom, but I don't have to."

"That must be nice."

Su'ad smiled at the ungentle sarcasm. "I never took dancing serious, you know that. Finally it just looked better than what I was into, you know? I mean, all those years in school—to wear a whistle around my neck, teach fat kids to play dodgeball?"

They turned left into a room filled floor to ceiling with shelves collapsing under the weight of sloppy mounds of molding ledgers, ancient scrap metal, broken bottles, the dusty legacy of some bygone Barbary Coast saloon dug into the old stone foundation; a half-hinged wooden door led to a one-stall, two-urinal bathroom, not very clean. Scarred metal gym lockers lined the opposite wall, dents and broken locks suggested that the clientele lost their keys a lot.

Su'ad removed her sequined bra and the belt with the glass fringe, her gauzy split skirt. There were deep grooves in her shoulders. "Here." She handed Reno her bra. "Feel the weight of the damn thing." At least a dozen pounds of beadwork. "Have to be a bloody weight lifter to wear it." Su'ad made a small throaty sound, her least amused laugh. "But there's a lot more money in dancing than lifting weights." Her skin was shiny with sweat and glitter.

"You still work out?"

"You just saw my workout." She pulled on a bright red tank top. Short black leather skirt.

Reno looked skeptical.

Su'ad frowned. "Irony. You know from irony?"

"Yeah, sure." Reno looked at her feet. "No. Yeah." Reno could feel Su'ad snickering. Irritated. "Well, how you mean?"

Su'ad smoothed dark stockings over her feet, up her legs. "I'm sick of everyone assuming I'm a whore because I dance here. Things aren't what they seem." Su'ad sighed. "I'm a dancer, an artist, a professional. Not a whore."

"What's the matter with whoring now?" Reno knew from whoring, wasn't so sure about this artist business.

Exasperated. "Nothing's the matter with whoring except it can kill you. But that's not the point."

Reno lifted her left eyebrow, superb arch, months to get it right. "I hoped you'd be situated a little more secure."

"Security? Who you kiddin'?" Su'ad flipped the jeweled costume bra into her case, pulled out another one. "Architectural engineers should be designing these contraptions. But no. Crazy old Egyptian seamstresses cornered the market a thousand years ago, charge six, eight hundred dollars for an authentic costume, still cut into your shoulders." She held up the new one, green satin, gold beaded fringe, turned it so it glittered in the light. "Domestic workmanship. Weighs half as much." She slung it over the back of a chair. "Lasts half as long."

Reno's tentative fingers played with the fringe. "You enjoying yourself though, huh?"

"And why shouldn't I be? Listen honey, I got sixty dollars my first night, for twitchin' my ass. Thought it wasn't a bad deal." Su'ad snorted, remembering. "Never made that much money so easy. Hey, it's all illusion, you know that, same as

it ever was. Seem to come natural." She smiled, her pointed
tongue flicking the corners of her mouth. "Mr. Huntington
was here my first night, circling like a lazy hawk." Sibilant.

"That old pervert?"

"Not old. No no. Not old. He writes a column in a snobby
West Coast arts mag. First-person cultural commentary—you
know, if he isn't there it isn't worth attending. He thinks he's
the new age arts guru. Told some rich broad he was channel-
ing Noel Coward."

"Say what?"

Su'ad moved her face forward to peer at her friend. "Your
cultural education hasn't exactly been expanded these last
years has it?"

"Culture? I got culture. Right between my legs."

"Should see a doctor about that then." Su'ad poked Reno
in the ribs. "Yeah, and the rest of you isn't in such great
shape either. Touch your toes?"

"I'll work on it."

"Hell, girl, what they do to you in there?"

"Aw, you don't want to know." Reno had important matters
to discuss. Connections. Credit cards. Addresses. References.
Maybe, Reno thought, we get something going, a little thing,
on the side, the way it used to be.

"Okay, I believe you." Su'ad wrapped her long arms around
Reno in an impulsive hug. "Glad to see you out here among
the savage civilians anyway. Even if you are one of the walking
wounded."

Reno made a face, pushed her away. "Not me. I ain't no
wounded. I seen 'em, Susanna—there be some sad desperate
creatures beddin' down on the streets." She shook her head.
"Some fuckin' world you got out here."

"When'd you get so concerned about the homeless?"

"Soon's it seemed I might be joinin' 'em." Reno intended
to go on from there, bring up some of the difficulties one has
when one tries to establish oneself in the proper socioeconomic
circles without money or an inside partner. "Tell me what

your situation is here. Why you bother with that creepy old fart?"

"He's a powerful man, Reno. Unscrupulous. But they all are. Did you notice his sharp little teeth?" Su'ad looked up as she wiped the sweat-smeared makeup off her face, her dark eyes twinkling. "Vicious. And vain. He fancies himself a benevolent demon, you know, one of those guys who leave women devastated, yet uplifted. A real gentleman." Laughter.

Reno sniffed, she knew how susceptible Susanna was to gentlemen. Reno always had trouble with gentlemen. It gave her a certain amount of satisfaction to realize Eddie made Hunt buy her a drink. Still, that wasn't enough. Reno needed more.

"My first night here Hunt offered to help my career, make me a real woman." Laughing again. "I was respectful, you know, hand over my heart, head down." Su'ad did her "Aphrodite on the half shell," then lifted her face up, her own canines glittering in the light. "When I demurred, he said my career could struggle along without his help unless I was willing to—"

"To?" Reno's voice rose with suspicion, a protective reflex.

Su'ad leaned over the sink, gargled some water, her mouth open wide at the mirror. Spit. Wiggled her tongue at her reflection. Admiring. "Hey now. I'm a professional dancer. We're talking art here."

"Art?"

"Right. Not whoring. Shit, Reno." She started to say something more, "I'm so bloody sick of people." She shook her legs to release the muscle tension, bounced on her toes.

"Okay, sure Susanna, anything you say." Like herding turtles.

"Seriously now." Stretch. Plié. "I'm talking business. My business. Dancing. And my name is Su'ad now." A small glint in her eyes to take the sting out of her words.

"Sure. Call me Mata Hari."

Su'ad stuck her tongue out.

"Whatever. So, how much you say your costume cost—that ol' man pay for it?" Reno kept her face turned away, watching her friend from the side.

"He wanted me to dance at his parties. Just for tips." Su'ad shook her head. "I refused."

"Tips. I can see how that'd be rough." Reno's sarcasm didn't make a dent.

"Hey. I don't perform for chump change." Injured dignity. "Real money talks."

"I heard that."

Lecturing, Su'ad raised her index finger. "Middle Eastern dance is a special art. Even when it's called belly dance rather than Raks al Sharki it's still sacred. It's all about the fertility of the earth." Finger dropped, pointing symbolically down, she expected Reno to imagine perhaps the earth beneath the cracked concrete floor. "It goes back as far as the birth of culture." Pause before the revelation. "Back to birth itself." Su'ad looked like she was repeating the pledge of allegiance.

"Birth. Right. Fertility of the earth." Reno figured Su'ad had gone soft in the head. She'd seen it happen often enough in jail.

"It takes years to learn. There's a whole mental-physical discipline that goes with it." Su'ad was really serious. "An immense amount of skill." She curved her arms toward Reno, newly boneless, beckoning, the shape of her body undergoing a perverse metamorphosis. A mermaid. "See? That demands skill." Her body rippled again, a fountain, a flame. "Spiritual, you know?"

"Oh? Oh. Okay." Reno slid her shades down her long nose, looked at Su'ad over the top. Just looked at her.

Su'ad shrugged, fighting a smile. "Don't be so jaded." She stopped. "Anyway, Hunt's interested in me for culture, not sex. Art. I'm not into the other thing."

"Sex? Not into sex?" Reno wondered who was interested in what as she checked out Su'ad's long luscious body. "Hah." The ground slipped away when it should have been rock solid.

Sex? Art? At this rate Reno figured they never get around to serious issues. Credit cards. Bank numbers. Necessities. She tried to remember how she used to maneuver Su'ad. Another blank, eaten away by all that time in jail.

"I'm celibate. Have been for years."

Reno wiggled her eyebrows in mock horror. "You? I thought I had the celibacy thing to myself. What's the matter?"

"I'm not sick."

Reno thought celibacy itself was pretty damn sick. She wanted to spend her first weeks out in a state of continually reciprocated lust—Su'ad's attitude was stranger than raisins in ice cream. Reno knew little or nothing about love anyway, but if even Susanna wasn't fucking, it would seem Reno's chances of getting it on were pretty damn slim. She'd probably never get laid. Instant gloom. Might as well kill herself.

She pulled herself up; maybe she would give it some time. She wasn't that ugly. Someone was sure to find her attractive. Right. Some terrible fat accountant who wouldn't even take her back to his flat so she could case the place. Bah.

"Everybody thinks it's so cool to be an exotic dancer, nobody bothers to take it to the logical conclusion."

"Which is?" Great riotous sex.

"Celibacy. Fantasy and sensuality are my job, I sell the illusion of pleasure. But it's not real life—"

"Sure it is. If it's not, it beats the hell out of real life." Great riotous sex.

"Nope. The dance is fascination. Seduction. Not animal arousal. But to most men it's all one." Su'ad curled her lip. "Real life on their terms is a lotta bangin' around, greasy breathing, an ache between my legs and some huge jerk messin' up the bed." Su'ad applied fresh lipstick. "Isn't worth it."

Reno thought ever more seriously about great riotous sex. "Well. What about women?"

"The women I've loved haven't loved me. Like I said, I been celibate for a long long time. I like it that way."

Reno couldn't stand it. "C'mon back upstairs, we gotta call about those lottery numbers." Exasperation. Disbelief.

Su'ad pulled a comb through her thick hair. "Okay. I could do with some amazing unearned money grace right now."

Reno muttered, pointedly, "We all could." She wanted to follow that line of conversation. "Never enough to go around."

"Right." Su'ad's mouth drooped. She mumbled. "I'm really cash short now, just quit my day job."

Reno thought having a day job and a night job was excessive. "Why?"

Su'ad pulled into herself with a small frown, remembering the beautifully wrapped gift someone left on her desk at the office: a pair of crotchless panties. Her boss remarked with calculated innocence that he knew they'd be something Su'ad could use, being an exotic dancer, wink wink. "Tell you about it another time." Su'ad faltered, looked like she wanted to say more but stopped. Shook it off. "Once I learned more about Mr. Huntington I decided to be accommodating."

"Translation of 'accommodation' here is not to be understood as horizontal activity?"

"Don't harp on it, Reno. I figure the man will be incredibly useful." Su'ad raised a hand to her mouth, dropping her voice. "He's got a ten-year lease on the flat above the club here, probably owns a piece of the club itself."

"Probably? Or he does?"

"Either way. He's the chance I can't pass up. I have to be nice to him. Be nice, you know?" Su'ad never could resist the lure of potential money or power.

"What else is there to do with a powerful pervert besides fuck him? You claiming artistic privilege for that now?"

Su'ad stiffened. Hunt was rich. Rumor and her own experience seemed to indicate he was both impotent and fascinated with her. She never denied her weakness for that kind of man. "Put a bag on it, Reno."

Eddie called down from the bar: "Hey, what you doin' down there? Bring me up some towels, willya?"

In silence they each took an armful, trotted upstairs. "So, come on Su'ad, tell me." A pushy giggle in Reno's voice, unbelieving.

"There's nothing to tell. Absolutely nothing." Su'ad shook her head. "We're at an economical impasse."

Reno licked her lips. "Seems to be the condition of the moment."

The Ectoplasmic Eva was strolling around the showroom with an alarming leer on her face as tiny dark men pasted dollar bills lovingly across her quivering belly.

"Barbie goes Egyptian!" Reno's penetrating whisper got an amused glance from Eddie.

He mimicked Eva with a pelvic thrust. "Miss Tits from Hell."

Eva's eyes were heavy, hungry; she performed a slow grinding figure eight before a rigid eighteen-year-old. The blush spread from his navel to his ears; he licked his lips, chewing on nothing. Eva flexed herself all over for him, climbed back onto the stage smiling shyly; a quick couple spins then wiggling flirtatiously she shimmied back into the audience, collected many more bills. She finally swished out of the showroom stumbling on her veil. The youngster stood up, swaying. He turned to follow her.

"Oh boy." Reno knew about sluts. She wasn't sure about the Art thing. "My sacred twat. This gonna be interesting."

The musicians reached for their shot glasses and cigarettes.

The youngster collapsed back in his chair, called for another bourbon. On the rocks.

Eddie grimaced, poured. Put it on the bar. "Come get it, buddy." Waiting for the cash, Eddie looked to Reno like a sad twelve-year-old in someone else's clothes. She felt a sense of kinship—he had those seen-too-much-eyes, that heavy grown-up voice—Reno wondered how he'd ended up as the Istanbul's all-purpose bartender/barker. His eyes never quit counting the house, the drinks, calculating the potential take.

Eddie shook the ice water from his hands, waved them at

the stage like a magician: away went the children sailors, away the slimy beer stains, away the nosy bosses. Ritually chanting a counterpoint razz to the hypnotic Arabic music: away the last-minute ice delivery, away the heavy beer kegs, away the asshole customers, away the ego-driven dancers.

Eddie hadn't collected enough money to go back down to Slowmotion's end of the bar yet, he turned to Su'ad, maybe he could borrow a tenner. "Say, you cocktailing or dancing this weekend, Su'ad?"

"Dance tonight, waitress this weekend. Fabulous doesn't want any competition from the local talent." Venom in Su'ad's voice. "You know, women."

"Ah-huh. Ah-huh. An' that's the way he likes it." He set up two glasses. The fate of the Western alliance rested on his thin shoulders. Muttered. "There isn't a cocktail waitress on the face of the earth who can get it right three out of five times."

Su'ad was quick. "You wanta bet, or what?" She looked to Reno for approval, but Reno didn't give it to her. Seemed to her the wise money was on the bartender.

Eddie waved a negligent hand. "You? Bet? Hell, you don't even drink. I never bet with people who don't drink." He poured Su'ad a soda water, lifted a questioning eyebrow at Reno.

Su'ad pointed a long finger at his in-curving belly, growled. "You won't bet me because you know I'll come up winners."

"No way. You won't get half the orders right. It will be hell." He poured Reno another Johnnie Walker Black.

Slowmotion jabbed the tape deck with a vicious finger, apparently glad to see the back of the Sexotic Eva. Middle Eastern elevator music with a sanitized rhythm eased out of the speakers.

Reno saluted her with the glass behind Su'ad's back.

chapter six

Reno's guarantee-win lottery ticket had a couple right. Not enough.

"It's rigged. I tole you."

"Life's rigged, Eddie. 'Bout time you noticed." Su'ad turned to Sinclair as he shouldered his way through the crowd at the bar. "Hey. What was the meaning of all that fancy drumming up there for my set?"

"The man was proving my point." Grave. Sincere. "You dance, you blow Fabulous off the stage, he breaks his contract, the customers blame the club, we lose tons of money, have to close. Disaster. You see?" He ran his hand over his beard, hiding his smile. A man of the world ready to explain the celestial tilt.

"Oh, go fuck yourself, Sinclair." Su'ad dismissed him but he didn't dismiss so easily. He stopped. Eyed Reno. Up and down. An alphabet of need that starts before birth. "Hel-lo."

Reno shifted her weight from one foot to the other. She was rocked by unremembered, unexpected hormonal activity; she supposed it was hormones, couldn't be food poisoning, she hadn't eaten anything. Taking another long swallow of her drink she returned Sinclair's measuring stare. "Be damned if I can't do the hairy eyeball better than some fancy dude."

45

The corner of his mouth twitched.

Su'ad attempted rescue. "Did I tell you about the disaster this man caused last month when he tried to book country and western bands in here Monday nights?" She looked from one face to the other. Hopeful. Expectant.

Unsuccessful. They were oblivious as stones.

Sinclair, always on top, took Reno's cool hand in his huge one. "Permit me to introduce myself."

"Okay." Reno wasn't sure that was the proper response but it seemed a reasonable thing to say since she couldn't get her hand back. She shook her head to clear it; her eyes, unable to focus, rattled around in her head. Lovely. She wondered, a lot too late, what the hell she thought she was getting into; should've stayed holed up in the Royal, got sloshed in private. Safe.

Su'ad stepped in, flat-voiced. "Reno, this is Sinclair, the worst boss anyone could have." So much for rescue, good manners. "He also tried reggae-Moroccan fusion. Two weeks of that, the club was ready to file chapter eleven. Again." Su'ad's eyes flashed warnings.

Sinclair's grip measured Reno's hand her arm her backbone. "I'm glad to meet you. I manage this place. I'm the best boss in the world."

Reno took a breath. Blinked. Spoke smaller than she wanted. "Then I hope you're satisfied with the inventory you're taking." Desert sheik music boiled away parts of her brain.

Sinclair perfected the Middle Eastern glance: infinite regret that he couldn't possibly manage to make love to all the women he wanted. "I think you need a job." Intense under-currents in the phrase.

Reno pulled her hand away like it had been flamed. A job was not what she had in mind. Getting laid maybe. A couple drinks, a night out, a reassuring chat with a beautiful friend, a connection for some credit. Small things, but important.

Su'ad stepped forward. "Wait a minute. Since when we

need another cocktail waitress?" She tapped him on his broad chest. "Sinclair, you know we don't need nobody. Anyway, I thought you had something to do upstairs." Su'ad pushed him toward the stairs.

He didn't budge. "You can handle a tray fulla drinks, uh, Reno?" Another deadly glance from his wicked eyes.

Reno stood there like a deer in the headlights, didn't answer. Hell, Reno thought, not a goddamn waitress again. She knotted her fingers into themselves, security of a sort.

Sinclair motioned to Eddie, he filled her glass, she unclenched the hand, grabbed the glass, drained it.

Sinclair waited until she started breathing again. "Listen, it's better than a nine-to-five. Believe me." An odd worried kindness showed in his handsome face. "It's easier."

Reno thought about that. She liked easy. So she neither moved back from him nor closer to him. Still clutching the glass she glared in a distracted fashion over his shoulder. What she wanted and needed weren't connected. She blinked again. A job. For so long the point had been just to get out of prison. A job. She wasn't ready for that.

"Hey everybody. We just hired on someone new. Reno starts tomorrow night."

Eddie made eyes like an old beagle. "Another one can't count, make change or tell a Gin Fizz from a Tom Collins."

"Right." Reno agreed with him, eager. "Right." No reason to set herself up for more work than she had to.

Su'ad shaped her lips. "Ooh." Her eyes thoughtful. Stepped back from the bar. "Sinclair, come over here." Su'ad wore her matron face. "What you doin'?"

Sinclair lifted his chin. "Eva can't work this weekend so we need someone. Not that it's any of your business."

"It all my business. Why isn't the elegant Miss Eva working?"

"She gotta callback for the lead or something in some play they're casting at some little theater." He looked smug. "Girl's gonna be a star."

Slowmotion choked out a sputtered, "What? You shittin'."

Sinclair strolled away, whistling.

Su'ad stood for half a breath, the color rising in her cheeks. Stiff, she turned on Reno, all her anger aimed at the wrong target. "Listen, girl, I don't know what game you playin' at but I got a bad feelin'."

"Oh, me too, Su'ad. Me too." Reno nodded, agreeable. "But, hey, if I don't come up with eighty dollars by Monday, I'm on the streets. Curled up in a doorway with camel dung on my feet." That angle got her nowhere with Su'ad. Su'ad's sources of sympathy were never deep; over the past few moments they seemed to have dried right up. Reno put a lot of reassurance into her next line. Confidential information. "Hey, I'm not gonna rip off the damn club, honest." That seemed a little better. "Thought hadn't even occurred to me." Su'ad's eyes glittered, filled with distrust. "Well, damn it all anyway, Susanna, I didn't ask for the fucking job, that big old Arab just gave it to me."

Distracted. "He's an Armenian."

"Well, what's he doin' running a place named Club Istanbul?"

"Poker game."

"Oh. He win or lose?"

"What you think—hey, don't change the subject." A flash of sharp irritation. "Listen, Reno, nothin' says you got to take this job. Since when you just do what someone tell you; everyone 'cept me, that is?"

"I don't just do what people tell me to do. I make up my own mind about things." Proud of herself for it too. "What'd the other guy get?"

Automatic. "Sinclair hadda lunch counter. Gyros, dildos. Magazines."

"Wuh. Sinclair won this place?"

"No, you stupid bimbo! Sinclair lost. This place hasn't broke even in months. The sailors won't come 'cause we ain't naked, the yuppies won't come because it's not a fad anymore,

the Muslims won't come because he's a Christian—" Su'ad
spun around in exasperation. "It's a loser's proposition. You
don't want anything to do with it!"

"So why you work here?"

"I like it." Her eyes slipped sideways.

"Bullshit." Reno glared at her.

"Listen to me. You got to get yourself together, stop simply reacting to the first thing what happens." Toe to toe,
nose to nose. "Shit. If you had a original thought it would
die a loneliness." Su'ad's face was all harsh edges sharp
angles. Breathless. "Your life's a bloody soap opera, Reno,
but you not the star."

"Fuck you. Don't want to be no star. Don't need to prance
around on stage naked like you all the time." Reno stepped
back a pace, checking along the bar for an equalizer, something to belt the taller woman with; she wasn't a violent
woman but her reactions were still tuned to maximum response. Through her teeth: "Listen girl, I came to see you
dance, say hello, maybe discuss a small business venture, something to help me get back on my feet."

Su'ad's face remained closed. "Yo. A small business venture. I'll get right on it." Smooth as marble with that same
glassy gleam. Pulled inward, sucking on a lime. "Listen girl, I
can't help you that way, I don't do that anymore. Whyn't you
go home, take a aspirin, have a good sleep, call your parole
agent in the morning, have her get you a job."

The hell with it. Reno stood very still; all that time in prison
hadn't rotted her reasoning faculties, just warped them a little.
In a soft voice, metal in every word, "I don't have to call no
parole agent about no job. I got a job. Right here. You can
take your paranoia and stick it up your ass. I'm a felon, I'm
not an AIDS victim. It isn't catching."

"You near killed a man—tried to cut that guy's eye out."

"More'n one. More'n once. Do it again too. Some assholes
deserve it. You *know* that."

Frozen in time, in space, they glared at each other until

Slowmotion told Su'ad she was up in nine minutes—unless she wanted to dance in her tank top she better get into costume.

Reno left the bar with a booze headache, a job she didn't want; another night shot all to hell, even the stars hid out behind a leaden layer of fog.

It began to rain. She stared up at the dripping clouds as if it were a personal affront. Wet urban streets smelled different from wet cement prison yards. Big deal. Difference isn't enough, it's merely an overlay, a confusion. She decided she hated rain. Dainty reluctant one damp foot other foot down the streaming sidewalk she trotted, searching for something/anything familiar in the urban swamp.

She was wrapped in psychic cellophane, trapped inside a protective numbness that wouldn't retreat. She tried to remind herself she was *free:* this was real life. Freedom. At last.

She didn't feel free. What did she know about free. Shit.

She still had no money, no credit cards, no prospects. One step closer to crashing homeless on the streets or going back to jail. She grumbled: the only difference between the Royal Hotel and the joint was that no one leaned out of any of the cells at the Royal to greet her as she chuffed up the hall.

She fished in the pockets of her windbreaker, her mind on other things. She dumped the items she'd boosted on top of the rickety dresser. Like a magpie she was attracted to shiny things: a shot glass, an ashtray with "Club Istanbul" in cursive script, a glass candle. Half surprised she noticed they looked nice. She lit the candle. Tomorrow she'd put some flowers in the glass. As if she lived there.

She placed her boots at the foot of the bed, folded her clothes, piling them up in the order that she'd use if she needed to put them on in a hurry. Even if she led a messy life she still kept a tidy cell, ready, things packed as if she be gone anytime. Old habits die hard.

Reno hadn't wanted to stay in prison, but she wasn't ready for the streets. Wasn't half the way she remembered. Working at the Club Istanbul wasn't quite what she had in mind either. Huh. Didn't remember what she had in mind. Fuckin' ridiculous life anyway. What ya gonna do. She blew out the candle.

chapter seven

"Don't hurry or anything, hey, Fabulous still hasn't shown." Su'ad's large eyes were solemn dark holes in her face, her voice satin-ribbon sharp. She posed against the red curtains of the Club Istanbul, smoking, scowling, wearing a tiny black sequined dress. Gave Reno the once over. "Ain't you got any nicer clothes?" One hip jutted to the side showing an unbelievable expanse of leg. Her hair tumbled around perfectly modeled curves. Didn't seem nearly as pleased to see Reno as their long friendship might lead one to expect. "People don't expect to be waited on by some renegade, you know. They come here for a good time."

Reno grinned at her, showed all her teeth. Perhaps Su'ad would get cheerier as the night wore on. Or this could be the high point of her evening. "I'll show 'em a good time."

"Hell, girl, you look like you just got outta jail." Su'ad shrugged, lifted her hand to her mouth, foolish. "Oh, sorry."

Reno glared at her.

"Really. Go downstairs—see if there's anything in the lockers that'll fit you."

"Ain't gone kiss no one's butt. I'm dressed well enough for

a goddamn cocktail waitress." Huffy. Reno stomped into the club. "No one told me to dress formal. Damn."

Slowmotion smiled briefly at Reno, her broad mischievous face throbbing blue in the empty stage glare. "Blue. The dumbfuck wants blue. I'll die of boredom before the second set, you can believe that." She flicked the lights to green. "Eddie's in the basement, setting up the medicine. G'wan down."

Pausing at the landing behind the bar Reno stared up the carpeted flight of stairs leading to Huntington's flat. Poor perverts, she thought in a brilliant flash of irrelevance, don't get half the perks rich ones do. Money talks. She listened to the small secret noises, the invisible flexing machinery of the night club—she didn't intend to be a cocktail waitress forever: she wondered if Hunt had anything interesting in his flat. Slip in there, remove a couple valuable things, bingo! Cocktail-waitress problem solved. Also, her mouth a grim line, be nice to fuck with his head. Someone need to show these people they not god.

There was an old hatch-cover set in the outer wall of the stairwell; behind it she discovered a sturdy dumbwaiter that slid silently, well oiled, when she pushed it. Half-inch cable. Might be able to hold a small person's weight, make a handy private elevator. She wondered how much weight it would take. There was too damn much she didn't know; what the streets need, she sighed, are wise old cons to tell a person these things. Ah, they probably lie. She supposed she could go to the library. Right. Truth was a relative kind of thing. Libraries lie too.

Next to the hatch were a set of double fire doors opening into the side alley. Guarded by a primitive alarm system so simple an amateur could defeat it with a screwdriver. Didn't need no library to know that. The Istanbul began to look like it might have real potential.

She trotted down the stairs, whistling, tapped Eddie on his shoulder. "Hey Eddie, I don't know a Singapore Sling from a Rob Roy." Goofy smile. Never let on you have even one coherent thought.

"That's okay." Eddie put his wiry arm around her shoulders, handed her several hundred towels, two sacks of ice, put a coffee pot on top. "Neither do I. Don't worry about it." He gave her a gentle shove back toward the stairs. "You gonna do just fine."

There was at least six hundred pounds of stuff.

"Why don't we put this stuff in the dumbwaiter?"

"Broken."

"Oh yeah?"

"Well, Hunt said not to use it."

"No shit." Reno thought about that as she started up the stairs.

"Hey Reno, you got 'ny pot?"

She stopped. "Who me? No."

"Know where to get some pot?"

"No."

Eddie paused. Hummed. "Wull—you wanna buy some pot?"

"You nuts Eddie, you know that?" Shaking her head. She trudged up the stairs struggling with the awkward load. Seemed to Reno the place would be improved by an elevator, any elevator, even the dumbwaiter. She wasn't used to all this upping and downing; the prison had been dead flat. Her lungs burned from the effort to carry and to breathe. It was probably a genetic thing—she wasn't made to do any kind of labor, it wasn't healthy for her, her destiny couldn't be to slog around in cocktail lounges. Spas. Classy health spas maybe.

Reno found a nice bottle of unblended under the bar, poured herself a scotch, lit cigarettes for herself and Slowmotion. The club filled with the smell of incense, with the soft sounds of rain, smooth as the Arabic masmoudi rhythms coming from the tape deck. "What say, Slow, is this paradise or what?" Reno waved her scotch, didn't spill it. "An oasis in the urban desert."

"Huh." Eddie scowled his way across the room, a blast of cold air. "You best get those glass candles on the tables before people start arriving." Eddie muttered something about the place bein' a fucking desert, period, no oasis; he dashed out the door. "Be-back-inna-minute." Looking for a biker, someone, anyone who might sell him some speed. One step closer to paradise.

Slow hummed to herself, slid her eyes over at Reno. "Right. Right." Her voice slid down the scale, scornful. "Just wait a couple hours, you'll witness up front and personal the veritable ruination of paradise." Slowmotion shrugged, motioning at the street door. "Eddie still don't know how to score."

A cadaverous man in an old leather jacket leered in. "Yeah, so, what it is. You got naked girls tonight, or what?"

"We closed."

He followed a young well-dressed couple into the club. "Hey." He addressed their backs. "You can't just walk in here without payin', you know?"

They ignored him, ordered an Anchor Steam each. Reno poured. They left a quarter tip for Reno on the bar.

The skinny man pointed at it. "Pretty damn cheap." His voice was as thin as he was.

Reno clutched the quarter in her fist. "You think you take my quarter tip, you got another thing coming." She opened her hand, peered at it, sighing. "Pretty damn cheap is right."

He grinned. No bottom teeth, sold for dope. "Don' worry." He leaned on the bar. "Things'll get better." He labored over each word, turning his blank mirror-shade eyes toward Reno. "Want to have a drink with me now, or later?"

"I don't drink with strangers and neither should you."

Slowmotion cranked up the decibels on the tape deck. Music like a cat getting its tail twisted. She shut it off. Looked for another tape. Grumbling "Free advice ain't worth much," she put in a new tape, turned some dials, the tempo picked up, the stage lights began to pulse.

The skinny guy sat on a bar stool, leaned his cane on the

stool to the left, put his newspaper on the counter to the right, staking out some territory for himself. "Come on. How 'bout that drink for me?" There wasn't much expectation in his voice. He kept scanning the room. "Where you say Mister Huntington is?"

"I didn't."

A few more people wandered in, ordered drinks, Reno poured, they tipped small.

"Well, then, pour me a drink and we'll talk nasty about him."

"Show me some money."

The man shook his scruffy head. "Can't find a good heart anywhere these days." His nose was runny as he peered around. "My money's good." Stoned on some private psychosis, he tightened, lifted his shades; the pupils of his eyes had expanded like cosmic black holes. No trace of iris. "My money's good. Hunt will tell ya. We do business together."

Reno was familiar with those eyes, didn't like them; freaks were a lot more trouble than ordinary junkies. If this guy was the caliber Hunt associated with then she'd sussed the old man out correctly. Basic sleazebag. But hey, what did Reno know about the way the upper classes conducted their affairs—she'd only been in their places of business when they were absent.

Reno picked up a bottle of Irish rye whiskey, feeling the weight of it, sighting a spot on his head just above his ear. "Show me the long green. Or it's time to get gone." She stepped out from the bar feeling the weight of her chosen weapon.

"She think she hot shit, now huh." Addressing Slowmotion, rude thumb at Reno. "All's I want is a few words with my man Hunt." He looked sad, stood up to lean on his heavy cane. "We got business together." Thumped the floor once, twice like an irate old lady. "I got some special information for him. Shit." Twisted his head to the side, almost weeping.

"One a you should go get him—he wants to see me. Meantime, I'll have a beer."

Reno tiptoed up behind him, a straight shot to his left ear. Gonna have some fun now.

Sinclair slipped his huge bulk between Reno and her target, protective, he suggested to the man that he take his business elsewhere.

"AA-aah. You Arab *scum!*" The fellow roared out, arms raised. Cane swinging. "Aaah." He rose up dancing a grizzlybear dance, spittle blowing from the corners of his mouth. "Wait till Hunt hears how you treat his associates—"

Sinclair whacked him a few times, pirouetted him out the door. Professional. He pointed to the bottle Reno still held. "Unnecessary. That."

Reno shrugged. "Hey, what do I know? Was the first thing came to hand."

"Sixteen dollars a bottle, Reno. Next time grab something cheaper."

"Right boss. I'll douse 'em with that terrible beer you got on tap. That'll kill 'em."

He didn't crack a smile. "Call me when the star gets here, okay?"

"Star? Star?" Reno waved the bottle at Sinclair's back, spilling a little just to show her sincerity. "From what I seen no star be caught dead here."

Sinclair didn't answer but he sort of shrugged. Doubting his choice of careers again.

Reno was doubting her own choice of careers as she poured and swallowed another scotch in one go. Might as well get plastered, didn't look to be the kind of night one should face unaided.

The Istanbul continued to fill up with thirsty people who had left their main wallets at home. Quarter tip, no smile, no thanks. Standard. Reno couldn't believe it. Maybe, she thought, I don't look like the type who needs the money. Too well dressed. Hah.

Su'ad came up the stairs, long legs taking them two at a time. "Gimme some ice and a couple bar towels. Eddie's bleedin' like a stuck pig."

"What happen?"

"Cheek got stuck to the floor."

"What?"

"Glue. Sniffin' glue. The man likes to make paper airplanes. Come on. Gimme the ice. Quick."

Sinclair growled his way through the showroom again. "Hell fuck damn shit cocksucker. Where's the Sufis? Where's Eddie? Where's Farouk?"

"Dunno boss." "Dunno boss." "Dunno boss."

He glared at them, suspicious. "Well, keep pushin' drinks." He put his fists on his hips. "Maybe they won't notice there's nobody dancing." Stomped his way back up the stairs. "Maybe we'll just cancel the damn show. I'll move to Las Vegas."

"What's bugging him?"

"Men don't handle pressure very well."

Pressure wasn't bothering Eddie, passed out on the cracked cement floor, snoring, his cheek married to one of the few remaining black linoleum squares. He didn't mind. He dreamed pretty dreams in his own cheap-ass glue-sniffing technicolor garden of delights.

Su'ad rummaged out some ice, wrapped it in a towel. "Eva just called Sinclair. Says she needs twenty-five hun for an abortion." Casual. Wicked.

"Twenty-five hundred dollars? I thought abortion was still legal, simple, cheap?"

Slowmotion guffawed. "It is. Sinclair fall for that he one hell of a fool."

Su'ad nodded. "Didn't seem to be goin' for it—"

"How you know?"

Dignified. "I listened in on the other extension, naturally." Su'ad gave Reno a quick smile. "Fact is he didn't seem all that eager to help. Didn't sound to me like he believed it was his baby—or that she was even pregnant."

"Think maybe the guy's wising up?"

"No. I think he's against abortions." Su'ad paused, towels and ice in her hands. "Cheap-ass muthafuck against spending money." She spoke to Reno. "Listen, this is no kinda place for you. You should get outta here. Now. Another job come up. Listen to me, I got this bad feelin'."

"I got a feelin' too, and it's a itch here across my knuckles wantin' to pop you if you keep on with that shit." Reno spun away from her, high-stepping across the room to wait on a table of sailors sitting up by the stage. The boys had loud slurry voices, wanted another three pitchers of beer, three new mugs. She glared at them: going to get drunk and throw up all over everything.

"Hey Su'ad, lighten up on Reno, okay?" Slowmotion's voice was hardly more than a whisper. "It's her first night and we need her. I can't have her quittin' halfway through the damn show, now."

Su'ad whispered back. "You don't know her, Slow. She don't have good sense. Attract trouble like a dog draw fleas."

"Hey. Everybody wants to get over. Give the woman a chance."

Su'ad's mouth pulled down. "We got enough trouble around here. You wait, just her being here will aggravate matters." Glum. "Never fails."

Reno took a big breath, pulled her back straight. Some pal. She glared, pushed Su'ad aside, filled the three pitchers, took two to the sailor table, demanded a five-dollar tip before she brought the third pitcher. Flat rate.

It wasn't extortion.

They gave her the fiver.

It was art.

chapter eight

The pale blue robes of the Surfing Sufis flapped behind them like the wings of angels as they bounced into the club. More like birds than angels, they were noisy, arrogant, thirsty. "We gotta tab. Give us a couple pitchers."

"Thought Muslims didn't drink alcohol?"

Voices all in a jumble, one on top of the other. "Sure they do!" "We're from LA." "We got a dispensation from the Big Mufti."

Reno pulled herself up to her full height, looked down her long nose. Stood silent.

"Okay, give us a couple bowls of hash." This from a bright, helpful fellow with a braid down to the middle of his back.

"Sinclair didn't say nothin' about runnin' no tab." She gave the boys one evil little smile; this looked to be fun.

"Aw. Come on." Their faces sad, pleading. "Tell you what, we'll dedicate a song to you?" They gleamed at her, filled with hope, nodding encouragement. In unison.

"What if I don't like the song?" She already started to fill a pitcher. "What if it isn't such a good song?"

"We do you another."

Put the cold mugs on the bar. Held back the pitcher. "What if everything you do sucks?"

As one they wailed, "No! No! You'll love us, we promise."

The same bright one smirked, "You'll love us better the more we drink." He put a dollar down.

Reno was a quick study, peering at the bill as if it were a used Kleenex. "Not a chance."

They put several bills on the bar, inhaled their beers, leaped on the stage, filling it with boy-cheery noise. They banged large metal castanets in what was either a very complicated esoteric rhythm pattern, or none at all. They wandered around passing one another left to right, back to front, droning, chanting, hopping on one leg. Other instruments came out from under their cloaks: odd flutes, a stringed instrument that looked like a zither and cried like a child, small drums, medium drums, huge goat-skin tambourines.

A couple late arrivals grabbed beers, muttered about the tab and rushed to fool with the amplifiers and electric guitars at the back of the stage.

Reno fretted about tips. Swore. She was already getting an attitude about the customers. Men. Arabs. Yuppies. Musicians. Been at work a half hour, had it all figured: work sucked.

Something very like music began to emerge from the chaos, Su'ad came up from the basement smiling and clapping her hands.

"Oh. Hey. Not bad. Makes me want to dance—"

"So go on up there."

"Nah. No room—just look at those lunatics."

They stopped staggering around. "Something just for you, pretty lady." They began again, slowly, as if they were dreaming, light taps on the tiny tom-toms, rain on date palm leaves; then a woodwind began to whisper, each note dropped soft as a feather on top of the gathering rhythms, the tambourine players rattled their drums: "The breath of Allah." They motioned Su'ad on stage.

She hesitated. The drums called. Dum tekka tekka dum chek.

Reno pushed her toward the stage. "Fuck Sinclair tellin' you not to dance. Fuck Farouk—the man ain't even here yet, Su'ad. Go for it. Shit."

Slowmotion cut the boring blue spots, gave the stage the hottest bank of red amber. Su'ad grabbed a long glitter scarf, tied it around her hips, hopped to the stage barefoot, her toes gripping the floor like it was the earth itself, she put her hands on her hips, shimmied her shoulders, a fragile movement, canny, flirtatious.

The sailors put down their beers; greedy-eyed they watched her, trying to calculate how much she charged.

Su'ad smiled at them. A flower opening. Her slim foot lifted, toe-tapped, stepped flat down again; knees bent she stepped to the side, lift tap step, lift tap step, loose, authoritative; the drummers flanked her, the woodwind poised, waiting. She slid her head side to side, smiling; she was comfortable; her belly rippling gently she rocked on her heels to the clear North African rhythms filling up the room, the universe; she seemed to glide across the stage; holding up one hand palm out trembling, as if gathering power from the music; the other hand covered her mouth. She tilted her head back and a wild unearthly trilling, the zaghareet, shrilled like an arrow from her open throat.

She was answered by several voices from the audience; encouraged, Su'ad tipped her pelvis, rolled her shoulders; flipping her long hair in a whipping circle she issued a challenge, a blessing from her heart, her head, her belly—she blessed them all, blessings blessings. See what a woman's body can do.

As if attached by unbreakable lines the men leaned forward, clapping, reaching for a splash of the invisible nectar she dispensed with such liberal hands. One of the Sufis began deep swooping turns; he framed her with the wings of his blue robe, hid her until she exploded free in a whirl of arms. Long legs. Smiles. A mosaic of colors, bodies, shouts.

Reno stamped her feet, forgot where she was, who she was—hell, the boys put on a show like that, they entitled to free beer. All they want.

A small shiny man dazzled his way to the center of the showroom, clapped his fat hands, many rings, some were real—Reno could tell even from that distance. He stopped the performance with his too-much applause.

"Farouk! Faaaabulous Farouk!" Slowmotion's voice held only the minimum of professional approval.

Su'ad bent forward, her hand to her heart, flourishing curves in honor of his arrival, her face down, her lips pinched.

Farouk acknowledged her bow, vaguely, careful, his eyes sharp as shriveled black olives. He was attended by half a dozen lissome female acolytes: two carried his costumes; another had a grocery sack of health food, Cheez Whiz, and taco chips; one short stocky woman seemed to be a bodyguard; another woman was perhaps a chauffeur—black leather and studs.

He directed the procession toward the stairs up to Hunt's apartment.

Reno stopped them at the service door with a cold stare, told them the performer's bathroom was in the basement. "Don't leave none a yer valu-ables around neither."

Nervous titters from the flock of women and a sputtering imperious glare from fabulous Farouk. "Don't you know who I am?"

"You ain't nobody to me, bud."

Icy. "Get out of my way."

"You got five dollars?" Grinning.

Farouk pudgied his way past her. His horrified flock followed on his heels, bustling, rushing up the stairs, peeking furtively over their shoulders at her.

She winked at the black leather and studs one. The woman's

mouth made an unconscious O that set Reno to laughing so hard she got the hiccups. "Buncha fish-faced prudes."

Su'ad unpinched her mouth, smiled, licked her chops. "You're asking for it."

"Never get nothin', ya don't ask."

The Surfing Sufis played a military drum riff, looked around like they wanted another beer break. Slowmotion shook her head no, pounced on the microphone. "All right, ladies and gentlemen. Welcome to the show of shows. Put your hands together for the Stupendous Surfing Sufis."

The boys picked it up, played a steady six-eight, made an untraditional shift to ten-eight, rambled back to six-eight. Lazily spinning at the corner of the stage a tall ascetic fellow in baggy pants and a glitter vest put a tray on his head, bent nearly double, collapsed in a graceful loop to the floor. In the silence that followed, his hand lifted a few inches, shivering. The castanet clackers surrounded him with their metallic cacophony as his body began to ripple, boneless; the tray floated from one part of his anatomy to another as he rolled onto his belly. He was humping the floor, the tray continued to spin, rising and falling as if on wings, or wheels. The drummers formed a line on either side of him, stepping forward with a body wave: shoulders chest belly hips knees, then all together back again: chest belly hips knees, whack! Again. The man, in a shuddering spinning dry-humping frenzy was surrounded by rhythmic blue waves. Hypnotic distortions of bodies in space.

Reno felt a shiver start at the back of her neck.

Eva slithered into the showroom, her bee-sting lips arranged in a greasy pout. She was wearing spandex toreador pants and a tight pink sweater. Nipples. Six-inch pink spike high heels. She stood directly in front of the stage, bouncing those big buns of hers. She tossed a dollar bill to the tray dancer; he didn't even pause in his writhing to acknowledge the gift from the darling little pink beastie, he just rolled over and the bill was gone.

More money appeared, magic, multiplying, it seemed pasted to the sides of a drum, curled at the neck of a blue djellaba, falling in a cascade from the long metal castanets. A Monopoly money stream.

"Ai-wah!" Eva tossed another dollar, faced the crowd with her hands waving above her head, tits aloft. Hopeful.

The Sufis did the now-you-see-it trick, only faster, more dizzying, louder. They ignored Eva.

Exasperated, Eva climbed on stage, put the tray on her own head with a girlish wiggle; shimmying coquettishly she managed to execute a couple simple steps before the tray was snatched back and she was edged off the stage. She stood at the side trying to assure the Sufis that Farouk was an old friend.

Reno muttered out the side of her mouth. "Thought Eva couldn't make it tonight?"

Su'ad curled her lip. "Maybe she already had the baby."

The far end of the bar held a couple street regulars unimpressed with the staged rehash of early-seventies tribal boys-on-a-bender routine. They glowered in true Middle Eastern fashion. "Hey. Play somethin' else. Come on."

The Sufis bowed, they were professionals; with a bright rattle of dumbek and tambourine they slid neatly into a cheerful version of "Selim Selim." Eva tried to lead the audience in the song, but the tray dancer, glaring at her, claimed that privilege for his own. At least he had a nice singing voice.

Eva saw Sinclair come into the room, jiggled her way over to clutch his arm; she had a particularly annoying bruised-flower look about her.

The dope dealers, the society queens, the glitterati vultures, all the specially invited fans of Arabic culture stood around smoking, stepping on one another's toes, spilling their drinks, mouthing unintelligible syllables. Feeling cool. Not tipping.

Eddie emerged from the basement, small bandage on his cheek, muttered about the way the bar was set up, growling because Reno hadn't put any money aside. "How we gonna make it through the night if we don't got the wherewithal to score the you-know-what? Never think. You women never think." The glue-crashing blues.

"They ain't comin' across with no wherewithal tonight."

"Got to know how to handle 'em, Reno." Condescending. "Just got to have the right attitude."

"I got the right attitude, Eddie." Reno walked away, leaving him to deal with the bar himself, he think he so sharp. She told one arrogant fool who accosted her for a refill: "Small tips are no way to get a free round." He had cocaine powdering his nostrils. She took it as a personal affront.

The fellow, more cash than brains, tweaked, "Oh, I can pay for it."

"Yeah, but I can't deliver it without you tip me first." Reno figured subtle was no good; outright extortion seemed necessary for these hambones.

His droopy doper mouth dropped open, his hand fumbled to his wallet. Retreated. He frowned, unsure of himself. He didn't think that was the way these transactions went.

Reno left him to figure it out—he'd come around when he got thirsty.

The tall thin fellow slipped back into the club; subdued and sly-eyed, he cozied up to the far end of the bar. Put a twenty down. His raspy voice mentioned to no one in particular that his "Uncle Harry back in town." Directly to Reno. "I took care of my business in spite of yer unhospitable attitude." He nodded, pleased with something. Big breath. "Now bring me a beer an' tell me where I can find Eddie."

Eddie jerked slightly, his sad eyes lit up; a carefully choreographed unconcerned mosey down to that end of the bar brought him close enough to check out the thin man: not young, just pickled, his skin unwrinkled—fat with junk molecules. It's a cellular thing, right down to the DNA, a fountain of youth and good humor. Until things go wrong of course, then it's instant Methuselah. Eddie noticed the man's hand shook as he played with the twenty on the bar.

Eddie drawled, "I been known to know Harry. Haven't seen 'im in a long time though." Casual.

The silly rituals of the secret brotherhood. Dope kinship. What a crock. Eye to dilated eye, they measured each other's credentials in silence.

"Hey. How about another beer over here?"

Eddie didn't look up, his manhood riding on maintaining eye contact. "In a minute pal. I got someone aheada ya."

Reno got the beer. Another quarter tip. Went back to Slow-motion's end of the bar, four quarters in her palm. "Hey, with money flowing like this I can retire in another hour."

The skinny man broke eye contact, muttering things about brotherhood. Sharing. Honor. Mister Huntington. "Being there." Eddie muttered the proper responses. Small smiles all around. The thin man shoved the twenty at Eddie, moved slowly away from his new friend, coughing and shaking his shoulders. "Hunt says yer a good man so I'll see you later bro."

Eddie was happy: hope springs eternal, once again there was the possibility of bliss. He practically danced on his way to take care of his thirsty customers. His life had purpose, his smile had grease: he'd bring a sparkle to those flat gleamy barfly eyes, silence those great wet complaining mouths. Fish. He sighed a superior sigh, pulled a series of draft beers, spun around, slid them down the bar. One two three. "Comin' atcha." Snatched up the couple dollars on the bar. Put them in his pocket. He'd earned it.

"Now we cookin'." Into overdrive, all smooth practical motion, spinning, bopping, grinning, Eddie banged the cash register just to emphasize his terrific sense of rhythm. "Keep 'em comin'. Oh yeah. Allll right." Boom a whocka. Down the bar. Zip-po. Rocket money.

Reno approached a table of rich smooth handsome men, crisp white shirts, dark glasses. They ordered scotch, smoked Camels, tipped small. "Ah Sidi," she said, "such a little tip for so much service?" She was thinking about the twenty Eddie had just received.

"More later. You'll get more later."

Reno fingered the fifty-cent tip. "For those of us who live entirely in the present it is so often the case that later never comes." She moved in front of the table to block their view of the stage.

They didn't mind. They ignored her, tallying up the crowd, talking in Arabic, trading secrets of the Sphinx and Cheops.

Reno walked away. "Die of thirst in deserts of your own making." She was still wondering about the twenty.

"Not much luck, huh?" Slowmotion sounded sympathetic.

"Screw them."

"Listen, Reno, these guys aren't oil sheiks—those men spent all day humping boxes of canned soup off trucks for the corner grocery."

"Oughta have some compassion for a fellow wage slave." Her lips pursed. "For sure oughta tip better than that."

"Ever occur to you they can't afford to tip better?"

"Then they should stay home." Reno's mouth turned down. "Play checkers." She flicked her fingernail against the rim of a wine glass in irritation, picked it up, put it down. "What's the deal with that junkie?"

"Doesn't pay to examine Hunt's business too closely."

"If I don't examine it, do I collect a twenty?"

No answer.

Su'ad sashayed past, a superior smile. "Told you you wouldn't like it here."

Reno didn't even blink, just reached under the bar for the bottle of scotch.

Eddie came over, "Take it easy Reno, there's another show after this one."

"Oh boy." She walked away, drinking.

He turned his eager calculating face to Slowmotion. "What you think we bring in tonight, Slowmotion? Couple grand?"

"Maybe." She measured out the two syllables like she was weighing out gold. Or heroin.

"What say we don't deposit it directly? I gotta way to turn it over a couple times before tomorrow."

Slowmotion nodded her head up and down once. "Eddie," she smiled, "that's stealing."

"No, man. It's borrowing."

Reno listened. Twirled her empty tray on her extended middle finger, glared at the money-covered men on stage. She had ten dollars in tips. That, plus the hourly five didn't add up to Monday's rent. Didn't even add up to food for the weekend. Nobody should work so hard for so little reward.

chapter nine

Nothing ever slid into the smooth groove.

Club Istanbul was a horrible bar filled with sleazy creeps: arrogant no-talent dancers, lazy money-grubbing musicians, a bunch of doped-up employees busy stealing everything not nailed down. No-class customers who wanted to hang out and drink for free. No surprise the club was still in the red. Even if (Sinclair searched for the smallest glitter of hope) it was less in the red than when Omar ran it, he didn't want any part of it.

Sinclair sat in his closet-sized office, thought about a job at a bank, a gas station, maybe he could get work as a garbage man. No more touchy dancers or snooty customers. Hell, everybody's garbage stank the same.

He fingered the club's liquor license. Registered in his proper name: Mugurditch Soghomonian. It was a great, an honorable name. He needed to spell it for the clerk at city hall three times. Another reason why he never used it—spell it?—hell, no one bothered to learn to say it. He couldn't re-member when he gave it up, settled on Sinclair. In any case, here he was, Sinclair: an upper-class white-boy kind of name, a black satin jacket, fancy embroidery on the back, silk shirt, blue-dyed lambskin boots kind of name. Surrounded by racked bottles of fine wine, to his left a shelf held impressive books in French and English, and casually displayed on top of a neat pair of oak filing cabinets was the OED. His soul was not soothed by these artifacts from his intellectual front.

Sinclair propped his head on his hands at his real antique bleached-oak desk, ignored the blinking lights on the three-line designer phone at his elbow, ignored the small pouches of medicinal substances on either side of his arms. He groaned. Wished he was somewhere, someone, else.

If everything went smoothly over the weekend they might pull marginally into the black. But everything wasn't going smoothly. It never did.

Wasn't his fault. He'd been dealt another bad hand.

Sinclair sighed as Hunt's voice shrilled through the common wall the office shared with Hunt's flat.

"Keep your silly women out of my house, Farouk. What is it with you? I didn't expect the muffin man and his harem, for Christ's sake. You're fat, you're sweating rivers. Are you sick?"

The question carried the swallowed terror that always touched Hunt's voice when he dealt with disease. Any disease. That disease. The terror of AIDS in the arts community had kept Hunt celibate for several years. In the middle of tragedy there was that much at least for which to be grateful.

"I'm fine, Hunt." Farouk's well-fed voice held a trace of derision. "What's the real problem?" He cut Hunt's response off with a mean snicker. "Haven't got laid since my sister died, uh sweetie? Is that it?" Another calculated pause. "People your age shouldn't even want to."

Hunt's voice was sharp with a deadly edge. "I made some promises to get you this gig. You could show a little restraint if not gratitude. Or you gonna cancel again?" Hunt hissed. "Were the New York reviewers right—you too fucked up to dance?"

"Damn you, Hunt. You worried you won't get your cut?"

Farouk didn't hide the venom. "I don't have AIDS. The New York papers are hardly a reliable source—they mention me because I make their papers worth reading. Examine your own conduct, you greasy old hairball."

Hunt spoke in short panting breaths, a vicious smile in the words; his voice didn't waver, shaved ice pleasure. "Want publicity? I'll give you publicity in headline-size type: 'IS FABULOUS FAROUK, EGYPTIAN LOVE GOD, FALTERING?' Smaller type, but not too small: 'Unable to dance because of failing health, drug problems.' Easy to continue, how about: 'Showing criminal disregard in his mad search for solace he's infected multitudes with an undetermined virus.'" Hunt's creamy laugh boomed out. "You know how it goes. The world loves perversion."

There was the heavy sound of furniture toppling, a sharper noise, maybe a vase smashing. Hunt's laughter. "In all its myriad guises." Another pause. "Oh, get up. We could start booking you into porno palaces? Probably bring in more money."

A knock on Hunt's door. Eva's trilling voice: "Hel-lo boys. Don't let me interrupt."

Sinclair would have pulled his hair out in handfuls if he hadn't already shaved it off, another gambling debt. One long finger rotated the skin on his temple, the little muscles in his jaw jumped as his strong teeth ground slowly against one another. He wondered if Farouk would make it on stage at all. He tugged at his ear, reached for a cigarette, pulled his hand back, twitched it forward with an effort and grabbed the Camel unfiltered, lit up.

Deceit had never been Sinclair's strong point. That might be why he made such a mediocre gambler. He liked honest confrontations, the whole dramatic scene, shouting, arm waving, delirious frenzy—these things were familiar to Sinclair from the households of his youth. He enjoyed loud arguments, especially if they weren't about anything important; he seldom caught the urgency, or the lack of pleasure, in other people's raised voices. He never recognized the real pain, the under-currents. The danger.

Eva would be upset if she knew he was smoking again—that's why, he told himself, he only smoked in his private office. Eva seemed especially sensitive to his minor sins of all kinds lately. Maybe she was pregnant. He inhaled, dubious, he always used condoms. Perhaps, he told himself, it was the chance of working in a theater that put her so much on edge. Hell, the girl had to score somewhere soon—she wasn't getting any younger. Or thinner. 'Course, Sinclair rubbed his jaw, he liked big women. He liked women. Period. He just didn't like them to con him.

He stood up, intending to go next door. Something else crashed. Eva's giggle penetrated the connecting wall.

Sinclair shrugged. Maybe not. He heard Hunt shout, "Don't bump the mirror you clumsy bitch!"

Sinclair went downstairs to the showroom. "Where's Eddie?" He fixed Reno with a red-rimmed glare.

"Don't know." Singsong. "Eva went upstairs—didn't even offer to help us out."

Severe. "She tell you guys how the callback went?"

Slowmotion picked it up, nasty as a razor. "Nope. But after the Sufis pushed her off the stage for the second time she landed in that fat cop's lap over there." She pointed with her chin. "Claimed to be 'with child.'"

"Abused dancer finds true love in the lap of off-duty cop."

"She always said she wanted to make the Sunday papers."

"Anything to advance little Eva's ca-reer." Sneer.

Sinclair's jaw muscle began jumping again. "Come on you guys. Cut it out. Didn't she say anything about the play, really?"

"Didn't mention it."

"Get real, Sinclair. That whole thing something she made up." Low and mean. Slowmotion smiled to herself as she changed the lights to the bilious green she seemed to favor whenever she wanted to make people look awful. "She makes up things, you know?"

Sly. Slip it, bitches, slip the little silver knives up up between the ribs, peel the skin back, cut off a chunk of his heart.

Sinclair spoke through his big white teeth, his eyes gleamed red. "Shit." He walked to the side of the room. "Su'ad. Come over here." Nothing gentle in the tone.

Su'ad meandered over, looking at him from the side, dancer drama, innocence in every studied motion.

"Fabulous Farouk was not pleased to make his grand entrance only to be upstaged by you doing the shikhat."

Her whole body formed a big "so-what," her shoulders moved in a circle. "Shoulda seen Eva up there then. That would've delighted him for sure."

"What were you thinking of? You got to think what's good for the club. Got to put the club first."

She stared goggle-eyed at the rotating mirror ball on the ceiling, lips pulled forward in a silent whistle.

"Come on, Su'ad, use your head."

Su'ad waved a cigarette, Slowmotion leaned forward, lit it; Su'ad radiated in the reflected light, flames in her eyes, a little medieval spontaneous combustion right there at the bar of the Istanbul. Sinclair shivered in unconscious envy as Su'ad inhaled. Smiling a little she sucked on it longer, slow, deliberate. Exhaled two streams of dragon steam.

Reno positioned herself near the cash register. Never know when it might need to be emptied because of an administrative riot.

Sinclair was master enough of the subtle move to maneuver Su'ad back into the stairwell. He closed the door to the showroom in case they needed to yell. "Listen—"

Right then Farouk's hot-oil voice poured from the upper landing. "And if that high yaller bitch of yours gets on my stage again you can bet your ass that someone will pay. It's in my contract. Someone will pay. You can bank on it, Hunt."

Eva's giggle was a tinny counterpoint to his words.

Su'ad started up the stairs. "High yaller my twat."

Sinclair, frantic, grabbed her. "Oh, shit, Su'ad, don't do that. I'll make it up to you." He pulled her back into the showroom. "Honest."

"You and who else?"

"C'mon Su'ad." He was sweating.

She jerked her arm free. "You best go tell that fat queen to watch his mouth or he'll hafta buy himself a whole new set of teeth."

chapter ten

A long the perimeter of the showroom Farouk's simpering fan club swayed to the music, clapping softly in unison. Calling the rhythm changes in feline tones: "Wahadeh. *Dum* tekka tekka tekka tekka *teka.*" All together they swiveled to the left, right hip drop. Clap hands.

Fabulous Farouk, imperial in black and gold, strutted around the stage with his arms raised, his fingers spread. The band formed a military half-square around his pudgy figure, their worshipful eyes never leaving his undulating form.

Reno's voice rang out again. "What's he gonna do now? Bless us?"

"Shhh. Shhh."

"Fuck you." Reno hadn't stopped serving drinks in hours. Her feet hurt all the way up to her armpits; even her mind, what there was left of it, hurt.

Farouk, balancing delicately on his small feet, performed some complicated steps, a couple wide-armed pirouettes; mincing backward he lifted his chin with a small smile as if pleading for approval; sly, flirtatious, slippery, he waited near the rear of the stage for the audience to beg him to come

76

forward again. His cat women obliged. On a rush of musical energy he thrust himself to the front, a bold man conquering every willing heart. He posed, flamenco arrogant, filled with blood lust, cocksure.

As the image of a frowsy fat queen fell away, he gave his audience a glimpse of that cold power that had earlier in his career won him such praise.

Too little too late for Reno. She grunted. "Cheap-ass audience—breathe in the smell of artistic sweat, breathe out nickels and dimes. Nickels and dimes."

An impatient woman dressed in a professionally ripped eight-hundred-dollar dress waved a taloned hand at Reno.

"Kiss my twat." Reno said it twice to make sure the woman understood; went behind the bar, poured her ownself a big scotch. "Gonna dress like that, should be kinder to the servants." Reno headed for the stairwell sanctuary, muttering, "Think she's better'n me just because she some kinda oil-rich A-rab."

The alley doors were open to the winter night, rain spattering into a pool of greasy light. Su'ad spoke without turning. "She just a housewife from the 'burbs. Works as a legal secretary, left the husband home with the kids, come out here looking for ro-mance." Su'ad leaned against the wall; pain and exhaustion on her face, she spoke through tight lips. "Even when it's good it's bad. They wanta go someplace nice, get a dose of culture, maybe get laid. End up with a dose of somethin' else. Exotic." Anger flaming the edges of her words as she lit a cigarette. "Everyone wants what they ain't got. Fuckheads."

"You sounding like me." Reno sat on the steps, stared at the dusty shoes encasing her brutalized feet. "Not good."

"Cocktailing is the worst." Long drag. "It adds up to getting fucked, Reno. No matter what you do. Fucked. Don't tell me I didn't warn you." Su'ad's voice oozed bitter satisfaction.

"Yo Su'ad." A big swallow. "That's why they call it work."

If it wasn't fucked they'd call it fun. Or crime." Reno waved her glass in a cheerful fashion, comrade to comrade.

"Oh, Reno, shut up."

Reno lifted an eyebrow.

Su'ad continued. "Assholes worship they own pricks, want nothing more than a warm clean hole to shove it into. I hustle my butt around here every night of the week, people care bloody less if I'm a dancer or a whore."

It was difficult to carry on a conversation with Su'ad when she was like that. "What's the problem, Su'ad, long as you get paid? Hey, think of the untalented multitudes of us who like to watch." Reno didn't understand Su'ad's attitude. "After all, it's not like this really is the magical Middle East. Hell, the Middle East isn't even magical anymore." Swallow. "If it ever was." Second swallow, quick on top of the first. "So it's all pretense. So what." Swallow. "Makes you wonder." Reno put her glass down, ran her fingers through her sweat-tangled hair. "Fantasy works good long as there's enough shiny flesh. Come on." Finger raised. "Problem ain't art *or* whores. Problem is these folks don't tip worth shit. There's the problem."

Su'ad glared out of the corners of her eyes, muttered. "People just wanta see cheerleaders falling out of their bras up there."

"Sounds good to me."

"Oh, Reno, shut up."

Sinclair attempted to tiptoe behind them, invisible.

Su'ad ripped the headscarf off her head, threw it at his retreating back, hollering, "First time in months there's a crowd in here. High-energy music instead of those lazy sleep-walkers you're so tight with. You a sorry prick, Sinclair. You getting sucked off by that pisshead or what's the story?" Her voice slipped up a notch. "All you A-rab cocksuckers got some kinda cul-tural affinity, what it is, man." A vicious harpy, claws unsheathed, hair writhing around her shaking figure in great cascades. Hecate herself. "The great A-rab brotherhood. Too stressed out about their manhood to let a woman dance."

Sinclair hesitated, his back to her. Continued up the stairs. "Mujahedin takin' over, Su'ad? Western Wahabi botherin' you? The PLO here again?" He growled to himself: "Brother-hood. My ass. Skin members of they own family alive if there be an advantage." It had seemed like such a good idea to hire Farouk when Hunt brought it up: bring in a classy crowd, unify the community; he shoulda known better. "Hey, you don't like it here, Su'ad, go work somewhere else "

"Fuck you, Sinclair. Fuck you! I gotta job here you god-damn bald-head freak, I gotta good job, and nobody's gonna take it away from me, not you, not that strutting maggot on stage!"

Su'ad had a strange perspective about loving her work.

"Good. Good. Then do your job, get back out there. Hustle drinks." He sounded like he was smiling.

Su'ad made an inarticulate strangling sound, started up the stairs after him.

Reno flicked out a professional hand, tagged Su'ad's leg as she went past.

Su'ad flopped down on the steps. "That asshole promised Farouk that the local female talent—that's me—wouldn't set foot on stage. It's the most fucked thing I ever heard of."

"Didn't realize you led such a sheltered life."

"Shut up, Reno."

Reno tried to remember how much she had to drink. Couldn't. Probably should stop. Couldn't see why. She sighed. How little the free world resembled her memories of it. "Seems to me that Hunt's the one did the promising."

"What you still doing here anyway, Reno? I thought you would have pocketed a small fortune already."

There was something between them, an anger in the not-quite silence when words didn't fill the space.

Reno tried to be discreet. "Told you I wasn't gonna rip off the club." A small sip of scotch. Nice: "Want me to get you a soda?"

Su'ad shook her head. "Sodas make me sick." Glum.

Reno tried to stare deeply and sincerely into Su'ad's eyes, missed by a quarter inch. Left her focus on automatic, put the sincerity into her voice. "I'm not really interested in ripping off the club. What I really need is some plastic." Hint.

"It was important for me to dance tonight. Open a whole new world to me. Those tight wads out there," rude thumb, "are the ones who set up shows, choose dancers to showcase at small halls. Concerts, performances in good clubs, other cities, parties paying hundreds of dollars. It's the opportunity I've been hoping for." The lines in her face seemed harsher. "The future ain't so far in the future anymore, you know what I mean?"

"Why you dancing here anyway? I mean, why not go in for something else—musicals? Something? Like Eva?"

"Eva's full of shit. She's a good dancer, but not very inspiring, you know?"

"What about—what about—" Reno reached into the depths of her television viewing—"the Opera Corps de ballet?" She said it *corpse*.

"Eva didn't get no callback for no part." Su'ad stared at the floor. "She's playing Sinclair for the fool, trying to get Hunt to set her up at the same time." Shake of her head, hair jumping like electricity.

"So what's the old man doing for you?"

"Not old." Defensive. "He's offered to do a lot of stuff for me."

"Like what?"

Su'ad stretched but it didn't revitalize her. "Says it takes time." Direct. "Okay. I've come right out, asked him for help." Shaky sigh. "He got angry." Su'ad moved away from Reno. "Said he didn't want to be pressured." The conversation was over.

"Well what's the problem? Nothin' about you bein' a high yaller, huh?"

"Reno, I'm no more color than you are—alls I fucking know about Indians is what I read in school." Grumbling.

"What you want then?"

Su'ad took a deep breath. "I want to be a good little bourgeois. Before there's no middle class left." She turned her sharp glare on Reno. "I want my cut, goddamnit."

"This is the way you're going about it?" Reno waved in a general way at the showroom.

Su'ad grabbed Reno's hand, pointed it at the ceiling, indicating either some sky god or the unhelpful Mr. Huntington. "I got plans."

Reno frowned at the other woman. "Bein' Indian is something to be proud of."

"What you know about it?" Su'ad stood up, jiggled her ass, left hip, right hip. "Nobody likes us. We make people uncomfortable. Either they feel superior, call us lazy animals, drunken savages, or they feel sorry for us, wrinkle up they faces like they be constipated." Shrug. "I don't give a shit for their pity." Flames. "What's worse is those bastards who hear I'm Indin, say wull whyn't ya dance Indin-style." Anger rising as her voice shifted lower. "I don't know any Indian dances and even if I did it wouldn't put food on my table." Hands on her hips. "What good it do me? You tell me that. Hah."

"What about pride and self-respect. Honor?"

Walking away into the alley. "Them ten-dollar words can't beat cold cash."

Slowmotion filled the doorway. "Ah. Fresh air. Sweet Jesus." She tipped her head back, opened her mouth to the rain. "That putrid sack of pus on stage drivin' me nuts." Her extra-large sweatsuit trembled with private mirth. "Hey, yer a cheery lot. Well. Stop whatever you be doin'. I been thinking. You guys will love this. We bound to make a pile a money."

Reno held her breath, waited for Slowmotion to say Eddie planned to double his income with the bar's cash and Hunt's pet junkie. Su'ad would never believe it wasn't Reno's idea. An ugly destiny tap tap tapped at Reno's shoulder.

"We need to take the initiative back from Hunt. Teach

him a lesson. The club's dark on Mondays. Why not open it ourselves?"

Su'ad snapped. "And do what? Comedy? It's been done. It's embarrassing."

"Comedy? Embarrassing?"

"Yeah, people standing up there ripping open they souls, saying it's a joke. Makes me sad."

Reno had a feeling they'd had this conversation before.

"Nah." Slowmotion leered happily. "You be the barker. Who could resist?" Her pudgy hands made a wavy curvaceous outline in the air. "We put a new twist on 'talk to a naked girl.' Girls stay clothed, customers strip, Reno here steals their clothes, wallets. Good huh?"

Su'ad started to smile, very small. "Why you always come up with stuff like that? Doesn't have to be that way."

"What? You wanna do some artsy peep-show thing again?"

"No. No." Su'ad's eyes got dreamy. "We could rename the club 'The Hammam,' you know, 'The Baths.' We'd have exotic dancers, classy strippers. Professional Middle Eastern dancers. Us. Live music." Su'ad smiled, with a glance up the empty stairs. "Women only."

"Oh great." Reno was too familiar with women-only scenes. "They'll want child care, you know. And have meetings. Lots of meetings. Then, of course, there's the huge monetary resources of dykes and single mothers we can tap into."

"Shut up, Reno."

Like the Royal's phony Hindu with his mantras, perhaps Su'ad found some spiritual comfort in the repetitive phrase.

Reno tried to move her various body parts; her lower back felt like it had been welded together—she'd never be able to fuck even if the opportunity arose. One night's work crippled her; soon she would be tossed on the streets like yesterday's garbage to sniffle in the icy cold. She leaned against the wall and croaked. "Doom."

"Oh, shut up, Reno."

Reno closed her hand on eighteen dollars in tips, nearly all of it in quarters. She didn't put any warmth in her voice, let it slide out dead ugly. "You know what you can do with your attitude, Su'ad." Pause. "Die."

Su'ad put her face in her hands. The woman knew from Drama. "Sorry." She tugged at her hair. "Sorry sorry sorry." She rearranged her face, her voice, looked around the stairwell for her head scarf. "Oh, Reno, I'm sorry."

"That's better. Even if you don't look sorry."

Slowmotion said, "Well, think about Mondays."

"Women only. Ha." Reno made an ungraceful snorting noise in the back of her nose. Another one of her talents.

"Reno, that's disgusting." Su'ad frowned and smiled all at once.

Slowmotion continued her pitch. "If it ain't Mondays, it got to be somethin' else. The man needs to rediscover who's boss around here."

"Yeah. Right." Reno didn't know what she was agreeing to.

There was no music. The customers were stretching their legs, looking for a waitress, the Sufis were crowding around the bar looking for a drink. Farouk, charming as a python with a mouse in its belly, dripped sweat on everyone from his position on stage as he looked for his entourage (who were looking for the bathroom).

Eddie stared woodenly into the sink, didn't raise his head as they approached. "Hi there folks. I just broke a glass in the ice."

"Oh shit. Whyn't you call one of us? You ain't been servin' it have you?"

He looked up, dreamy-eyed. "Well, not to anyone we know."

chapter eleven

Slowmotion put on a tape of Algerian rai music. Ghetto rock and roll. "Chaba Zahouania. 'Nights Without Sleeping.' " Her voice held promises. "Nights without sleeping. I can dig it."

Farouk frowned.

"Hey, Slow, that's allll right." First time Eddie approved. "Not Sinatra, but not bad." He poured boiling water in the ice sink. Watched the ice tremble and disappear. No pieces of glass surfaced. "Maybe I just imagined I broke it?"

Slowmotion turned Chaba Zahouania up. Closed her eyes.

Farouk's thin scimitar mouth curving down, his stomach pulled in and up so it transformed itself into a semblance of chest, he started to come over to the sound booth but Eva moved to intercept him.

She patted him on his arms and shoulders with her little delicate hands. Cooing.

Hunt sidled up to Su'ad, thigh to hip, real tight. "I'm sure Farouk meant no harm, Su'ad." His eyes floated over her body. Gloating.

Su'ad leaned into Hunt, pliant as ivy. Hunt smirked with pleasure. He ran his hands along the edge of his belt, carefully put one hand on each of her hips. Su'ad shifted her weight. Left. Right. Smooth as a cash register.

Shoving off into the crowd, Reno hollered, "Drink or Die." Poured some ice water down an obnoxious woman's silky back. Reno wished, without knowing she wished it, just for a moment, that she could play the game as well as Su'ad. Couldn't imagine how they'd stayed friends for so long, Reno herself being honest and straightforward as an angel.

"So, enjoying yourself?" Eddie nuzzled Reno on her shoulder, oddly cheerful.

"Oh hell." Reno figured he was maneuvering himself into scoring position; she didn't see why she should care. "Fuck you, Eddie."

He planted a kiss on her cheek.

She ignored him.

Sinclair interrupted. "Hunt's going to give a party after to-morrow night's show." Undercurrents in his voice.

Hunt fancy-stepped in their direction, Su'ad pouting by his side. "It'd be the perfect thing for you all to come."

Su'ad's lips turned up a quarter inch at each corner.

Hunt purred, "I'd be so grateful for your help."

Liar. The man hadn't been grateful since birth.

Eddie made a rude noise at the back of his throat, even better than Reno's. "Grateful. My dick. Fuckin' sold myself into bondage that's what I done." He clattered away down the metal stairs.

"Eddie knows I couldn't do it without you." Hunt's limp hand addressed and dismissed them with a small curling wave. He wafted away, his voice drifting back like the scent of expensive cologne. "You know how it is. I need someone to hostess, to serve the liquor, take care of the buffet, keep the guests happy. Five bucks an hour. Good, huh?"

"Eight." Reno didn't stop to think. Hunt's shoulders twitched as she called out to him. "Or you can do it yourself, Mis-ter Hunting-ton." What the hell. Arrogant bastard.

Sinclair hid his face, might have been laughing.

Hunt hardly paused. "Seven it is then." Hearty, heigh-ho and away, through the crowd like a ship under sail, off to try his charm on Slowmotion. He used a conspiratorial tone. "You'll provide something more aromatic than oregano, eh Slowmotion?"

Slowmotion didn't glance up. "Eight bucks an hour for each of us. You're getting a real deal. Talk to me about the other shit later, Hunt." She changed the tape, finally looked at him. "You know nothing aromatic comes cheap. Now get away from here 'cause it's time ta play you bet ya life."

She punched up the stage lights; her voice dropped a little, thickened, rich with sarcasm, oozing over the sound system. "Let's hear a big welcome back for everybody's favorite band: those marvelous Beach Boys from Beirut! The Surfin' Sufis! Annnnd the Big Kahuna! Yes folks. The Big Kahuna! Tonight right here on this stage! The Fabulous Farouk and his bouncing bundles of joy boys!" She sucked on a cigarette. "Fabulous Farouk! Put your hands together, ladies and gentlemen. Let's hear it for Farouk and his joy boys."

The applause was strong, ready, wasted, eager. It was only the workers that were left out in terms of a properly festive attitude: the goddamn stiffs wouldn't get up offa their goddamn wallets.

Su'ad wrapped a possessive arm around Hunt, her charm burning like acetylene. Her voice dropped an octave. "A party, how sweet. And I'll dance." Hunt looked vague, irritated. Su'ad reached over the bar, poured him a Johnnie Walker Black. She never stopped moving, rubbing against his arm, his shoulder, his hip. If you got it, use it. The full frontal flashing-eyes treatment. "My usual rate for dancing at a private party is sixty dollars for a fifteen-minute show, Hunt." Her lips got warm and full. "For you I would do it for free, but I know you wouldn't want me to drop my professional standards."

Hunt continued to clear his throat, cough into his hand. Avoid her eyes.

"So, for you it's forty-five. A good deal." Clinging to his

arm, bending her knees so she didn't loom too far above him Su'ad took him away from the bar crowd. "A great deal."

Hunt looked shaken, but taken. Murmured something about he'd have to discuss it with Sinclair. With Farouk. After all it was a party for Farouk.

Su'ad leaned away, one of her warm hands lingering on his arm, she seemed reluctant to leave him. "Ah. Well. If you need Farouk's permission to put on parties now Hunt, you can count us out."

"Well done. Leave me out." Reno was all for that. She wondered if the old pervert knew what a pro Su'ad was. One of the best. A little thick about men, but one of the best.

A dozen expressions zipped across Hunt's bland, sophisticated mug before he caved in to Su'ad's ministrations. "Of course, of course."

Eva bustled between them then, chattering. "Come on over here, Hunt."

Su'ad clung to Hunt, her long body in her little black dress sending sparks directly at his crotch.

Hunt, shifting his weight, uncertain, grinned. Ran his hand down the front of his suit jacket as if he wanted to make sure his fly was zipped.

Eva's voice was thin, unhealthy. "Come on. We have so much to talk about."

She took Hunt's other arm; Su'ad didn't let go of the one she had. They each tugged.

Reno had never seen anyone torn asunder but she was up for it. Couldn't explain these sudden urges. Didn't fight them either.

Su'ad smiled. Tight. Her eyes blinked once at Eva, slow. Die bitch die. Smiling, graceful, effortless as a swan, Su'ad let go and floated to the far side of the showroom. Hunt followed her.

Reno whistled. "Whatever she has, I want it."

Eva gave her the up and down. "Forget it."

Eddie came up behind them. "Beat it, Eva, you stink like

a cow." He smiled at Reno. "You don't need to be like Su'ad; she's too tall anyway. You got other qualities." He nodded. Reno looked blank. He continued, jovial. "What say, Reno. Take the edge off the night?" He was an eager one. "Met a man earlier this evening. A direct line to some ver' nice her-on."

Slowmotion hooted. "I seen you tryin' to score, now, all of a sudden Hunt's junkie comes in, you drop right into the pocket. Didja already give 'im money to score for you?" Hooting again. "Good luck. You be sniffin' glue for all eternity you keep tryin' to deal with Hunt's people."

"Hey. Wasn't talkin' to you." Injured dignity. Eddie fingered the forty dollars in his pocket. He'd show Slowmotion. He'd show all of them just who he knew, what he could do. He squared his shoulders. "Later for y'all." He went out into the night looking very young.

Soon after that Sinclair bundled up a disgruntled Eva, told Slowmotion to watch the setup. "Gonna give Eva a lift home, she's not feelin' too well."

Reno said that she wasn't lookin' too good neither.

When Eddie hadn't returned by last call Reno and Su'ad shut the bar down; they vacuumed the pockets of the last customers as Slowmotion forced them out into the street with a loud rendition of "Shittin' on the Dock of the Bay" by Loydie and the Low Bites. Su'ad stuffed some money in the mutual tip jar, poured unblended scotch into a tumbler; swaying her hips in a practical manner she carried the scotch up the stairs to Hunt's flat.

Reno had serious doubts about Su'ad's celibacy.

Slowmotion counted out the register, fingers flashing as wet crumpled paper money piled up by the hundreds.

Reno washed up the last of the glasses, put her head down. "Gone sleep right here, that way I already be here when it come time to work tomorrow night. No interim nonsense about living. Never make enough to pay the week's rent anyway; lucky I got me a job at a place with a nice soft bar."

Reno stretched her arms out, rubbed them around the surface. "Nice. Soft. Bar."

She had twenty-three dollars in tips, part of that was for Eddie; Reno peeled off five ones, put them on the bar. "Here, Eddie, grab it while it's hot."

He wasn't there to hear or pick it up.

"Too . . . bad . . . sweet . . . heart . . . Another time perhaps?" She spoke to air, put the cash back in her own pocket, thoughts all twos and threes. Graft. This petty plodding was no way to live.

Slowmotion scooped the cash out of the drawer, tapped it together with one chubby finger, palmed it. She filled out the bank-deposit envelope. "Wanta come with me to a friend's house, Reno? Got some people just dyin' to meetcha."

Reno opened one eye, itchy, sawdust must have gotten under the lid. Closed it again. "Can't be. They don't know who I am."

"They still be glad to meetcha."

"Okay. Sure thing, Slowmotion. I'll follow you anywhere." Somebody, Reno figured, had to know what they were doing.

Su'ad came downstairs, her mouth twitching with secret pleasure. She tapped Reno on her shoulder. "Hey you there, glued to the bar—had enough? How about I lend you some money, see you through till you get yourself a real job?"

Reno didn't lift her head, her cheek flapped on the bar as she spoke. "Got a couple grand stashed for me?"

"Well, no, I was thinking maybe fifty—"

"Won't even pay my rent."

"Shit girl, you need more 'n that, you ain't gone get it here."

chapter twelve

Slowmotion whistled for a cab. "Where the fuck do they all go at closing time?"

Reno had one eye closed, touched her nose with her index finger. "Couldn' tellya." She counted up the nights' drinks, without success; it was a series without end, an infinity of booze. She couldn't decide if that was a good thing. Or not.

Two big fellows driving a clean late-model Ford braked to a neat stop at Slowmotion's knees. The passenger-side window rolled down. "Hey, where ya goin'? Wanta lift?"

Slowmotion hopped back on the sidewalk, prim. "Buzz off."

The man's unfriendly eyes had a shine as smooth as two freshly shelled clams. "Hey, big girl, you wouldn't know where we could get some action?"

"Nope."

He got out of the car. "Mind stepping over here, showing some identification?"

Reno concentrated on her breathing. In. Out. Every waking nightmare. Her hand crept toward her pocket, her fake driver's license; she moved her thick tongue along the backs of her teeth, tasted arsenic, aluminum. Breathe, girl, breathe. In.

Out. The muscles in her legs jumped as if she were running but her feet stuck to the pavement.

Slowmotion didn't even shift her weight. Solid. "Yeah, I mind. What the hell for? Who're you?"

He took her arm. "I'm Officer O'Malley, vice detail."

"Get away from me." Twisting free with an unladylike jerk.

The clam-eyed man stepped toward Slowmotion as if to make another grab.

Reno took her courage in her mouth. "You don't have no cause to be hasslin' us." Her voice sounded firm. Brassy.

The driver lit a cigarette, smiled to himself. The flare of the match didn't illuminate much, but Reno could see that there wasn't any cop radio or miscellaneous cop paraphernalia in the car. A bottle of Early Times, some beer cans, fast-food wrappers.

The man on the sidewalk wore old ripped-up sneakers, sagging tan slacks, a mustard-stained T-shirt. He said, "We'll just have to take you down to the station." This time he didn't quite reach out his hand, but his mouth shaped the words in a mean hungry manner.

"Station? What, the gas station?" Reno stepped to the left forcing the man to put his back toward Slowmotion.

Slow gave that grin, a cross between a chipmunk and a ghoul, lowered one heavy eyelid. She gripped her shoulder sack by the leather strap, let it swing. "Best put your funky ass back in yo' car b'fore we call a real cop."

Reno felt her stomach quiver, allllright. She rocked on her toes. Light. She wasn't much of a dancer, but as a boxer she knew she did just fine. A left anda right anda quick jab to the nose. She coulda bin a contender.

The man seemed undecided until the driver leaned over, opened the passenger-side door. "Come on, man, these two probably got razors in their cunts anyway." He popped the clutch, they smoked up the street.

"Don't know if that was a compliment or not." Slowmotion shrugged. "Most likely not."

"Hope they got some full-body condoms, tryin' so hard to get laid." Talk's cheap: Reno hadn't seen a condom up close and personal in six years. "Only natural I guess." Expansive. "We just have to extend ourselves to the outer limits of our resources." Nice set of words there.

"What?"

Reno had a small thought, it seemed at the time to be an important one. "You know those people, Neanderthals? What if instead of humans today bein' an improvement, what if we're the degeneration, you know, like we're just some crummy remnants left over from divine Neanderthal ancestors?" Both hands waving, off in her own world. She stopped. "Oh, never mind." Slowmotion was looking at her funny again. "So. You wanna turn that money or what? I got an old friend, in South City, makes book, gives me good odds." He did some years back anyway. "So. Whattaya say we go see him?" Reno linked her arm through Slowmotion's.

Slowmotion shook her head.

"Loan-shark it?" Slow said no. "Well then how about makin' a down payment on a car, drive it into Mexico, sell it for double? Pay for our trip and then some." Slow said no. "Steal a car? Wait! Buy guns, then steal a car. Steal those guys' big ol' Ford!" Reno waved up the street in a loopy fashion. "Drive to Canada. I hear BC is beautiful in the winter. Sell everything to the Quebec Separatists."

"Quebec the other side of the continent."

Reno jerked her arm free. "What d'I know about this shit?" What she should do, her mind chugging along in low gear, was go home. But first she should ask Slowmotion if she could borrow a couple hundred dollars. Call the bookie, see if he was still in business. Reno staggered in two directions: down the street toward her hotel; simultaneously, with a circular swing of her leg, back to Slowmotion, mouth already open, planning her pitch.

Slowmotion met her halfway. "Don't worry, it'll be easy."

"Easy? Easy? It should be easy, certainly. But it won't be

easy. I know that much." Reno nodded to herself, dancing a little. "Connections. All anyone needs." She gave a hopeful glance to see if Slowmotion was following her drift.

Slowmotion spotted a bus way up the street, jumped around signaling to it. "I got some people, they know how to handle emergency supplies. We'll stick with the usual. Score some dope, yunno." She stopped hopping up and down. Breathed for a while. "Sell it to Hunt for his party at double. Easy."

"Dope? Dope? Damn." Reno crossed her eyes. "Not very creative." She thought of Eddie scouring the streets for a skinny junkie. "We got to do better'n that. The night's still young."

The bus rattled closer.

The young night was split by the familiar night sounds of glass breaking, screeching tires, horns and angry voices.

Reno paused. "I got it wrong. The night's already old; if we live through to the morning then through tomorrow day, a night might come that could maybe be considered young, but now—"

A siren began blasting from the same Ford that hassled them earlier, the same two hornballs leaped from their vehicle hollering "Stop," pointing guns at a couple of young shadows that raced away down an alley.

Slowmotion hustled Reno aboard, the driver so busy looking into the alley he never asked for their money.

"I be damned. They were cops," Reno whispered. "That does it. Good night, sweet thing." Reno headed for the back exit. One foot in front of the other. Doing fine. Goin' home. Yes, sir. She waved at Slowmotion, dismissed the dreams. "I be lucky if I manage to stay out of jail another week the clever way I be handling myself. Listen, Slow, I'm not allowed out after dark—perhaps it's something to do with vampires. Good night. I'm gone."

Reno pictured herself, already on her way: she'd use her contraband key on the sweet old front door of the Royal, climb up those stinky stairs, nip into bed, pull the covers up over her head. Wonderful. Reno closed her eyes tight, wishing the bus would stop.

Slowmotion grabbed her arm. "Ah. Come on." A slow wink. "It'll be fun."

Reno fell into a seat by the back doors. Staring blindly at the ceiling she told herself she shouldn't pass up a chance to learn something new.

"Oh boy." Slowmotion fished around in her sack. "We got to go to . . . let's see . . ." She handed Reno a spur. "Here, put this on your shoe." She smiled at Reno. Wicked. "House we goin', well, they can be particular about who comes in, after hours." In the streetlight strobe Slow was a chubby evil gnome with a lot of teeth.

Seemed to Reno to be a peculiar sort of particularity. She handed the spur back. "Don't like horses, they too damn big and they bite."

A man behind them began to puke. Cheap red wine foamed up in the bus-floor grooves as the bus went downhill; it rolled back again as the bus went up.

"Wuh. Let me out."

Slowmotion laughed and laughed, her face all prunish and wrinkled in the streetlights. "You funny, Reno. Here. Put the spur on. It's not nothin' to do with no horses—it just lets people know where you stand."

"I never was much for standin' with cowboys."

"Oh come on, Reno."

"You wear both of them. Should be enough they think you like horses or don't like them, whatever. I never felt any compulsion to climb on large bad-tempered animals and poke them in the ribs." Reno slipped lower into the plastic seat. Pulled her feet up, tried to ignore the puke. "Wouldn't even bet on horses if I hadda ride 'em. Listen, Slowmotion, I got to get off on the next corner. Got to rest up, you know, for the remainder of my life. I'm not gonna get my rent together this way." Slowmotion wasn't listening, just kept on pawing around in her big purse. "Or maybe I will. Hey, who am I to make plans?" Slowmotion nodded absently. "I'll tell you one thing right now, what you see is what you get. Your friends don't like the way I look, they can fuck themselves."

"Sure Reno." Slowmotion settled back, looked out the window chewing her lips. Corners sucked in. Giving things some serious thought.

GIRLS NEON GIRLS NUDE GIRLS SUPER 8 HARDCORE GIRLS, quick commerce, greasy bills, small packages, thin gray faces, nimble fingers. Dante, signifying in one of his fevers, would be right at home: the whole city was set up with the bath down the hall no guests no drugs allowed. All the doors lock at nine-thirty. You either in or out. Dog collars and spurs the latest ticket out. Or in. Gone get bust-ted for sure keep this up. Bust-ted.

"You known Su'ad long?"

Took Reno a moment to realize that she was being addressed. "All my life just about."

"You guys always go at each other like that?"

"Yep."

The first wet drifts of fog slimed across the window as the bus nosed out of the tunnel, crossing into nowhere. Creatures swam out of the murk, threatening, pleading, waving their skinny arms as they died.

"Su'ad said you were a polymath—"

"No I ain't." Short break. Frown. "What's a polymath?"

"Good with numbers." Slowmotion smiled to herself.

"Oh. That. Sure. Okay. Yeah."

"You know about computers."

"Some. Sure." Reno didn't bother to point out that being locked up had a lot of disadvantages, only one of which was that she was years behind the newest computer technologies. Polymath? Polygoof.

"Good." Slowmotion's smile got wider. "Good." She licked her lips. "Su'ad mentioned you was a guest of the feds."

"Did she now."

"Yep."

Reno stared without seeing at the puke river rolling up the aisle. Kept her voice easy: "Shouldn't maybe believe everything Su'ad says."

chapter thirteen

"Woo." Reno rocked forward on her toes. "Terrific neighborhood."

A damp wind whistled down the street. Not a star in the sky, the near-full moon merely a small bright hole someone had shot in the dull gray canopy overhead. Menace lurked in every shadow, seeped out of every broken roof cornice, dribbled from each cracked window.

Reno squared her small shoulders, bounced from one foot to the other, scowling. "Not the kind of place I woulda chosen to finish up a pleasant evening. Not a place for a respectable burglar neither. Look around, Slow. It's already been cleaned out." Sniffing. "Nothin' left but the garbage."

From the cosmic depths of black infinity, a raspy voice called: "Hey, girl—you got a extra cigarette?"

"Don't come no more'n twenty to a pack. Never been a extra one yet. Get back, asshole." Reno looked for an equalizer, found soppy newspapers, chunks of glass, weird gray lumps of take-out food packaging, nothing even remotely like a nice piece of lead pipe.

Shrieks from the shadows. "Fuuuuck you bitch. Fuck you."

Bulky figures huddled in doorways; no one ventured into the piss yellow circles of light.

Hurrying to catch up with Slowmotion, Reno stumbled over several pairs of dirty feet sticking out onto the sidewalk from a dark alcove; they didn't move. She lectured the comatose forms: "Oughta keep yourself to yourself. Looks like ya took a shit then staggered on down here to die."

One of the feet twitched, the long toes climbed up the hairy leg, gave it a good scratching. A moan of almost sexual satisfaction came from the shadows.

Reno backed away. "Savages."

Slowmotion pulled her across the street, laughing.

Reno was sorry she'd drunk so much. Marooned in a classic backlot horror-movie set, an urban desert. "Listen God—" She glanced up. Through the thick stuff that was her mind certain thoughts wormed their way into the light: God never had listened to her, sometimes Hail Mary Fulla Grace would condescend to deal her the Ace. But that was about it.

Reno puffed at Slowmotion. "I can't remember the Pledge of Allegiance either."

"Come on." Slowmotion tugged her toward the glow of a red-and-white plastic Coca-Cola sign, the "Cola" part painted over by a sloppy red flowerlike thing. They went down the wet cement stairs. "This is it." Slowmotion gave the buzzer on the metal gate a couple sharp jabs.

Reno felt a cold warning shiver start at the base of her spine, work its way up to her brain. "Cops and bounty hunters sweep through neighborhoods like this one just to see what shakes out." Casual. "It's been a lovely evening but now I really must say good night." She looked back up the street, saw a late-model Ford cruise by. She grabbed Slowmotion's arm. "Oh shit. It's those weird cops again."

A grimy boy opened the door, Reno pushed her way into a trendy-scummy basement. Didn't look to see if the Ford slowed down. As she took in her newest surroundings her hopes for potential safety disintegrated. Dull gray pipes crossed the cracked ceiling, a couple black plastic sofas, their dingy white guts spilling out, were arranged to face a small makeshift stage. "Atmospheric sort of place, eh? Or what should one say?"

Slowmotion gave her the elbow. "One shouldn't say anything."

Odd ambisexual people roamed around, rolled their eyes, wiggled their ears. The talk was postmodern, anticulture, machine economics. Deconstruction. They had purple hair, no hair, scraps of hair, chains, bangles, tattoos, shades, dark lips smiling around pointy green teeth. Terrific crowd.

At one end of the room a tidy dyke with a lot of papers read poems and used an electric keyboard like a percussion instrument. Which, she explained with a neat smile, it is.

At the other side of the long room there was a bar: a plank set on top of two nuclear-waste canisters, coffee three bucks, Bud in a mug four bucks.

Reno said she'd pass, the bouncer-bartender said there was a one-drink minimum. Reno said she be damned if he was going to get his beery hands on any of her tips. "I ain't that thirsty."

The boy looked annoyed, confused. Tired. "There's a one-drink minimum."

Slowmotion went through a set of shiny black lacquered swing doors. A sign, "The Answer Is No," hung above them, a couple sheets of tattoo flash were stapled to a nearby wall.

"Look, I'm just waitin' for my friend to finish up some personal business, then I'm outta here. Pretend I'm not here, I'll do the same for you some day, okay?" Reno propped herself on the nearest nuclear-waste canister, looked around.

Overflowing summer-camp clay ashtrays were set out on wooden crates. The walls were punctuated by goofy paintings of pink avocado trees, yellow tigers, protoethnic figures in baggy pants and turbans. Someone had lifted the wall decorations from a Sambo's restaurant. From an alternate universe. Next to the erupting couches a couple silk cushions, stolen from some Zen-do, were occupied by solemn pie-eyed people.

Reno's stomach rumbled; she considered graceful ways to exit. Such an hour, such strange company. Why weren't all these people home in bed? Why wasn't she? It would be a long cold walk. She lifted one foot, it was numb; she pretended she was halfway home. Tried to. Tried to remember which direction was home. "Home cement home."

"Never seen you here before." Voice nasal, coke thick. Dull.

"You see everyone who comes in?"

"Yeah. Sure. So, where you from?"

Reno was sick of it. Tired. "State prison." Stupid.

"What?" The grubby boy drew the word up up up. Edgy.

Reno sang to him. "My family comes from a little village on the north coast of Ireland; everyone is very small there, their houses are very small and their animals too. They spend all their free time making pizza. Um hm. Um hm." Suck on it you silly prick.

"Huh?" Nasal again. Half smile. "Huh?" Not so nervous.

Reno turned a direct gaze on him, eyes wide and clear. "Doesn't anyone understand irony?" Pleased with herself.

"Huh? Where you from anyway?"

The bartender made an excellent wall. Reno thought she'd bounce ideas off him for a while, then go to sleep. "Everything's just in limbo until I win the lottery." Slid her voice into a whisper. "The numbers game isn't good enough for 'em anymore—been a rebirth of Catholic prudery." Wasted wisdom. "Bigotry has got to proliferate. Propagate. Perpetration of seduction's worse than communism. But pollution is okay." Reno smiled. Her head throbbed in perfect time with the percussion piano.

The bartender stepped back a pace.

"Well, what is it, dude? Never learned to talk philosophy?"

"Huh." His mouth dropped open so Reno could see all his cavities.

"You ever consider goin' to a dentist? Whyn't you go see a dentist? That must hurt." Reno tried to point but her hand was stuck to the bar. She gave another conversational shot, a freebie, one of the major secrets of the modern world. "You know you can't ski on fresh snow anymore?" The fellow didn't respond. "Know why? Because it's radioactive." Reno hunkered down, confidential. " 'Course the radioactivity evaporates pretty fast from snow. Has to, the prices people pay to break their legs and freeze their tits off."

He backed up until he came to the wall. A lime-green tiger grinned over his shoulder. He made one very pale Sambo.

Reno leered after him. "Hey, honey, what time you get off work?" She bared her fangs for the quick shot to the throat.

Slowmotion popped out of the back room. "Yo, Reno, come on back here, the boss wants to meet you."

"Why? Who they think I am?" Reno didn't move from the bar, didn't stop leering at the boy—together they formed an essential part of her environment, holding her upright.

Slowmotion laughed, a deep cough. "From what I tole her she figure you a master practitioner of some esoteric discipline."

"Hoo. Some big multisyllable words jammin' the air waves now. Well, anyone want to meet me, they can come over here, buy me an overpriced underproof after-hours can of Bud." If someone else was buying Reno figured she be able to swallow a Bud. "But whoever they thinks I am, I ain't."

"You're just what the doctor ordered." A lean Afro-Asian woman with long shiny professionally straightened hair slipped gracefully in her direction. Mandatory dark glasses, patterned raw silk shirt hanging out over a pair of bright baggy pants, kung fu shoes. "Hi. Name's Poppy." She offered the back of her long hand as if Reno were a stray cat. Gold fingernails.

Reno ignored the hand in spite of the fact that the woman avoided the cliché of crimson nails.

Poppy patted her on the arm. "Pleased to meet you. Come on back into the office, I've got something nicer than Bud." When Reno didn't move, Poppy lifted her shades. Large slanted eyes, pale blue. Quizzical. Cracked ice. Contact lenses?

Reno thought the woman looked too pleased with herself—the place was making Reno itch. She scratched. "Thanks, but

I never drink after midnight anyway." Fuck her. "You the boss? Why only Bud? It's politically unsound."

Poppy laughed in a friendly way. "I seem to be in charge here, at least tonight. I won't make you drink if you don't want to." Her voice was devious. "Come on into the back room." Intrigue.

Reno levered herself off the bar, bared her teeth at the bartender frozen against the wall like a diseased ice cream cone. "Waitin' for some one to pop peanuts into that mouth or what? Maybe you get yer teeth fixed, have a nice smile like mine someday." As Reno was led through the black swing doors she wondered if she'd ever come out again. It was that kind of night. Morning.

The back room looked more like an interrogation cell than a punk Zen-do. Maybe a faint trace of cop stink—Reno didn't know if it was real or simply the recurring paranoia she'd been feeling since she got out. She tried to check for tape machines, hidden microphones, spy cameras; grim, she realized she wouldn't spot anything even if it had blinking red lights and a siren, she was that spaced.

Poppy motioned for them to sit on a couple of the little pillows, poured three coffees, proffered a chipped plate of marijuana cookies. Slowmotion dove right in, growling with pleasure. Reno bit, the sweet pastry stuck, smeared to the inner sides of her teeth. Swallow as she might it wouldn't go down; she felt her throat close, swallowed swallowed and swallowed hoping she wouldn't choke.

All the time she was locked up they talked about food, morning to night they talked about the good things they'd eat when they were free: strawberries and ice cream with a shot of amaretto poured over, pasta and pesto, salads of sweet peppers with cucumbers and sesame oil. Barbecued chicken. Cornbread muffins. Ribs covered with a blazing hot sauce. Sunday-morning champagne. Cinnamon cookies with a quarter inch of white frosting.

Reno's appetite was dead, her mouth numb. The cookie

kicked into her gut with a twisting nausea. Been two three days maybe with nothing but taco chips and salsa to eat. The coffee burned the roof of her mouth, her eyes watered. Food in the free world was not all it was cracked up to be.

Poppy produced an expanded aluminum briefcase, all silver curves like a small Airstream trailer. Her long precise hands worked easily at the combination locks, folded back the lid with a quick flourish. She smiled then, small pointed teeth evenly spaced, puffy blue eyes guileless as a cat's. She turned the case toward them.

Attached to the lid was a sheet with governmental stamps: USA, Hong Kong, Belize, Algeria. Something that appeared to be a diplomatic seal, a roll of official red-and-white stickers reading CONTAMINATED. In the bottom were many small, neatly labeled glass jars nestled in pink plastic foam: rocks of cocaine from the Bolivian chaco, ancient acid crystals from some long-defunct Sausalito lab, *Cannabis ruderalis* from the Russian steppe, small dark brown vials of seeds from Yemen, dirty brown weed from North Africa, green-black plant material from Nigeria.

"Mexico's in another case. You want to look at that, you come back another time." She picked up a clear vial filled with what looked like dried white corn. "These are from Uganda." She shook it to let them hear the rattle. "The plant itself is harmless, but the seeds are deadly. They call these the teeth of Idi Amin." Her head tipped back, a laugh gurgled up from her throat.

The woman's teeth turned into corn, flames danced in her cracked ice eyes; Reno stretched out on the floor, closed her own eyes. Too much was more than enough.

Slowmotion fingered one of the strange little jars. "I remember Idi." The vicious chuckle. "We bin through some strange ones, huh, Poppy."

"Got some ways to go b'fore we be home free." Poppy lifted the vial out of Slowmotion's hand, tucked it carefully back in the case. "Check these out: Laotian opium poppy seeds. Unfortunately the plants are terribly fussy about climate, soil, water, altitude. Tried to grow some here in the city but they came up sad. Spindly. Sapless." There were undertones of something more than words in her voice. "Not everything immigrates successfully."

Reno moved her head; there were sharp objects loose in there.

Poppy fondled her bottles, purring a little. Muttered prices. Slowmotion countered.

"Don't waste my time." Poppy turned her wrist with an abrupt movement. Gold Rolex. Reno tried to remember where she'd recently seen another one. Couldn't. Two, maybe three in one day. The world was lousy with Rolexes. Who woulda thought. Reno didn't care, she rolled over on her back and stared at the ceiling. Animals lived up there.

"I've got an hour more before I'm off. The prices only go up."

Reno murmured, "And the price only goes up."

Poppy saluted the sarcasm with a quick lift of her long hand. Too many Fu Manchu movies. She clicked the briefcase closed. Irritated, she spun the combinations, slid it back behind the cabinet. "C'mon Slow, ole girl, quit fussing. There's too much to be done without you haggling over price."

"You figure we still can get over?" Slowmotion made it sound less like a question than some obscure bargaining gambit.

"Sure. The dude's not invincible. Shit. Remember when he tried to have his wife committed to Langley Porter?"

Bitter laugh. "Called the police, said Aisha was nuts—said she believed she spoke with spirits."

"Jealous 'cause they were better company'n him, eh?"

"Whole relationship was screwy: he thought she was the daughter of an oil sheik, she thought he was some rich-and-influential columnist."

"Shows how wrong first impressions can be, eh?"

Slowmotion spoke into the thick air about a foot in front

of Reno. "Hunt made up for that mistake though—I've always believed the bastard offed her. Maybe for the insurance . . ."

The conversation began to sound like an elaborate performance to impress Reno, but she couldn't follow the action. Perhaps, she thought, it would all become clear in time. Time. Something there was too little of.

"You got any proof? Hah?" Directly to Reno. "The scumbag had her cremated."

"Ya can't test ashes for traces of poison. Or heroin."

"Maybe if there'd been any family around other than Farouk—"

"Now there's a useless prick."

"Ah. He was just a kid when they hooked up—besides he adores Hunt. Still kisses his ass."

Poppy gave Reno a big smile. "But maybe we can change that." Out of a felt sack she pulled a tidy Black & Decker cordless drill, six different bits including a sixteenth-inch tungsten carbide one, silver as moonlight. The whole thing was no bigger than her hand.

Reno's stomach knotted, she rolled over, eyes hooded. "Nice drill. So what." The floor wasn't all that comfortable but it beat standing up. Reno didn't take her eyes off the drill. Didn't touch it either. She was not a violent person.

These things are always multilayered, push-me pull-you negotiations, either designed to impress or designed to frighten. Built out of the basic need: greed. Nominal topics shifted but the subject remained the same. The thing behind the thing behind the thing. Plato throwing the shadow of Socrates on the cave walls. The way to get over.

Slowmotion got up off the little floor pillow she'd flattened. "I'll be back in ten?"

"Fifteen. Your friend and I have a lot to talk about."

Plato's cave vanished. "Me? I haven't got anything to say. I don't know anything. Don't know from drills." Slowmotion left the room. "Hey. Don't abandon me." A feeble plea.

Poppy put the drill on the floor near Reno, took a small

smooth crystal plate, a couple lines of cocaine already laid out. Pretty. "Here. Do this, it will brighten your outlook. We actually do have things to discuss."

Pretty woman. Pretty drill. Pretty dope. Reno snorted. A line for each nostril; she judged the toot to be excellent, reminded herself that she was no judge, told herself to keep her mouth shut, her eyes open. Sniffed the powder deeper into her nasal passages. Decided not to tell the woman she was pretty. Decided not to tell her she was also an asshole. Maybe Poppy would lend her the drill. A world of possibilities. Ah.

"I hear you have some exceptional skills."

Reno tried to marshal her scattered wit. Singular. The only one she could find on such short notice. "Right." She wasn't so clear about what it was they were discussing. "But the law takes exception to them so I don't use them." Reno glared at the floor, her eyes an eighth of an inch to the left of the drill. There weren't many mechanisms that could stand up to it, no place she couldn't get into if she had that dainty little tool. If wishes were fishes.

The coke didn't give Reno enough energy to get up off her ass or she would have walked out right then. The mind grease was churning. But churning wasn't enough, she didn't need butter in her brains. Reno tried to make do with what she had, couldn't remember what it was she had. Other than a headache and an additional ten years on top of her time if she was caught doing whatever it was she was doing. She choked back a groan.

Poppy's voice penetrated the fog. "I understand you have just been released from the tender custody of the government."

"You understand? Not likely." Only thing anyone wants with some unknown convict is a patsy, a victim. The hell with that. Reno started to her feet, got about halfway. "This is the shits." She grunted. "There's hundreds of places I'd rather be right now, but I'm not, I'm here stuck to your floor. Soon as I can move, I'll be outta here. We can pretend we never met."

"Oh come on, I'm offering you a job."

"Well, I already got a job. It sucks, but that's the thing about jobs: they all suck, so I'm not interested in your stupid job, babe." Seemed to her that the free world had heavier gravity, motion was very difficult. "I don't give a shit about your phony corn pellets from Uganda, that bogus international collection of stems and seeds." Rhythmic pounding in her head. "I don't know nothin' about drills."

Poppy looked amused, disbelieving.

"And you," Reno swayed forward until their noses were an inch apart, "don't know nothin' about me."

The woman's cat-blue eyes didn't blink. She nodded slowly, smiling. "Whatever you say."

"Shit." Hey, Reno thought, I can be a one-syllable huffy bitch when I wanna be.

"Another time then. Perhaps when you're not indisposed."

"I'm always indisposed." Plaintive. "Why the hell you want to talk about this shit with a total stranger at dark-thirty in the morning?"

"Here we both are, seemed logical."

Standing. A whole new perspective, being upright. "Don't want to talk about it." Whatever it was.

"Okay. Fine. But time is short. When will I see you again?"

"Don't like meetings." Mule. She needed to get out of there; she patted herself, all the parts seemed to be in their usual alignment.

Poppy remained cross-legged on the floor, placid as only a happy little despot can be. "Believe me, you could be an immense help to Slow and me. Perhaps a line of credit on the Centurion Bank would interest you?" She rummaged up an American Express Gold Card.

Reno glared. Of course it interested her. She felt her saliva glands start to work.

"Guaranteed to seven thousand dollars."

The edges of Reno's mouth crinkled with disdain. "No way you can guarantee me that." Disappointment.

Poppy smiled as if she knew better, put it away. "What you know about computers?"

"Nothin'." Reno put her hands in her pockets. "Why?"

"I need you to get some information, a simple matter of downloading a few files from a hard disk. A snap. All you need to do is tap a few keys, pop a couple disks into a portable computer. Fifteen minutes' work. No more."

Reno moved toward the door. "Just tap a few keys? Anyone could do that. You could do that."

"I can't get at the computer. I know you can."

Reno didn't bother asking how Poppy knew. She slid one foot gingerly in front of the other.

"Access and timing are the keys. Together we can, like, hijack the data, hold it for ransom." She twinkled. "Life can be beautiful."

Reno was only three feet from the door. "Hijack the data. Right."

"It's in a good cause. What you think about Mr. Huntington? He has some things we need, we intend to get them. You can help us. Why blow the chance to get your own American Express Gold Card?" Her smooth voice floated in the room, bobbing gently, a weather satellite.

Slowmotion came back. Poppy nodded to her. "In all our years together we've never had such a deserving target. And all the players just seem to be showing up on time." Poppy looked smug. "See? Here we all are."

"I don't have nothin' against Hunt." Reno heard Poppy's murmur that it was only a matter of time. Probably true, but she wasn't about to say so.

"Think about it." Poppy stood up from the floor without using her hands. Show off. She gave Reno a stiff rectangular white card which read "New Age Tattoo. By Appointment Only." A phone number was handwritten on the bottom left corner. The flip side had a black-and-green square like an old computer screen: "PCrypto. Archivist." Another number.

Reno pushed her chin forward. "What is it with you people?"

"Who people?" The Buddha remained unperturbed even when small flames burned in her cold blue eyes.

"You assume a lot, don't you?"

"Yes." Perfect assurance.

"Well. Who would I ask for if I ever decided to call?"

"You wouldn't have to ask. I'm the only one answers the voice line." Tapping white card.

"I see." But Reno didn't see.

"Other one's modem. Password's 'PCrypto.' Then you're into the system. Leave me a message."

"I see." Reno didn't see at all. What kind of message? We who are about to die salute you? Attempting to be social: "There's a party at the Istanbul Club tomorrow night. Featuring your dope. If that kind of thing gives you a thrill you shouldn't miss it."

"I'll be there." Buddha smile.

Oh. Terrific. Reno couldn't decide if she was glad or not. Poppy was a damn interesting woman.

chapter fourteen

Slowmotion pranced on the street, eager as a puppy. "I thought you guys would get along." Pretending to be oblivious to Reno's discomfort. "You liked her, huh? I knew you would." Moving things from one pocket to another. "So when you gonna get together?"

Reno looked up the empty street; all kinds of disasters waited for her approach. "People get these weird ideas, weave their night dreams in intricate patterns, expect someone else to make their fantasy come true." Reno snorted. "I got intricate fantasies of my own."

Slowmotion wasn't as oblivious as she seemed. "Poppy's really great. Connected. She's getting it on with some guy in the DA's office." Sharp-eyed, watching Reno.

"Some guy? In the DA's office? Jeez."

"What's the problem? She's tight with everyone. Needs to be. And she likes you. I can tell." Slowmotion shifted her sack from one shoulder to the other, searching for something. "You play it right, she'll hand you this town on a platter." Found and lit two cigarettes. One to Reno.

"Don't want the town on a platter." Reno turned a full circle trying to orient herself toward home. "Never trust a woman with an obvious sense of style." She didn't mention the eyes. "Never trust a dyke who's fucking the pigs."

"Oh come on, girl."

Reno pulled a stiff lip. "The only skill to running an after-hours place is the ability to bribe the police to stay away. That's too close to licking ass and liking it." Reno looked sideways at Slowmotion. "The place stinks of cop. Queers and cops are a very bad combination."

"You can't carry that attitude around with you forever."

"The hell I can't. Oh, forget it. The only question of the night is, Which way is home?"

Slowmotion punched Reno lightly on the arm. "You like her. I can tell."

Reno squeezed her eyes closed. Opened them. Same place. "No I don't." She remembered Poppy's long cracked-ice eyes. A whore for the DA. Reno thought she would puke. She shivered; she wasn't cut out for this marginal existence, unsuccessful scrabbling. At the rate she was moving up the socioeconomic ladder she should forget parole, making plans, instead she'd simply get loaded as often as she could, boogie until she was shipped back to jail. Take pleasure where she would.

They stumbled together past the graffiti-stained walls of a bombed-out hospital district littered with crimson, black, and green comments about recent and historical whores, wars, dead heroes: "Born To Mack." "RIP The King."

Reno rubbed her hands together, pulling on her gloves. "We going to walk all the way back home or what? What we doin' around here? Looks like The Creature's home turf." Pleasure? Hah.

"You talkin' about Fangs?" Slowmotion capered on the sidewalk, her shadow Godzilla-huge. "Oooh girl, I saw him the other night, diggin' all around in the garbage, growlin' and snarlin'. Yes darlin'." Slowmotion's voice dropped lower, her head angled forward, swaying side to side. "I felt the icy tomb breath just a-risin' up from the sidewalk." She raised her arms in a spooky fashion. "Yes now, I turned around, there he was, practically on my neck. I thought I be his dinner, yes I did."

Reno looked over her shoulder. "Really?"

"No." Slowmotion chuckled, an eerie unpleasant sound.

"You a real thrill. You and your business associates." Reno stared straight ahead, one foot other foot, just another greasy-robed slum warrior with a newspaper helmet, an antenna whip for protection. Every few months the bums were jerked off the street, dipped in Lysol, heads shaved, pair of socks, pants, shirt, maybe a tie, cardboard shoes—dissolve soon as they get wet. After a few days the bums regained the protective color-ation of the professionally invisible. Reno wondered if they were fingerprinted. Wondered if she were picked up if she'd ever get out again. . . . The shadows of hunting cats moved at the edges of perception, tails high. "Where in hell are we?"

"Here."

"Lovely." They stood in front of an old cement-block hotel. A couple window blinds flicked back into place as they looked up. Not a sound. "A real palace."

Street door was open. They slipped into the narrow lobby, padded silently down a short hall to the freight elevator: out of order. "Naturally." Up three flights of stairs, dark hall, Slowmotion used a key on a scratched-up lock that looked like almost any key would work. They entered a small messy room filled with old guitars, drums, out-of-style boom boxes, VCRs, piles of ruffled cloth obscuring a sewing machine, a television. "I seem to know this decorator. Same one as did the basement of the club."

"Sit over there on the mattress if you want. This'll take a while, but I need to put it together now, got to move some of it in the next couple hours. Hey, you know how it is."

Reno didn't know how it was, had no idea. Didn't care. The mattress was lumpy but it gave in the proper places.

Slowmotion placed the dope on the floor, dug out Baggies, scales, straws, pipes, screens, papers from behind or under things. She pointed to one of the piles of pot. "Tell me what you think. Got to start it movin' tonight. When Eddie gets here he can put some of it on the street; the rest we'll hide in the alley behind the club with the garbage—no one bother it there."

"Tonight? It's already tomorrow, girl."

"No one goes back there in the alley anyway. They think it's filled with the club's radioactive garbage."

"They're right. The free world's one big garbage dump."

"Mmmmn. Listen, I'm gonna get stoned, get me some energy before movin' on. Want some?"

"No." Reno pulled a pillow over her head, searched through the darkness for the loose end of the ball of string that her mind had become.

"Hey. Wake up. You could at least talk to me while I bag this shit up. This is gonna impress Hunt, oooh yes honey. He be ready to pay double what it's worth when I'm done."

Listening was work enough.

Slowmotion warmed to her topic. "See, first I show Hunt the dynamite ugly weed, get him blitzed on a sample. Let him roll it up himself so he be sure that I didn't doctor the pipe or the papers, you know. These rich guys so devious, they always lookin' for the scam."

"Ain't no way a rich man gonna give a poor woman a deal." Her voice came out thick, muffled by the pillow.

"Right. So I got to, well, you know, con him."

"Con the con man." Reno wanted to sleep.

After a pause filled with rustling Slowmotion's voice took on some coke strength, husky. "I turn him on to the ugly shit, he gets wasted, then I sell him the beautiful stuff, the stuff that's not nowhere near as good, for triple what we paid. See?"

"Uhnf."

"Come on. Wake up. Appreciate."

"No."

Eddie staggered into the room then, an ancient man with a throbbing head and the taste of vomit in his mouth.

Slowmotion greeted him. "Hey Eddie. How'd it go? Save me any?"

"Ha ha ha. It's long gone. Having fun is hard work, no one appreciates that." He peered at Reno curled up on the mattress. "Who's that?"

"Reno. Leave her be, she needs to sleep off a fit of bad temper."

Reno waved a couple fingers.

"Sure, Slowmotion, anything you say. But that's my bed she's on."

Reno curled up even smaller.

"Doesn't take up much room. Take a hit off this here, that pile yours. I need the cash before three this afternoon."

Reno opened an eye, pushed the pillow to the side as Slowmotion gathered up her paraphernalia. Weak whisper: "Hey. Don't leave me."

Slowmotion opened the door, looked back with a wave and a cheery grin. "Aw. Go to sleep, you guys can work it out in the morning. I got people to go, places to see. You know how it is." She closed the door behind her.

Eddie had to throw up.

Reno looked over in time to see a clear stream of puke pour from Eddie's mouth, most went in the sink in the corner. Some dribbled ugly to the floor. "Nice shot. But no points."

Eddie looked up, bleary-eyed. If he hadn't been so loaded he might have been embarrassed, but he was so he wasn't. "Can't win 'em all."

Reno crawled around, found a towel under a pile of shirts, wet it, wiped his mouth, pushed him back onto the mattress, mopped up the puke on the floor. Trying to be a nice guest.

A loopy grin wobbled across Eddie's face. "Amazing how much better I feel after that."

"Amazing how awful I feel seein' you do that." Reno waved her hand at the crummy room. "This your home?" There wasn't anything much of a personal nature there.

"One of 'em." He gestured at the walls, imitating her. "A

place to crash when I'm in the neighborhood, you know? Hey, since you're here." He sat up, junk beneficent. "I got a little dope left, enough so we can both get off." He puffed up with importance, pulled out a leather pouch, untangled his works. Lecturing. "It's a duty, a necessity, to maintain the proper antisocial posture."

"The proper what?" Reno was awake, but wasn't lucid. There is a difference between the two, unfortunately; one state complements the other, but the whole consciousness doesn't work without both parts. Back down on the mattress. "Posture?" She wasn't in shape to do any more dope. Needed to get into training for that kind of action. Then again, she thought, she probably wouldn't be on the streets long enough to get into training, may as well do it now. Do it all. Tomorrow may never come. Or it may, but it be worse. "So. What you got there, bro?"

The syringe popped from its protective plastic sheath; he plunged it into the bleach, squirt, into the bleach, squirt, into the glass of water, twice. He put it aside, lit the candle, melted the tar in his spoon, looped the cord with a slip knot around his upper arm. He looked over at her. Proud. He concentrated, fading in and out of focus as the reluctant vein began to swell. "Should be guests first, but I waited long enough for this, you know?"

His foggy eyes wandered over her face, back to his arm, his mouth folded into a smile; the minuscule point pressed against the skin, with a subliminal pop it slid a careful angle between the microscopic ridges of the vein wall. "Yup yup yup. That's the ticket." Drop by drop he fed himself, warmth beginning at the back of the head, the hollow bones themselves heating, expanding, absorbing the smooth dope like a sponge. He put a cotton ball over the tiny wound, bent forward for a moment then straightened up with a sharp breath.

His eyes were suddenly clear. "Amazing, huh?" He expelled the syringe into the cotton, wrapped the cotton in a Baggie, dropped the syringe in the bleach glass. "Your turn now." He moved the candle toward her, proud. "I saved you some." He got busy cleaning his kit.

"Thanks, Eddie, but count me out. I don't share needles no matter how much bleach you use. My mamma didn't raise me to be no fool."

"Hey. This is elixir, this is angel piss! The stuff the news-boys like Hunt dream about but never see."

Why the hell not. Four in the morning as good as any time. "Okay, but I'll pass on that needle."

"Sure. It's your problem if you want to get off the staircase halfway to heaven." He wiggled around. "Listen. Hunt's such a cheap fucker—" He stopped to wallow in some memory. Reno listened to him with one ear, her attention focused on the dope. Eddie's voice slipped, he curved his shoulders forward, protecting his story. "When he and my dad were in Vietnam together Hunt sold his army rations, hey, sell any-thing he could get his hands on, spent it on dope." He leaned over to check the amount in Reno's tinfoil. Sly. "Hell, my dad said the asshole never ever turned anyone on." Solemn. "I'm not like that. But still, I wouldn't offer this to anyone but you."

"Why not?" She continued peeling flakes off the lump of tar.

"There's only you here." He giggled, impressed with his own humor. "Figure it might improve your disposition."

"Don't count on it." She snorted a line, lay down on the mattress, waited to pass out, deal with it when the sun came up. "One more thing: you best not throw up again or nothin' improve my disposition."

He put one arm on each side of her, holding himself above her, smiling down into her eyes. "I promise."

She hadn't looked into a face that close from that position in a long time.

Eddie wore a cat licking cream crazy smile as he lowered himself to stretch full length on top of her. He rocked his hips against her. Slow and easy.

Reno responded without meaning to. To her surprise Reno didn't toss him off; her fingers, as if they had a mind of their own, walked up his spine, exploring the forgotten contours of a lean, friendly male body. Carefully she spread her hands across his back.

Eddie rolled to the side, slow. His eyes never left her face as he placed one finger on her lower lip. His hand trembled, delicate as the wing of a moth. Serious.

Reno closed her eyes, opened her mouth. She tasted salt.

Much later Reno fell asleep, her face buried in the curve of his neck, his arms around her, his leg flopped over her hip.

chapter fifteen

Between three or four A.M. and the first light of actual morning a babbling river of thought sludge flows through the back alleys of the city, unhampered by civilized, rational boundaries. Decisions based on private fear-filled hallucinations, postmidnight delirium, made and unmade with a facility seldom equaled in daylight hours. It's the wellspring of creativity, the genesis of shallow calamities.

Su'ad perched on the edge of the bed in her studio apartment, rubbed her favorite cat on top of its round little head. Chasing elusive worries, she listened to it purr. After leaving Hunt's flat she waited a long time for a bus to come along, couldn't shake the feeling there was something symbolic in the event. Time was growing short and she had too few options.

Every spare moment of her time was spent dealing with basic survival, life maintenance; it left her unsatisfied. While she still had her office job she could fool herself into thinking she was building a security, a legitimate foundation for a normal life. That fantasy finally collapsed with the gift of crotchless underwear. She shoulda seen it coming.

Her only release was in performance; the best part about

dancing was it made her feel beautiful. Desirable. She knew she wasn't beautiful in any traditional sense but she had a certain kind of feminine power, and with it she courted the false testimony of applause, chasing after that lie with every gesture. She could believe while she danced, believe many impossible things. In her life she should be as direct and powerful as she was in her performances. Ho.

She was more potent on stage than she ever could be elsewhere. She was good, she was an artist, she knew it. But the small stage at the Istanbul was getting crowded—she was sick of Sinclair's inability to see beyond Eva's white-girl posturing. Seemed like every man wants a blonde for his very own. Su'ad grimaced. "High yaller."

She would not resign herself to second place, not behind a slut like Eva. She didn't care if Eva was up for some part in some play or not. She didn't believe it anyway. But the suggestion woke some desperate thing in the back of her mind—the fear that her present every day every night world was the best she would have for the rest of her minor-league life. Nothing more.

Hell. If these were the eternal boundaries of her world, the future evaporated into sweaty nights of bump and grind, empty days, empty nights, then she'd grow old alone: she'd be nobody special. To anyone.

She should settle into simple self-absorbed survival? Get another day job, clerking again, somewhere dull? Smile, coy as any Eva, when the next boss put a pretty package on her desk containing edible underpants, nipple rings, multicolor condoms with smiley faces on the tip?

No reason, she said to herself, to settle. She never settled.

The cat shifted on her lap, dug its claws into her thigh, purring. He looked up at her: Pay attention to me. "Me." He said, "Me."

Her answering machine switched on, its red light blinking brightly in the dim studio; Hunt's voice oozed from the speaker. He was calling from the pay phone at the corner. "I must see you. Now. How about it?" She listened, hugging her cat, didn't pick the phone up. "I'll be over in ten minutes." His voice was thick, rich. "Make us some coffee, I'll bring sweet rolls. We need to talk." He breathed a while. "Please." He disconnected, certain she would do as he asked. Everyone did.

Su'ad and her cat exchanged looks. "How'd you like to live in a big fancy flat above the club?"

"Mine?" Her cat asked. "Mine?"

"Of course. Hunt loves cats."

The cat looked dubious, stretched down off her lap, stalked stiff-legged over to the lower bookshelf and scratched at the books.

Su'ad didn't notice.

The coffee was ready by the time Hunt arrived. Su'ad modeled her new costume. "Thought I'd wear it for your party. What do you think?"

He sipped his espresso, appraising. She looked like a captive dragonfly queen, glamorous and flirtatious. "It's okay. A little old-fashioned." His eyes were cold. He reached for another sweet roll. Su'ad was getting too confident; she wanted too much from him. Tomorrow night he'd see how she'd take a fall—he had no intention of giving her or any of these she-demons an inch; he simply enjoyed watching them struggle.

Su'ad half smiled, eyes down. The situation had not gone quite as she had expected. "Thanks. I guess." She sat across from him at her small table. "You really think that I'll get some serious offers?" She stood up again, turning; she held the edge of her pale purple skirt out, her long body displayed as if for sale, she tried to catch his eye. "Hotel work in Egypt?"

He spoke to the ceiling. "Certainly. Besides, all exposure is good." He held his cigarette, waiting for her to light it. "Even negative publicity can bring positive results."

Su'ad felt a thrill of unease, clung to his earlier assurances that he would help her, introduce her around, mention her in his column. He knew the manager of one of the hotels by the pyramids. Pyramids. No shit. She grabbed a stick match out of the holder, struck it on her thumbnail, lit the cigarette in her own mouth and presented it to him. "I don't expect any negative reactions." She sat across from him again. Dark eyes glittering. "I expect them to love me."

Hunt didn't respond, he watched the smoke from his cigarette curl up to the ceiling, musing over his plans. He snapped his sleeve back, checked his Rolex. "You'll be the party's big surprise." He smiled then. Narrow.

She didn't smile back.

He stood up. Standing, he could maintain a more powerfully seductive appearance. "Oh darling, please indulge my addiction to drama. To intrigue." He put his hand on her shoulder, fingers pressing lightly into her flesh. "Thanks for the coffee, I must be on my way." He appraised her as she took off the costume, held out his arm for it. "I'll keep this for you at my place."

Farouk sat alone in Hunt's flat. He'd sent his friends away to the hotel; they understood his need to be alone—that's what they were paid for. Unquestioning support. He worried in a vague way about the constrictions on his life in America. Getting respect wasn't easy. "Hell, I need a crowd around me. Doesn't work with only one or two. A crowd to watch, or to be sent away, at the royal whim—numbers enough to assure everyone. I'm an artist of international acclaim! Not some stupid towel head selling dildos in Times Square." He got up from the couch. Pulling himself up, tall, looking in the mirror. "I'm not some camel jockey who can be pushed around by every prep school graduate looking for exotica on the street."

He was not entirely unhappy with the night's performance. He couldn't say what it was that was bothering him; preferring not to delve too deeply into his own psychology or motivations, he fingered a smooth wooden box with rounded corners, an elaborately swirled enamel lid. Craft work, not fine art, but elegant. With a decisive movement he removed the lid, arranged the items with surgical precision on the coffee table's mirrored surface, placing the tiny tools in a strict row: blades, silver straws, packet of cocaine, packet of chicken crank, tinfoil square of Mexican brown, silver spoon. Farouk's hands were very clean, very steady. Craft contained things, art symbolized things. He took pride in the sharpness of his thought. Damned the necessity for mundane business concerns. Being an artist was lonely work.

With the concentration of a tea master he spooned some of the sparkling cocaine on the mirror, click click razor flash across and back, click click mix mix, the mound became a square, the square two triangles, the triangles two lines.

He listened to the shluf shluf of the stylus beating itself against the end grooves of a record. Hunt's continual mother hen criticism was unnerving, the man never could leave well enough alone; Hunt misunderstood so often, Farouk suspected he did it on purpose. Certainly Hunt never understood Farouk's sister Aisha. Even after he married her, Hunt never understood her.

Farouk's face twitched with a shudder. It was all a crock, that's what he wanted to tell Hunt. All a crock.

Farouk inhaled the powder. Slumping back on the leather couch, nose lifted to let every molecule penetrate, he looked around the room, moving over it first with his eyes, then getting up: touching, opening, peering behind things. No dust. He wondered if Hunt had a cleaning woman. He wondered if he fucked her. He wondered how old people fucked. He wondered if Aisha had enjoyed it. He hoped not.

He kept looking around Hunt's flat, looking for something private. Exposing. Real. The place was too clean, too orderly. People shouldn't live with that kind of precision.

Tidy to a fault. Impersonal except for the monograms—on underwear, sheets, cufflinks, glasses. Farouk envied these flourishes, flauntings; he grabbed a bottle off the shelf, poured himself a straight shot of supposed fifty-year-old something or other. Coughed. Hunt refilled his bottles with cheap scotch.

Farouk dove onto Hunt's satin-quilted bed; wallowing, reckless, he kicked his feet on the mattress, ho ho ho. It didn't satisfy. He leapt up, began opening drawers. Tacky shit. All arranged. Color-coded socks. He asked himself what he'd ever thought was so superior about the man, how he'd let himself be so impressed with those ever ready battery powered words, Hunt's desperate verbal toys.

More than food or drugs or sex Farouk had wanted to live inside Huntington's words, wanted, at some point even to inhabit his bones, his muscles. Probably, but he never gave it a thought, probably he wanted to be Hunt and fuck his own sister. Then again maybe not.

Maybe, he let a new thought drift—careful, chase it, it's gone—maybe Aisha discovered something about Hunt she couldn't live with. Broke her heart. Hunt said she died of a heart attack, but it didn't have to be some flaw inside her own body that killed her. Maybe—it wasn't the first time he had the thought—it was something evil in Hunt himself that moved her beyond a person's normal desire for survival.

Perhaps Aisha wanted to die, wanted Hunt to come home to an empty body, sprawled limp and ugly. Show him what he'd done to her. She'd be absolutely no good to him anymore, no longer beautiful or amusing; far too big to flush down the crapper.

The old gossip that Aisha overdosed, or that she'd been whoring out of Hunt's apartment, one of her tricks killed her, or that Hunt did it himself out of jealousy, frustration, never impressed Farouk. It had taken Hunt some fixing to get out from under the stigma of that dead mermaid wife. That impressed him.

Hunt skewered them all, exposed all of them, over the years, like dead nerves pulled from rotten teeth. Denying nothing, Hunt just pursed his lips, looked suave, ruined careers, blighted marriages. At first Farouk was grateful for Hunt's apparent concern about Aisha's honor, the family unit, maintaining the necessary public respect. But eventually Farouk noticed that Hunt was thriving on the controversy; he watched, incredulous, as Hunt merely smiled, gravely, at the suggestion that Aisha was the mystery woman high up in an international drugs hierarchy. Or a spy for Palestine. Farouk would have loved it if she'd been a real spy, dangerous, desperate, brave.

Too silly. He recalled the gossip that Aisha was mad, talked to spirits—if she'd known about her namesake, Aisha Kandisha, the most infamous seductress-demon in North Africa, she would certainly have played that up, mentioned it to Farouk. "Look, little brother, I'm destined to be famous." But she never did.

Aisha was vague about everything, especially the Middle East—a creature of appetites, her usual response to anything was a puzzled giggle. He wished she'd actually spoken with spirits, might have learned something.

Farouk leaned forward, curling into himself, head to knees, belly tight to thighs, toes curled. Curled: a bud a fetus an egg, shuddering.

Too bad, it was too bad, so sad, sad sad just too bad—up and down back and forth artsy-fartsy—who was he trying to kid: Aisha was a junk whore, lovely and poisonous. In spite of that, everyone loved Aisha. The quintessential woman. Mystery in every gesture.

No one can live with someone like that.

Farouk took it further. Higher. Richer: Hunt had lived with the sense of his failure as a man—while she'd been alive Aisha was the living proof.

No one can live like that.

Farouk grasped one of the red silk tassels on Hunt's black lacquered bureau, pulled out a drawer. Photos of naked people he didn't know, taken by a photographer with a nasty streak. People simply didn't look that ugly on the natch. Farouk started at the upper left drawer of the chest, working down, if he didn't find anything in the first five drawers he'd go back into the living room, do another line. Pack it up. Go to his hotel.

The next drawer didn't slide out easily. The photos were in an old envelope. Farouk had forgotten how very beautiful Aisha was: long silky hair, skin so pale as to be silvery, her black eyes had seemed, he remembered, silver too. Her eyes were closed, she was posed naked, nipples painted. Shot after shot, different poses. Ending on the bathroom floor.

Farouk stood still, his heart thudding uncomfortably. It hadn't taken him more than a moment to realize she was either dead or dying when the shots were taken.

He imagined Aisha decorating herself, then slipping into that shallow-breathing heart-stumbling cyanotic phase, she waited for Hunt to come home and save her.

Hunt simply took pictures.

Farouk put the pictures back, except for one that he slipped in his pocket. His features quivered then smoothed into the round placid planes of river-washed stones. He took the dope with him, locked the door behind him, left the flat and spent the hours until sunrise pacing the streets.

Hunt lay back, dissatisfied. He held Eva's head steady between his legs, his breathing remained uninspired.

Her large butt stuck up in the air, a provocation.

"Oh never mind." He whacked the highest part of her. "The timing just isn't right." He untied the laces around her wrist.

Eva came up for air, wiped her mouth with the side of her hand, licked a finger and used it to clean off the mascara smudged below her watery blue eyes. She reached out for him once again. "Oh please, I want to—" Begging. She knew he liked that. "Please let me do you."

This wasn't simple S & M between pals; this was a war they each believed the other to be capable of losing. Both were mistaken.

"Fill up my glass for me first, that's a good girl." He zipped his pants. "I've got an idea for my party tomorrow night, a way to add some drama to the evening. I think you could help me out." He watched as she froze in the middle of her pirouette. "You've got a really fine costume stashed somewhere don't you?"

"Of course, Hunt. Just promise me I'll have the proper audience for it." Eva balled up her fists, pushing them together, her false devotion unwavering. "So long as I get the applause, and the publicity, I'm ready." She went to his sideboard for the bottle of scotch.

"Publicity?" Hunt murmured, exhausted. "What ever happened to art?" He lay back on his couch, closed his eyes, motioned her back to his side.

Eva came with a quick gracelessness, her cherub face masking her hatred, her hands rubbed his chest through his silk shirt. "Tell me why I need to break out my best costume."

Grunting. "You'll see. Just make sure to bring it this evening." He arched his back like a cat, checked his Rolex. "You haven't got anything against petty theft have you?"

It wasn't a real question. Eva didn't bother to answer. Growling, she used her claws on his zipper.

chapter sixteen

Head under the thin pillow, Reno chased dreams— a moth to the candle flame—tried to move, tangled in the covers. Her arms wouldn't lift.

Some gray man flashed a badge, made a grab.

She was trying to bust open a cash register but her eyes couldn't focus, her fingers fumbled, unable or unwilling to slide the narrow blade into the tiny lock. She took out all the screws instead, they multiplied in front of her dreaming eyes as she worked. Dozens, hundreds of minuscule steel screws.

Uniforms slammed into the room, pistols drawn.

You pays your money, you takes your ride. Reno killed them with a perfect toss of the screws, silver bees, straight for their eyes.

She woke up smelling the fried hair cheap soap stale tobacco smell of prison. Didn't open her eyes, promised all the gods from everyone's deepest need that she'd never do whatever it was she'd done again. Vowed to improve herself with every shining hour, knew she wouldn't but felt it could be important to vow it, show her intentions to be pure.

Wondered what day it was. What place it was. The ever-vigilant Kazam X would throw her out of the Royal for sure.

One eye opened, scanned left and right: curtains closed, disgusting mess, a pile of clothes, she was alone.

Hadn't the foggiest. Wasn't hung over—she patted her face, wiggled her eyebrows, felt no bruises anywhere on the body. So, where was she, why was she—there, not somewhere else. Rolled off the mattress, pulled back the curtain. Faint daylight bounced painfully off a yellow cement wall three feet away across the alley.

Always one for taking the private exit whenever she could, Reno squinted for a way down. Felt bile rise in her throat. Perhaps she was a little hung over. She let the curtain fall, took a breath.

Looked again at the pile of clothes crumpled in the corner. Two bare feet glowed bluish in the morning light. There was a sort of ultimate not-there-ness about the position, and a terrifying familiarity about the studded jacket, the shaggy hair.

Reno leaned over the body. "Hey! Eddie! Time to get up."

A siren screeled a couple blocks away.

She shook him hard with a sudden fear.

He moaned, didn't open an eye.

Gratifying. But not enough. She tugged him into a sitting position. The sirens were closer. "Eddie. We got to get out of here." A quick glimpse of his face, pasty where it wasn't turning red blue green from bruises, made her suck in her breath. She pulled him upright, kept him standing by main force and a solid grip under his arm, but walking was one of those exercises he was unable to perform.

Dragged him to the sink, one of her hands hooked in his belt loop, he leaned to puke again. "Goddamn, Eddie. You spend more bloody time upchucking than anyone I've ever met."

Bleary, he muttered, "Isn't that the way it's done?"

"How in hell did you get all beat up?"

"Couple pals came by. Remember the skinny guy who came in the club last night? We went out to score and um."

She craned her neck to look at the street from the alley

window: Two police cars pulled up, couple uniforms, couple suits, half jogging into the building.

"So. You know another way outta here besides the stairs?"

"Maybe." He was unable to take it any further.

Back over to the window. "We got to get outta here. Now. You got a good idea how?" She motioned at the door. "They goin' to be comin' in here soon. What they gone find?"

"Underwear. Not much dope now." He grinned, winced at the face action. Put his hand up to the side of his face. "Hey, I sure can't afford to get picked up."

"No one can Eddie." Reno opened the window onto the alley all the way, listened for approaching leather footsteps.

His eyes got big, moonish circles in his swollen face. "The problem is, see, I'm a runaway, if the po-lice catch me they'll lock me up till I'm twenty-six, you know?"

"A juvenile?" Her voice cracked.

"Yeah. I turn eighteen next week."

She reached out a hand to steady herself, the window frame felt clammy. "Of course. A juvenile." The blood pounded in her ears, she wondered if perhaps this was the prelude to a stroke. Put her butt on the sill, swung a leg out. "A runaway." She stifled a laugh. Choked.

"Hey! Where ya goin'?" Eddie clawed his way up the wall to a nearly upright position.

"Las Vegas." Reno thought about simply jumping, a short flight down. Oblivion. Hell, she was going back to jail: breaking parole, dope, embezzlement, contributing to the delinquency of a minor, harboring a runaway. Things never worked out for her. Never.

The hallway on the floor below them echoed with heavy feet. She squinted into the alley, hoisted herself all the way out onto the ledge. Might as well give it her best shot. It hadn't been so long—she hoped these things stuck in muscle memory.

"Hey, Reno, wait for me."

She paused half in half out. Strategies snagged their way

through the muck of her brains. Worry, like mice under the floorboards, scratched, but her mind only made belching noises. Her heart was beating, which is a good thing for it to do at anytime, but it was beating in an exceptionally loud manner; her hands were sweaty, her stomach turned small flips, flat gray waves curled down her vision, an unpleasant sensation of her mind rolling over like a lazy whale. What the hell.

She licked her lips. The soft salt taste of Eddie's mouth on hers. Oh God, she should probably add sex with a minor to the list of charges. Probably. She didn't remember. "Okay, follow me and do everything I do." She wiped her nose. So did he.

She scraped her hands through her hair. Wondered. Time to go. Measured the drop to the ground. Wondered about condoms. "Okay, Eddie, remember, it's only the last ten feet that kill you." Three stories. She urged herself to move. Would be a good trick if she could pull it off. Stretched over to the next window ledge, hooked her hands on the open sill. Hung there.

Frying rice, babies crying, Chinese television.

Her shoulders screamed as she swung her legs to the next window's fire-escape ladder. The old metal rang softly as she scrambled down a floor. Two.

Buses rumbled past the mouth of the alley as she navigated the slippery metal steps; below her, simmering in filth were oil tins, broken bicycles, faint in the early light. Startled by a couple drops of liquid hitting her shirt, Reno moved abruptly to the next ledge, nearly slipped to splatter her own self on top of it all. With a strange sense of relief she realized it was blood—she thought Eddie was puking again. She knelt down, hung from her hands, dropped the last ten feet, didn't break an ankle. Eddie flopped next to her, moaning.

They hobbled out of the alley without speaking, headed east. Still a few sleepers in the next set of doorways, mumbling for spare change. Eddie left little spots of blood as they made their royal progress down the street.

"You gonna stop that bleedin' or we gonna do something about it?"

"Up ahead there's a drugstore. Some cotton balls stop it. Don't holler at me."

"Not hollerin'." Reno wanted to pop him one. "What the hell happened anyway?"

"Well, it's sort of embarrassing. Some people came by after we, um . . ."

"Never mind that now. We talk about that another time." She gave him a sharp glance. "Besides we didn't do nothin'."

He grinned with half his face. "Right. So the guy told me he had the deal of the century set up, you know?"

Shook her head. Sure, she knew. Noticed that he also had cuts on his knuckles just starting to swell up purple. At least he'd gotten in a few licks. Seventeen. Holy hell.

"Well." He squirmed a little. "It was a setup." He seemed to think with that he'd answered the question.

Reno wanted to know details, for some reason it seemed important. "You let that skinny old junkie rip you off?" Just trying to be helpful.

"No!" He wiped his nose, smearing blood everywhere, shrugged. "Well. Yeah." He looked at her like he expected her to belt him.

She spit on her fingers and cleaned off some of the blood on his face. Seemed he'd already been hit enough. "How much he get off you?"

"Everything."

Then she wanted to hit him. He sensed it, going rigid under her glare. She went into the drugstore without another word, got some peroxide, Band-Aids, cotton balls, pain killers. She didn't stop at the counter to pay.

When she came back out he'd disappeared.

chapter seventeen

Half hour to show time. Eddie, the number-one bartender and baby dope wizard par excel-lence, was still among the missing. Reno didn't care: people like him were just a whole lot of energy wasted on nothin'. Only reason, she told herself, she showed up for work at all was to get herself some traveling change. A dollar for the club, one for herself. She'd need it in Vegas. Didn't matter what Eddie did. Nope. Before the end of the second show she ought to be able to pocket enough money to hold her for a while, then she'd be on her way; there was more to life than slaving in some silly bar. Eddie. What an asshole. Didn't call or anything.

Sinclair hurried past, frowning. He looked very handsome when he frowned. Sort of sexy and distracted. Reno pulled her eyes away, moved to the far end of the bar, telling herself to get a grip.

Sinclair stood in front of her. His arm muscles had great definition. Reno thought, abstractly, that he also had a good line from his shoulders to his hips. Get a grip, girl.

He stuck out his lower lip. "Are you avoiding me?"

"Yes." She danced around him to put a red glass candle and an ashtray on a table.

"Oh." He hadn't expected such a short, direct answer. "Why?"

"Because I think stupid thoughts around you. I hate that."

Foolish grin. "Like what?" Preening.

"Huh. I make idiot noises inside my head and you expect me to tell you what they are? Right." She moved him to one side, grabbed another tray full of candles, went to the far corner of the showroom.

He followed. "Oh, come on, Reno."

"If I tell you will you forget all about it?"

"Nope." Bigger smile.

"Fuck you."

Cajoling. "Come on, Reno."

"Okay. If I tell you will you at least shut up about it?"

Pause. He figured he'd lied before, he'd probably lie in the future—this one wouldn't be much of a burden. "Sure."

She looked up at him, her eyes round with a mischievous sincerity. "You have a beautiful mouth."

He put a hand to his lips, puzzled: "Well. I don't see that's such a stupid thought."

"Thick as a brick, Sinclair. You are all cement north of the eyebrows." Reno smacked the last candle down on the last table. "Gimme a match, bonehead." She didn't look at him, held her hand out, palm up.

"What?" Sinclair patted his pockets, distracted, wanting to pursue the conversation but not sure where it was supposed to go. He handed her a pack of matches. "Damn." He saw Eva come in, ducked back upstairs.

Eva came up to Reno. "Seen Sinclair?" Suspicious.

"Nope."

"Su'ad?"

Reno shook her head no. Casual. She already knew the answer. "You cocktailin' in her place?"

"Seems Miss Fortunate isn't going to work tonight." Sniff. "Su'ad thinks she special, thinks she going to be the big star at Hunt's party tonight." Arch. "Won't she be surprised when it falls through." Eva slammed her soft fist on the table.

Reno measured the woman, a nasty piece of work, the kind of woman who made up in devious what she lacked in smart. Reno wondered how Sinclair could bear to fuck her. Shrugging, "Oh well. No explanation for some people's taste." Eva's petty plots weren't any of Reno's business; Su'ad could take care of herself. Besides, Reno didn't have time to attend to other people's troubles. Eddie, however, she might take the time to attend to, if he ever showed up: he deserved a good kick in the butt. She went behind the bar, started slicing lemons, wondered how it was that she ended up doing someone else's work. Again.

Slowmotion finished setting up the register; it was a little short. "Eddie didn't give you any money for me did he?"

"Hah." Never seem to get away from it. Reno shrugged, another couple hours she be on a bus, what she care. Fuckum. Reno poured herself a scotch. "All my troubles Lord. Soon be oo-over."

Eva swiveled across the showroom holding her tray in one hand, a martini glass carefully placed dead center, her brittle smiley-doll face tense above her doll body.

The sailor didn't tip her.

Su'ad stopped at the bar. "Pour me a soda?"

"Sure. Sure. Last chance." Couldn't hurt to tell Su'ad she was leaving, maybe get a couple bucks from her. "I'm outta here in a while." Reno smiled, preparing for the touch.

Su'ad scowled. "You can't!" Her voice a controlled wail. "You got to come to the party. You got to be there." She put what sounded like real worry in her voice.

Reno ignored the tone. "Seen you dance before. See you again someday." Grabbed a lime, made a neat cut, slid the slice onto the lip of the glass, pushed the soda across. "Sorry but we all out of little paper umbrellas."

Ignoring the small humor. "No, no. It's important." Hesitant. "I need you to be there."

Reno didn't answer, just wrinkled her nose. These people were all in a conspiracy. Probably all FBI agents. Even Su'ad. Especially Su'ad. She sighed.

Poppy strolled into the club wearing her usual bright silks, a pair of long diamond earrings, her blue black hair hung straight down to her waist. She cradled a trendy blue rubber briefcase as she drifted between the tables, pressing flesh, making appointments; she left the other customers pushing their heads close together and gossiping in her wake. Ignoring them, she headed straight for the bar. Smiling at Reno.

As if they were coconspirators.

Reno's head throbbed; she had forgotten all about the perplexing woman. Couldn't remember if they'd set up some deal—there was a nagging suspicion that they had. Reno watched Poppy's smooth approach, worried.

"Hello again." Poppy winked. "Are you in a better humor?" Her cracked-ice eyes wrinkled at the corners. Hard to know if it was amusement or a twitch.

Reno growled. "What'll it be? On the house." Didn't look at her.

"Unblended scotch?"

Reno poured from a bottle of Glenfiddich.

"Ah you're still sour. Good. I value consistency." Poppy slipped onto a bar stool, easy as royalty, she reached out one of her long thin hands, palm up. "Got a cigarette?"

"Just smoked my last one." Reno had to be careful. She licked her upper lip, tried to think of something clever to say, fumbled in her pockets. "Here's some change, buy us a pack from the machine."

Poppy didn't touch the coins, folded her hands like a schoolgirl around her shot glass. "What time did you say you get out of this place?"

"I didn't. I never leave."

"Thought there was a party?"

"Oh. Right. After the show. Through that door, upstairs."

"That sounds good." Innuendo.

Didn't sound so good to Reno. In fact the whole setup looked worse with every passing minute. Reno glanced at Su'ad, quick, from the corners; Su'ad wore her matron face, disapproving. Reno mumbled. For Poppy's ears only: "Don't know what you're up to with all this attention, but I'm tellin' you, Poppy, I don't know what to do with it. Makes me uncomfortable."

Su'ad put her glass down on the bar. Snap.

Reno continued. "I don't work for people who make me uncomfortable." Brave words, not the least bit of truth.

Poppy smiled. "Tell me what I can do to make you comfortable." Sea-tide undertow whispered in her voice, tugging.

Indignant. "You think you gonna pimp me off?" Forgetting to whisper.

More laughter from Poppy. The woman's idea of funny was beginning to grate on Reno's nerves.

"No no no." Poppy straightened up, squared her shoulders, looked Reno in the eye. "I'm not that easy to satisfy, but I have an idea you will do just that."

"Sex? I don't indulge." Reno spoke with a confidence she didn't feel; didn't look at Su'ad; told herself it could almost be true. Reno didn't remember last night with Eddie so clearly anyway. Sex didn't count if you can't remember. "I stay away from it. Something you should consider." A quick flash of Sinclair with his shirt off. She wished, not for the last time, she had more control over her thoughts. Perhaps she should take up meditation.

Poppy's tongue licked out, her eyes shot a mean glance at Su'ad.

Su'ad said, "Go fuck yourself." Over her shoulder, to Reno: "You best stick around for the party, and after. We got to talk."

Poppy echoed her. "We too must talk."

Reno grunted. "We are talking. But it doesn't seem to be for any purpose." She trudged downstairs to get a sack of ice. Wallowed in unbidden visions of Poppy, a blazing fireplace, a magnum of champagne, an aluminum case lying open. Reno thought about listening to that kinky silkish woman tell her lies. Her hands shook as she hefted the ice tray. "Where do I get these ideas? Bad movies. That's where. No more of this crazy shit." She would stick to her decision. A few more hours, she be on her way. Into a real future. Without innuendo. She turned toward the stairs.

Eddie came staggering into the basement. "Oh, Reno, you won't believe what happened." Rubbing the blue circles under his eyes with a tremulous hand.

"Don't tell me." She suddenly didn't want to see him, let alone talk with him. Oh hell. "Shouldn't you be upstairs working the bar?"

"Sinclair's got it." Eddie shrugged. "A bunch of angry women up there, too much for me. Eva's pissed, Su'ad and Poppy are glaring like gladiators. Good thing Sinclair knows how to get his hands wet." He moved up next to her, small sparks where they touched. "Uh, you got any, you know, pain killers?"

Reno put the tray down. "I can probably get you somethin'." He looked so young. She could stick around, keep Eddie in pain killers. Be accommodating to Poppy. Keep an eye on Su'ad. Punch Eva. Take Sinclair's clothes off. It might not be so bad. "Hey, Eddie, maybe you should consider taking it easy, give yourself a drug-free holiday for a week?"

His face registered the massive incredulity only a young stud would manifest.

"Well, a day anyway?"

"Who died an' made you God?"

Eddie wouldn't notice if there was a sixteen-ton weight poised above him ready to fall. Reno touched his cheek lightly. "No one. And I hope no one does. You know what I mean?"

Glum. Apologetic. Embarrassed. "Shit. Don't I know it."

"Come on. Back to the arena." Reno handed him the ice tray. "I'm going to hang out down here for a minute, okay? Let me know when the tigers upstairs have left the bar, okay?"

"Right." Half step. "Which tigers?"

"Any that you spot."

In a few minutes Eddie hollered that the tigers had wandered off, bickering; Reno trudged back up to the showroom.

Big rattle of drums. Farouk took his place center stage. Dancing with an otherworldly desperation, he let his body slide nearly out of control, pulled it back at the last moment into the realm of the human. His movements had a sharp dangerous edge, each motion precise beyond technique, a murderous accuracy in every fluid gesture.

Reno tried to figure out why his performances seemed so erratic. As if it were impossible for him to sustain his concentration. Hard to believe that other people had demons as strong as her own; she almost liked him then. Not enough to change her attitude, but she almost liked him.

Farouk's adoring harem stood once again along the sides of the room, clapping and swooning on cue. His bodyguard, the almost perfectly square little woman, hung around Slowmotion, giving her tips on lighting and sound levels.

Slowmotion had other things to think about—like a deficit of something over four hundred dollars.

Reno drifted over to Eddie; she didn't know why, maybe just to be near. Security of a sort. She thought about the bus ticket to Vegas. She thought about being all alone again, reminded herself that proof of adulthood was found in the capacity to take action; still she dithered. Maturity is overrated. She felt about as decisive as a puddle of warm piss. Glared into the mirrored ball, no answers there either.

Poppy reached across the bar, grabbed Reno's arm. "We must talk." Sibilant hissing jewel-toned words. All too familiar.

Reno let herself be lured back to the lower depths of the club; one made sophisticated moves, the other made sophisticated dodges. Reno was shaky: the streets were looking more and more like a strange interlude—real life was in jail. Poppy's long cool hand on her back woke thoughts of great riotous sex. In the cramped filthy basement? A going-away present.

To Reno's surprise, once they were alone in the basement Poppy became brisk instead of seductive. All business. Popping open the rubber briefcase, Poppy pulled out a small pouch. She placed it on the chair. "Here's proof of my sincerity. My bargaining chips."

"But I don't even know what the negotiations are about." Reno swallowed, clutched her hands behind her back. Whatever was in that pouch was certain to be hot—a gun used in a messy political murder, some banker. A senator. They gone try ta pin it on her. She knew.

"I need you to do some work for me, tonight."

Someone clattered down the stairs.

Reno hid the pouch in a pile of towels. Hurry. Paranoia. "Like what?"

Poppy was amused. "That must be yes." She leaned forward, whispered. "I want you to get me all the information on Hunt's hard disk."

Reno hardly heard, the sound of her own nervous breathing drowning every other sound except the footsteps approaching the basement. "Say what?"

Eddie came in, angry. "Why is Eva the only one up there? She can't take care of the whole damn showroom herself!"

Reno's breathing slowed. "Sure she can. She just a lazy cow." She smiled at Eddie with a very dry mouth.

Eddie looked from one to the other of them with a suspicion he didn't bother hiding. "You guys doin' a private deal down here or what?"

"Nope nope." Reno gripped the pile of bar towels to her belly with a false grin, patted Eddie on his tight little ass as she passed. "You two guys the wheeler-dealers, the bright hopes of a generation. I just bees the hired help. Got it?" She spun a little clockwork dancer circle before her exit.

Now her only problem would be to stay as far away from both of them as she possibly could. Find out what was in that pouch.

Reno knelt down behind the bar, opened the pouch, pulled

out a Makita portable drill—with that and a crowbar she could take the world apart. Some Greek philosopher said something very like that. There was also a very small computer thing, about the size of a checkbook. Her breath caught somewhere around her solar plexus. She shoved the pouch behind the rubble under the cash register, grabbed a tray, headed for the far side of the room. To think.

"Hey. How about some beer over here?"

She pulled her mouth down in a grimace, insulted. "See the bar over there? Well, that's where the beer is. You ain't lame or nothin'. Go get it yer own self." She rested her shoulders against the wall, stared at nothing, thought about important matters. Not the least of which was that she didn't know how to download Hunt's damn computer, didn't know what the little electronic gadget was. Hadn't even cased the damn apartment yet. Hadn't planned on it neither. Hell, she didn't even know what kind of computer he had or where it was.

Some mess she'd managed to make of everything. Without even trying. Hey: package that talent, make a bundle.

The customers were drenched in beer and sweat. Various men from various nations shuffled happily around the stage, shaking their shoulders, stepping strong, grinning in a beatific haze. The music never let up, pushing the energy higher, higher. Slim women in tight jersey dresses slithered around on their stiletto heels, cruising, checking out the potential for mileage later in the night. Eva leered from the edge of the vortex, her coke energy fragmenting in the smoke-thick air.

Poppy's voice came at Reno from behind her left shoulder. "The pocket computer belongs to Hunt. It's got the access codes to his computer. You might want to make a note of them before you give it back."

Reno choked.

Chuckling, Poppy didn't exactly soothe her. "I have some small talents of mine own—Hunt hasn't yet realized his pockets have been picked. Perhaps you should be delicate about returning his little gadget."

When Reno turned around, Poppy was gone.

The audience ethnics took the stage. Farouk went off somewhere to confer with his bodyguard—a handjob maybe. To stiffen him up for the next performance. The rest of his harem, involved in esoteric deals of their own, snorted the lines on the tables, waited in lines at the bathrooms, had tequila and limes and lines, rum and coke and lines. Everyone's favorite girls.

"Like being inside a lava lamp." Reno scowled on the sidelines, debating with herself about her life. About the unguarded purses littering the empty chairs.

Eddie slipped up next to her. "So, girlfriend, what's the haps?"

Reno jumped.

"Edgy tonight. How come?"

"No man. You got it wrong. I'm cool." Reno slid sideways.

Eddie followed. "Don't try to shit me. This place sucks so bad. These folks wouldn't give a starving man a nickel. Hey, check out the performance that miserable band is doing." He nudged her. "Sold the fuckers a couple bones, but they didn't even offer to turn me on to their other shit."

"Maybe don't have no other shit."

"Aw. What you know about it. Look at that guy over there with his hand down Eva's pants."

Reno gave her shoulders a little shimmy. "They're an inspiration to us all." Airy. She motioned with her chin at the crowd. A wiggling line of Farouk's femmes began snaking through the audience. "They seem to have less and less clothes on as the night goes on. You notice that?"

"Can't tell me they ain't loaded." Eddie grumbled, strangling a bar rag.

"Can't tell you anything. You don't listen." Reno hadn't meant to say anything at all, but once she started she couldn't stop. Hissing: "Where the hell you disappear off to this morning, you rotten asshole." Furious. "I worried all day." She had intended to be cool right through to the end. So much for intentions. "Well? How do you explain yourself, you little fuck." She spit her words.

Eddie looked pleased. "You were worried?" Real pleased.

"I'll rip your face off and feed it to you, you do me like that again."

Eddie didn't look at her or answer, just watched the women snaking through the crowd, hummed to himself; dancing a little, he listened to Reno simmering. "Hey. That must mean you like me." He leaned back against her, forcing her to put her arms around him to hold him up.

Vicious whisper. "I'm gone drop you right on that smart ass of yours, Eddie." He shook his head smiling no-you-won't. She let go and stepped back but he didn't fall down.

"Bunch of silly fools." Su'ad snapped her empty glass down beside them. "What they think, they gonna get discovered here? Bunch of two-bit whores. Hollywood bumps and grinds. Fan dancing. Makes me gag."

"Hunt makes me gag." Reno spoke without thinking, pushing Eddie away. "Anyway, what's the matter with fan dancing? What right you got to be callin' those women fools?"

Su'ad shifted her weight. "Mm. Listen to you now. Gimme another soda." Wrinkled her nose. "If you please."

Poppy came over, put her arm around Reno. "I know a silly fool when I see one." She leaned over to Su'ad, whispering, her voice thick with innuendo. "I'm sure lookin' forward to seein' you dance later tonight." Poppy licked her lips, let one eyelid droop closed. Lascivious, classic.

Su'ad wrinkled her nose. "Bah." She stalked away to the far side of the room, removing herself from temptation. She found herself doing that a lot lately. She didn't like it but didn't know what else to do.

Rapid, official, no longer flirting, Poppy said, "I need that information tonight."

"Oh sure." Reno scratched her chin, pretending. "But it'll cost you more than that cute little drill."

Before Poppy could respond, Eddie interrupted, maybe defending Su'ad, maybe angry with Poppy's arm around Reno. "Hey Poppy what you got to be cappin' on Su'ad for?" Maybe jealous of their hushed conversation; the smell of money. "She nervous as a cat about the party."

Poppy sneered. "What she think happen? Instant stardom? Hah. Not likely." She picked up Reno's scotch, sauntered over to join a table of rich inebriates. Invertebrates. They scraped their chairs making room for her. She didn't look back at the bar.

Eddie pulled Reno behind him. "What is it with you guys? Thought you and me was partners?"

"Partners don't just disappear without no explanation." Hiss hiss.

"I saw someone owed me some money."

"Bullshit." Reno forgot that she was counting down the minutes until she hit the cash register. "You did not. Or maybe you mean the money you gave your pal last night? Shit." Reno screwed up her face. "I don't wanta hear your dumb explanations anyway."

Eddie gave her his best big-eyed look again. "We in this together." He called over to Slowmotion, soft, cajoling. "Hey, Slow, if ya gimme some coke I could cook it up. Sell it in rocks; make us a little money." He looked eager, tried for casual.

Reno whispered, outraged. "Make crack? You wanna blow the place up?"

Whisper back. "Hey, I seen it done dozens of times." To Slow. "Whaddaya say?"

Slowmotion looked at them with disgust. "You mean you saw someone on TV do it." She focused all her attention on the light board. "Why should I give you some; whyncha use what you got. Or did you do it up already 'steada sellin' it?" She didn't even bother to look at him for his answer.

Reno's mouth grew tight. Solemn. "Tole ya." Hiss.

Eddie shrugged, smiling. Easy. "Wull, hey babe, just think

about it, okay?" He trotted back down the other end to pull some draft beers.

Slowmotion watched him go. "That subnormal comes up with the dumbest shit."

"He ain't subnormal." Reno couldn't understand why she was defending him.

"Oh? He thinks Frank Sinatra's a god."

"What if he's right?"

Slowmotion leaned out of her booth. "You guys got somethin' goin' on now or what?"

Before Reno could deny it, Su'ad came back. Worry. "Hey, I just knocked on Hunt's door—there's no answer."

"He got to be around somewhere." Slowmotion was brisk. "He probably just takin' care of his secret party preparations." To Reno. "He always plan some surprise."

Eddie interrupted, loud. "Yeah, he pour all the good booze into jars, drinkin' it all the while, then he fills the empty bottles with cheap shit." Eddie was suddenly Mr. Information. "Never never drink the wine from his cut crystal decanters— it's the worst."

Su'ad shifted from one foot to the other like she had to pee.

Reno said, "You tellin' me smart people bring they own booze to his parties."

"He ain't rich because he a nice guy, you know."

"Tell her that." Reno pointed at Su'ad with a rude thumb.

"Aw, she know it."

Su'ad spoke, prim. "Someone got to go up there soon, set up the place."

"How we gonna do that, if he don't answer?"

"Sinclair has a key. Besides, Reno." Su'ad looked sly. "You can open any door."

Offhand, Slowmotion reminded her. "Hunt's got more locks and alarms than a museum."

"That don't bother Reno." Su'ad showed all her teeth in a mean smile, then chewed on her knuckle.

"The man let people in when he's ready. It's his party, he not gonna want people poking around his house without him there." Reno edged down the bar, away from Su'ad.

"You can slip in there like you usually do—he won't even know you bin there."

Angry. "Stop that, damn it. Don't be playin' me like that behind some creepy party."

"You seen his place yet?" Su'ad sounded casual, watched Reno. "Some nice stuff up there."

Reno growled a warning.

Slowmotion flicked on the strobe lights as the Sufis began their dervish spins.

Farouk moved to the side-stage alcove. His females surrounded him, cooing.

Reno heard one call him "Daddy." Decided some things were simply not meant for her understanding. "Nope." Stared at Su'ad, still warning. "I'm looking forward to it though." Reno intended to be long gone before the damn thing started.

Su'ad pouted. "Knew it. You still got the itch."

"No man, I don't do that no more." Reno walked away.

Su'ad called after her. "You and Poppy puttin' something together, I can tell."

"You outta your mind." Calm. Keep calm. Low and inside. "What is it with you? First it's 'Go away Reno,' then it's 'Oh please stay an' see me dance, Reno.' Now you playin' this other song. I don't need this shit, b'lieve me, I don't."

Su'ad looked hurt. About to apologize.

"Fuck you." Reno stomped down to the basement, splashed water on her face, thought about just heading out the alley door, forget the cash drawer. She had some ID, maybe get a casino job in Vegas. What more do a young girl want.

Poppy followed her down. "Hey. Don't let Su'ad do you that way. We can have a good thing here. Security, Reno."

"Secure? Like maximum security?" She dried her face. "Okay, whyn't you tell me what you want me to do and I'll tell you why I won't do it."

"Easy as taking candy—get the 'access' code from the pocket computer, turn on the computer in Hunt's flat, go to the C drive, write 'copy star dot star,' dump the contents onto a couple disks. Take you ten, fifteen minutes. I'll handle it from there."

"What? What what? You're outta yer fuckin' mind." There was no way she was going to do this.

"Relax. Take a couple minutes to play with Hunt's little one before you give it back to him. It'll all become clear."

Clear. Only thing clear to Reno was that everything was comin' across the plate a little too fast for her. "Rippin' off that old dude's hard disk is worth a lot. It's an easy fifteen hundred." Reno paused. "No. Two Gs."

Poppy seemed to be thinking that over.

Eddie nipped into the bathroom. "Hi girls." Slammed the cubicle door behind him. "Don't stop discussin' me just because I'm pissin' back here." The toilet flushed. He emerged, didn't break stride. "Come on Reno. Back to the arena." Eddie grabbed Reno by the hand. "See you upstairs Poppy. Don't rush."

chapter eighteen

H unt lay on his leather couch, fly unzipped, drifting in an imaginary boat to the banal sounds of Haydn's *Water Music*. La la la, he conducted an orchestra, note-perfect like all the 1950 recordings.

Music was solace, but solace was not enough. He turned the music down, walked to the sideboard, poured himself a tumbler of unblended, wandered to his window. The rooftops stretched like a huge flight of steps down to the bay, a dark blue point sparking in the distance. The fog sat just above the horizon like desire: dense, threatening. No stars. He drank.

He suddenly couldn't decide if the party this evening was important, or simply part of the cultural trivia he'd involved himself in for so long. It was necessary for him to have a firm grip on the social-cultural pulse, he always kept his files up to date and in order. He wasn't sure what was essential anymore: things were slipping away, the game had gotten old, taken him with it. Nowhere.

There was a softness in his midsection, a slope to his shoulders, an unsettling sag to his throat. He tried to correct these defects by holding himself very straight, breathing the way he imagined athletes breathed, but he saw the signs of irreversible personal decay. When he touched his toes in the morning, grudgingly, he would stare at the swollen veins, snakes forming a lattice work on his calves; he got a shiatsu treatment once a week, he massaged his face with Retin-A at night, his scalp with special oil every third morning. He gargled with salt yet he continued to age. Something was missing.

Sex perhaps. Eva tried, but she didn't have the touch. Su'ad might. He didn't believe what Eva said about her. Professional jealousy, but it paid to be wary; he didn't want entanglements—preparation was half the battle. He'd see how the evening's entertainment proceeded.

Bitter. Criticism as a profession was essentially a thankless job: the acuity of his eye, the years of training his carefully cultivated sensibility, testing, weighing the shallow pleasures of those who accept things for their seeming. His greater talents were ignored because he made a good living, a very good living, dealing in uncommon information. The essential trivia of the private life of artists. Everyone fawned on the people he wrote about, too few realized where the real power lay. This had been some protection; now it was putting restrictions on the full use of his powers.

Pleasure. He hadn't had a proper lover in years, not since that mad beautiful wife of his had overdosed on his couch. He couldn't get rid of a sneaking suspicion that the impossible woman had planned it to spite him. Tossing his head he repeated to himself again that it didn't work. He was doing better now than ever before.

He supposed, although he didn't know, such emotions being foreign to his practical nature, that Farouk may have loved his sister.

Bitter. As if these "artists" would have amounted to anything without an appreciative, an educated, a literate audience. Himself. He *made* those people, that was his art. Bitter, because he was not given his due; bitter, he was underestimated. Bitter because he was growing old and suspected that people thought since his eye was educated to be discriminating beyond the common herd, his soul was composed entirely of rubble. He wouldn't be held accountable to anyone for the state of his soul.

He decided early in his career not to tie himself to the usual drudgery of securing rent money, drug money, the hand on the curve of the butt, scrounging, bartering, counting his change, counting it again. Not him. Mired in the mindless unprofitable camaraderie of lesser mortals—he'd used that phrase once concerning some actor but he savored it for himself, more appropriate. He knew the tyranny of talent.

Hunt created Farouk, each engineered show, each review, each apparently casual remark. Timing, timing and presence of mind were great talents. Yet at each turn Farouk twisted everything to suit his own desires, the complacent bastard.

People adored blood sports, always forgave the one who used the blade if it were sharp enough, entertaining enough. They wouldn't forgive a coward though. Hunt grimaced; so much depended on Farouk's mood. Thus, the drugs.

Farouk himself might think he'd never forgive Hunt, but he would, everyone did—they came around or they became irrelevant. Hunt shrugged. His thoughts were fragile, infinitely stretching things, but sharp and shiny, to cut or strangle.

He stepped into his study, frowned at his computer. It was all set to send the latest information to Zurich. Blinking idiotically, waiting for the instruction to "send." He had the whole hard disk open, undecided what he absolutely had to send, what he could still hold back. Accounts receivable. Accounts payable. And another account not yet billed—made no sense to threaten a district attorney with exposure if there was really nothing to expose. He needed to be sure. He sat down, scrolling through the directory.

A rapping at his door formed itself into a familiar series of knocks. He got up, unlocked the door. "Ah, Eddie." Hunt used his deepest voice, warm and kind. "I was worried about you."

"Get out of the way, Hunt, I got to put this in the kitchen."

Eddie pushed by him carrying two huge grocery sacks. "I don't suppose you got any pain killers?" He dumped the load on the sink counter with a groan.

"They really aren't good for you, you know." Hunt gave Eddie a couple pills, Eddie gave him his go-to-hell look. Hunt ignored it, recited instructions on the buffet, waved his hand in a circle, a magic gesture, pulled his cuffs and said he was going out for a moment to take care of some unfinished business. "Don't let anyone in until I get back."

"Bullshit. I can't set this dump up alone."

"All right, if you insist." Hunt smiled to himself. "I'll ask Eva to help you."

Downstairs the Sufis were hot, a circus of colorful acrobats and glittering music, topped with their famous hypnotic shamanic drum work—the audience was up, applauding, screaming, "Ai-wa!" "Alllllah!" The basic appreciative litany. Still didn't tip worth shit.

Slowmotion thudded around the bar pretending to belly dance, her hips going in dangerous circles, her arms waving like seaweed. "One of these days, baby doll, we be rich an' then some." A proper Farouk bump and grind. "All our worries be over."

Once again Hunt had missed Farouk's show. "Here Slow." Hunt peeled two hundreds off a roll. "I'll have the remainder for you in a matter of hours." Smug.

Reno watched him put the rest in his right front pocket. Pat it. Smooth his dick. Primed for the quick fade, Reno couldn't understand why she hadn't already left. She examined her motivations, discovered, among the weeds, a lurking desire to roll Hunt. Seemed to be a universal thing. Besides, it might prove to be one of her life's more lucrative pleasures. Better than the gossip on his hard disk. She wondered, spastically, how the hell she ever gonna live a normal life if those kinds of ideas didn't start looking less attractive? All she needed was some security. She deserved it but she didn't have the smallest idea how to get it. When she looked around for Hunt he'd disappeared into the crowd.

Farouk beamed from the sidelines, one arm around a glazed half-dressed acolyte. Daddy was pleased.

"Rolex," Reno said. "Another Rolex." Worth a lot more than the information—Reno couldn't take her eyes off Farouk: the wrist with the Rolex was attached to a hand that squeezed one young woman's breast, thumb across the nipple; his other hand made a dainty arabesque with his cigarette, emphasizing some point. A dozen heads nodded in complete agreement with him.

Selling a hot Rolex was always a touchy procedure. Jewelers wouldn't pay shit—they only wanted you to trade up to a more expensive watch. She was doubtful that she could connect up with a reliable fence until she'd been out for a while, got the feel of the market. All the good it'd do her to pick up a dozen Rolexes.

She'd know the time.

Su'ad was right, this was no life for Reno. She slipped another tenner into her pocket. No one noticed. Typical. She wanted to leave right then but there was no one around to take the bar. She pocketed a buck. Pouring shaking scraping sticking wiping washing. Dishpan hands.

Of course, she would be better off with a Rolex than without. Always pick up a little change from it. Or wear the damn thing, look like she was Someone.

A fool.

Eddie returned. "Hey, Reno, you get the feelin' Hunt's up to something?"

"Since birth. Man never do no one no favors." Reno folded her arms on the bar. "That's a bad sign in a human being isn't it?"

"Over seven years old, yeah." Eddie hit her arm lightly with his knuckles. "Right. Who knows what goes on in the depths of a deviant's mind, hey, Reno?" He pushed her toward the stairs. "Come on up. We best keep an eye on the old bastard's flat."

"Eddie, you much too cheerful. Pain killers?"

Eddie grinned.

Reno thought he probably swallowed a handful.

Slowmotion waved at them, fanned a wad of bills, thumbs up. "Hang on in there, babies. Things are looking gooood."

Poppy fought her way through the maddened crowd, whispered, "Tonight. I need it tonight."

Reno shook her head. "I don't think so—I got to—" She didn't like the look in Poppy's eyes. Time to get the hell out of there. Reno went to follow Eddie up the stairs but Slowmotion hollered: "Last call. Pickup starts in ten minutes."

"Shit." Eddie pushed Reno back to the bar, shouldering Poppy aside. "Handle the bar for me, okay? I'll finish upstairs." He didn't wait for her reply.

Last call was like a war behind the bar: all systems into overload, nuclear weapons, everything, billions of glasses mugs pitchers coming and going, bottles half full and entirely empty wet napkins limp celery stalks dried lemons olives folding potato chips. Bar origami.

Reno stood in the wreckage, wondering, not for the last time, if perhaps there really were some permanent damage done to the brain by all the various drugs, legal and illegal, that people pumped through their systems.

"Tonight. Before Hunt sends his column off to the magazine."

Reno jumped at the sound of Poppy's voice, waved her hand, shrugging, palm up. "Lookit this mess. The place is a disaster. I be lucky if I get this done before morning let alone play with that sucker's computer."

Poppy's icy eyes gleamed. "Here's two hundred. Before delivery." She slid the bills across the wet bar.

Reno picked them up, couldn't meet Poppy's eyes. She had nothing to measure the offer against. Nothing. She put the bills in her pocket. Getting quite a little collection in that pocket. She sighed. All the good it would do her when they picked her up. And she hadn't even committed any real crimes yet. But they'd come for her. The signs were all around.

Slowmotion's voice held gnomish innuendo as she spoke to Poppy. "Be sure and stick around for the party. It'll be something you won't want to miss."

Reno tried to clean up the bar around Slowmotion, fussing, hoping to make her go away, take Poppy with her.

Slow didn't move, rested her large bulk on the bar, casual.

Poppy laughed. "I'm looking forward to it." Suave.

Reno hated suave.

Poppy's long hand rested on the bar, manicured fingernails tapping. "I wouldn't miss it for anything." One perfectly manicured finger scratched Reno's arm. "I hear anyone who is anyone at all will be there."

Seemed to Reno that missing it would be the best thing in the world. "Right. Sure." She made a final circuit of the room, herding the unimportant drunks out onto the cold wet street. "They tell me the food's been poisoned."

chapter nineteen

The entrance to Hunt's apartment was blocked by bright people on the cultural cutting edge nibbling discreetly at the canapés; they filled the hall, they clung together, an impenetrable net of shoulders, sleek hips, well-modulated voices murmuring genteel witticisms and shredding reputations. They smiled at Reno, but they didn't get out of her way: they were waiting for an invitation to the bathroom or the kitchen or the bedroom; they played the game the way it was played when the stakes were high.

They'd had lots of practice.

Reno felt very much at a disadvantage. As usual.

The next room she wiggled her way into was small and full, the people in it were small—not in the physical sense, but in the mental—and full, again, in that other sense. The movers and shakers, the art world policy makers—they didn't seem so impressive when you looked at them up close and personal.

A very clean man bumped into Reno, he was small and full and wore a silver jacket. He said, "Excuse me." Teeth. His leg pushed against her hip. "Crowded in here isn't it."

Reno didn't even blink at him.

"So. Here we are. Might as well get to know each other. What do you do?"

Reno blinked. That was the lamest conversation opener she knew, but she had no response prepared so she didn't say anything. Didn't tell him to get out of her way, complimented herself on her discretion; he edged closer, she didn't back up, he was standing between her and where she wanted to be.

"Well." Coy. Closer yet. Millimeters separated them. Cozy. "If you won't tell me what you do—" He pushed his face into hers, smiling, eyes making promises Reno didn't like. "At least you haven't told me yet. But you will. I think we'll have enough time for all kinds of things. Don't you want to know what I do?"

Reno grunted, didn't have the presence of mind or glibness of tongue to say "No, please don't tell me I don't want to know."

So he told her. "I'm in the district attorney's office." Pride.

Without a second's pause. "That's a terrible place to be." She muscled past him, shoving herself through the crowd.

He followed her, hurt but smiling in a charming, puzzled way. "Oh. Oh dear." His arm reached past a fat lady to pluck at Reno's retreating back. "If it will make you feel any better about me, I'm not a very good lawyer."

She looked at his eager, expectant face. Remembered other lawyers. Other places. That's the thing about just getting out of jail—times places people bodies faces without reference points flow together. Not always appropriately. "Take your practice elsewhere, creep. I don't socialize with lawyers, sex offenders or cops." Reno moved sideways jamming an elbow into the cheerful drunk who was blocking her escape.

"Oh. I've heard about that reaction, but never experienced it. Oh." He was sincerely distressed. He'd had great riotous sex on his mind, Reno had looked like just the right one. "Oh. Oh dear."

Ships passing in the night. Bums pissing in the wind. Too bad.

Reno waved to Slowmotion, sixteen people away. "Sorry. I gotta get outta here, be back soon, this ain't gone get good for a while, I know how these things go." She hadn't the foggiest how these things go, but she knew very well how to make herself go. Away. She assured herself that Hunt would make Su'ad famous and happy so Reno didn't need to stay for her dance. Everything would work out great. Eva would choke on a canapé, Hunt would pay Slow the money he owed. Someone else would take care of Eddie. And Sinclair? Well, another time for Sinclair maybe. They'd all be fine, she'd be fine.

She wiggled out the door. Down the stairs. Took a last look around the showroom in the dim light. Groping her way behind the bar, she fished out the drill, paused over Hunt's pocket computer. Cute. Decided that both items were far more use to her than to any other human being. Hers by divine right. Fuck Poppy.

Eddie appeared, popping up out of thin air. "There you are. I bin lookin' for you."

It was a conspiracy. "Not now, Eddie, I got places to go."

"You can't leave now. It's just getting good."

Su'ad burst into their nonconversation. "My costume is gone!" Su'ad breathed in ragged gulps, bit her words. "Someone stole it from Hunt's bedroom." She was not quite panting. "That fairy musta stole it." Her movements were small, jerky. Distracted.

"Why he do that?" Reno spoke automatically. "Won't fit him." She choked on a sad laugh; she couldn't get out of that place to save her life. She put the pouch in her sack.

Su'ad glared. "I can't dance without my costume." She sat stiffly on the edge of a stool. "Might as well pack it in. Get a job at a fast-food outlet. A checker in a grocery store." Quiet desperate drama. "Or kill myself."

"Ought to try on someone else's problems once in a while." Reno had trouble working up sympathy over something so trivial as a costume. "Nuts. Wear something else." Reno put her hands on her hips in imitation of one of Su'ad's more familiar gestures. "There's all kinds of shiny stuff around here."

"Shiny stuff?" Su'ad shook her head. "I've got to be absolutely stunning tonight. My costume is very important. I want these people to see dancing like they've never seen it. I want to make them forget Farouk, all his trained puppies." She bit her lip. "I've got to look as good as anyone they might have seen in Egypt."

"It's a fashion show now?" Shit. Reno had to get away. Disappear. "Hell. Eva probably has something in one of the lockers." Shrugging. Damned if she do, damned if she don't. "Tell me which one's hers, I'll go down there, jimmy the damn thing for you."

Su'ad opened her eyes big; there was a shimmer of tears. Her voice was throaty. "I wouldn't wear one of her costumes for all the rice in China." Lower lip trembling.

Art: It's not enough to feeeel, everyone must know you feel.

"Well, fuck it then. Wear what you got on. You still the best." Reno felt better. "Sure. You'll knock 'em dead." She grabbed her bag, put the strap over her shoulder, edged toward the exit.

Su'ad moved her eyes slowly over to look at Reno. Nasty empty pools. "You haven't a clue have you?"

"Nope. I don't." What the hell. "But then, Su'ad, neither do you."

Hunt cat-footed his way over to their cozy little conference. "Missed you. What's the trouble, Su'ad?" A light scent of expensive men's cologne.

"My costume's been stolen." Flashing eyes. Drama to die for.

"How awful. And it was lovely. Don't worry, I think I may have just the thing. Come on back upstairs." He held out his arm, straight, commanding, palm open. She placed her hand in his, obedient. They left the room together.

Eddie looked at Reno, who looked at him looking at her. "What the fuck?"

"I dunno. You hafta wait an' see."

"Don't like to wait. Don't like surprises."

"Me neither." Reno was sorry she'd never see Eddie again. Something endearing about the boy. "Well, Eddie, I'll see ya upstairs. I gotta take a piss."

"I'll wait."

"Oh, no need."

"I'll wait." He followed her down, lit a cigarette, folded his arms, leaned against the wall. "I'll wait."

She wondered if she could stay in there so long he'd leave.

After a few minutes Eddie spoke. "I know you're up to something, Reno. Don't bother to stay in there forever thinkin' I'll go away. I don't like that look you got on your face. So you might as well piss or come out. I ain't goin' nowhere without you tonight."

She came out, ostentatiously zipping her jeans. "Don't do me no favors, Eddie."

"Wouldn't think of it." He held out his arm in imitation of Hunt.

"Fuck you." She took his arm. Grimacing.

They entered Hunt's apartment together.

Prawns on ice. Soda crackers. Green things pink things yellow crumpled exotic things. Little napkins with golfing pigs printed on them. Booze. Lots of terrible booze. The noise a room full of rich people talking with their mouths full can make is terrifying.

Eddie whispered. "Don't eat any prawns, they been frozen, thawed out then frozen again, now they thawing again." He grinned, pleased with himself. "People bound to get sick, eatin' them on this coast anyway." Solemn. "Fish is only good when it's caught fresh. Back home . . ." He stopped, not liking memories.

Fragments.

"I mean, my dear, it's the work of genius, yes, to decide what to put in, what to leave out."

"People are so touchy. They don't realize that any mention, especially a negative one, pushes the marketplace."

"Good for the political soul, dear. Keeps one honest."

Reno clung to Eddie, trying not to come into contact with any of the people in the crowded room. "Who are these people, Eddie?"

"Potential victims?" He turned his head in a slow pan across the room. "Diplomats?"

"Spies. Spies and agents for the DEA. Eddie, let's get outta here, okay?" She was sweating.

Slowmotion kept the lights low, pink to make the parchment complexions look better. The background music was low, bouncy, it would build up to a climax over the course of twenty minutes, half an hour. It was her job to prepare the slurpy crowd for the night's entertainment. "Hey assholes. Where you been?"

Music. Noshing. Backbiting. Distant buzzing voices: "Always good for business. To be mentioned."

"Yaz. Just to be mentioned in his column will bring in a certain amount of business."

"After that, it's up to you though."

Precise laughter. "Oh, we all know how to take advantage of what's offered."

Eddie pulled Reno through the crowd, planted her next to Slowmotion. "We been circulating."

Eva floated by, pouring André champagne from bottles with the labels washed off. Flirting. Pretending to have a good time. Her cat-in-cream smile slipped when Reno stepped in front of her.

Right up in Eva's face. "You know you can't fit in Su'ad's costume. Oughta give it back." Reno wrapped her rough hand around the champagne bottle.

Eva's mouth and eyes turned into big round Os, she tried

to wrench the bottle free, said she had no idea what Reno meant.

Reno turned the champagne bottle down the front of Eva's tight outfit. "This is only the beginning." No one saw what happened.

"Oh!" Eva whimpered. "Oh. You vicious little thug!"

Reno liked that. "Oooh. Look here. You pissed yer pants, girl." Loud.

Tightlipped, brushing at her crotch. "I'll certainly have some things to say to Sinclair." Eva's eyes shot tiny, red beams. "He only hired you because Su'ad begged him to—" Reno liked that too. "But I'll see to it that he boots both of you out on your ass." Grim.

"No you won't." Reno gave her a flat-eyed jail-house stare. "Because if you say one word you'll end up with that bottle up your cunt." Reno watched Eva's face crumble. "You best give Su'ad her costume back. Like, today." Strike at the eyes first. Or the throat. "Your ass is mine." Thin evil smile. Closer. Reno grabbed the other woman's shirt. "I know all kinds of nasty games to play."

"I don't know what you're talking about." Little shuffling steps back. Ineffective.

Something about the fear on Eva's face saved her, snapped Reno out of her hatred trance. "Shit. Get away from me, Eva."

Eva got.

Reno finally decided: she wasn't going anywhere. Not yet. She would see the night out, see what there was to see, steal what there was to steal. Maybe do a thing or two to Eva. Something memorable. "Hey Eddie. What's in that room?" Pointing to a closed door.

"Books. A whole lotta boring books. Computer. Lots of little parts to the thing. Copies of his columns and shit in scrapbooks. More on disks. All kinds of weird shit about people."

The rudiments of snatch and grab can be applied to any inanimate object. "How big's the computer?"

"One part's a laptop. Real tiny. Got another machine with a big screen he plugs it into." Eddie observed her face very carefully. Noticed that she was equally careful not to change her expression a millimeter away from benign disinterest. "You know anything about computers?"

"Me?" Reno raised her eyebrows. "Me?" She dismissed his speculation with a wave.

He continued to stick very close to her. "Clam and shell in the primal ooze."

"You nuts, Eddie."

"You're up to somethin'." Eddie followed her, unimpressed with her false disinterest. "Be damned if I know what, but you're up to somethin', Reno."

Before Reno thought of an interesting reply Su'ad rushed up to them, purring. "Hunt's lent me a lovely antique baladi dress for me to wear. It's got silver threads woven all through it." She smiled. "It's entirely covered with real silver beads. I'll look great." She didn't indulge in false modesty. "Come on, Reno, help me dress." Su'ad looked at the socialites crowded in Hunt's living room as if they were snacks.

Eddie, hard on Reno's heels, nudged up behind her, whispering, "No way, babe. No way. I'm not letting you out of my sight."

Reno ignored him. "Well, come on, let's get to it." Sooner Su'ad started dancing, the sooner Reno could break into the study, take care of her own business. Get gone. She moved away from Eddie. He followed as if attached by a rubber band, stepping on her heels. She elbowed him. He dodged.

Alternatives. Reno considered a couple of alternative plans she might try if Eddie insisted on continuing his silly surveillance. Push him out the window maybe?

Su'ad watched their impromptu dance. "Cut it out you two. This serious business." She made wavy motions down her body with her hands. "What a dress! Hunt asked me to have it cleaned before I gave it back." Shimmy. "But he said I could keep it for as long as I liked."

"You oughta have it cleaned before you wear it, just to be safe." Growling. Shoving Eddie away.

Su'ad used her magic mantra. "Shut up, Reno."

"Hey. Don't talk to her that way." Knighthood in full flower.

Reno looked at Su'ad, rolled her eyes, went into Hunt's bedroom, shut the door in Eddie's unhappy face.

He took up a guardian's position. "Broads. They don't know what they want. Bitches." He said it twice, it felt so nice. "Bitches." He assumed a very grown-up casual posture against the wall by the door.

"I'm so glad you're here, Reno." Su'ad flipped open the door to Hunt's wardrobe exposing a set of full-length double mirrors, lifted a dark cloth garment bag down from a hook. Reverent. "I'm so excited. This is terribly important."

"Oh. I can tell." Not enthusiastic. "Hey. You seem awfully familiar with Mr. Huntington's bedroom."

Exasperated. "Reno. I tole you. I ain't been fucking *any*one for years. Get off it."

"Well. I think you should know that I think your attitude is sick." Pout. There wasn't any windows in the damn bedroom either. Looked like the only private way out of the flat beside the front door into the hall was going to be through the kitchen window. Bummer. "Listen Su'ad." Touching the rich fabric of the baladi dress. "If Hunt's not good to you—I mean really good—" she motioned at the bed, at the expensive clothes hanging in the closest—"I'm going to rip his face off. Feed it to him—"

Hunt came in then, smiling; he pulled Su'ad into the strong circle of his arm. Ignored Reno. "Don't get into costume yet. Come, I want you to meet some special guests. You can get dressed later." He paused, pretended to notice Reno for the first time. "Oh, you can come along too." Dubious. Attention back on Su'ad. "The tall fellow I'm going to introduce you to books dancers into hotels in Egypt; the shorter one is a colleague of mine, works the Syria beat." Arrogant smile. "Of course there's no American dancers working in Syria now, but he'll be a useful, ah, contact for you." Hunt turned to Reno, made phony graceful host motions. "I hope you're enjoying yourself?"

Reno smiled through stiff lips, mouth gone dry. The man was nothing more than an ordinary pimp. She followed them out, watching Su'ad's face glow. Those special guests, they would love her.

chapter twenty

The Surfing Sufis finished stuffing their faces, opened their set with a slightly punked-out baladi tune, diddled around a little, did a couple folksy riffs, pretending to play simple background music as a prelude to a proper rocker. They slid into the chorus from a well-known tune making the rounds of the refugee camps during the Intifada that was based on a poem by Mahmud Darwish: "All I possess in the presence of death is pride and fury; I will my heart to be buried as a tree, my forehead as the skylark's nest."

"Not the usual love song, eh?"

Farouk scowled in the corner over his watered scotch, made snide comments to an older well-dressed couple about how cheap politics invaded every corner. He was getting plastered. "Always the Palestinians, as if there was nothing else going on over there."

The couple nodded, picked up a little girl dressed in a starched multilayer skirt, wide pink ribbon in her long curls. "Dance with me?" She bounced happily—music was music was music. She waved her chubby arms in the air. "Lookee, I'm dancin'."

Farouk stalked away, told the band to play something else.
"That's Palestinian."

"That's a good song, man."

"Come on, Farouk, brother, loosen up." The tray dancer
took him by the arm, into the kitchen, offered him a bowl of
hashish.

Nothing pleased Farouk. He didn't like the way the night
was going. He was on edge, afraid if something didn't break
soon he'd lose his momentum, be unable to confront Hunt at
all. He didn't like confrontations, liked delaying them even
less. "A lot of bullshit, a lot of secrets behind the party atmosphere, you know? I feel it, I don't like it." He walked to the
sink, wet his fingers, snorted water up his nose. Not discreet.
He was beyond discreet.

A man's voice, thick with a consciousness of his cultivated
accent, cut through the smoke. "A tragic loss to our community. When an artist loses the capacity to develop his craft
further in later life."

Farouk turned to see who was talking. The Syrian connection. The man had his back to Farouk.

A woman, expensive, elegant, responded with an educated
laugh. "On the other hand the mediocre ones fade into ob-
scurity, so we're seldom forced to see them." A small gesture, a gold-tipped cigarette held out for a light. "Diversity
is always . . ."

Gold Dunhill lighter. "So diverting?"

They chuckled together.

The Syrian, as if just noticing Farouk, held his arm out in a
motion both welcoming and disparaging. "Ah, but then there's
Farouk here. Our Farouk hasn't changed a bit." A smile like
a viper.

That's the lemon in the eye.

Eva, in a different pair of skin-tight pants, came in to the
kitchen, gave Farouk's arm a little squeeze, wriggled win-
somely against his hip. "Come with me, I'll show you some
real dancing." As they entered the living room she instructed

the band briskly: "Please. Debke." Imperious. "I hope you're familiar with Debke."

Dink dink dink. Du-uum. Dum tekka tekka tekka dum-tek. They began hesitantly; encouraged by what she supposed was their inexperience or timidity, she shouldered her way to a cleared spot on the floor. The Lebanese stomp needed lots of room. The Sufis pulled themselves together all at once, pitched a nice solid rhythm at her, hoping she'd pick it up. Nothing stirs a crowd up, gets them ready like a well-stepped line dance.

Eva didn't dance particularly well, but her steps were easy enough to follow. Spinning a handkerchief she slammed her heel once, twice; a half circuit of the room and Sinclair surprised her by stepping in, taking over the lead.

Elegant, stiffly regal, Sinclair moved with a courtly grace; lean forward, cross-step, precise, lean back hop step, slide and stomp; a line formed behind him, everyone doing their best Zorba imitations. Umf umf cross-step forward back umf umf stamp. Around the living room into the kitchen, down the hall and into the living room again. Umf Umf onetwothree, gathering up the reluctant stragglers, closing the circle. Sinclair and Farouk took turns fancy-stepping in the middle.

Eva, winded, dropped out, her eyes mean slits.

The Sufis, no slouches when it came to esoteric music, began to play in the more delicate Armenian style; with the graceful quick clarinet solo of the Sepastia Bar, the dance took another turn higher. Faster.

Because of his understanding of the intricacies of Armenian dance Sinclair could keep the lead steps smooth, apparently simple; he managed to give even the most reserved among them the courage to solo for a moment in the center, arms waving hips wiggling, then he took control of the floor again with a few moments of whirling expertise. Dazzling footwork. Beaming smile. His music.

Reno felt intoxicated when she looked at him. Stone-cold

sober. And intoxicated. She wondered if that was what love felt like. Maybe it was food poisoning.

When the music stopped, everyone fell down glassy-eyed with pleasure, exhaustion. Reno worked her way over to Sinclair—her mind was a blank as to what she'd say, but she knew she wanted to say something, be close enough to catch some of his pride and good humor.

Poppy cut her off, jiggled the scotch glass in her hand. "Not as good as what you served me downstairs."

" 'Course not. Hunt's an asshole." Drifting away toward Sinclair.

"World's fulla them." Poppy shrugged, her mouth in a speculative pout. "So. How's it goin'?"

"Uh. Okay." Reno tried to keep an eye on Sinclair. " 'Scuse me. I gotta take care of some business." Abrupt. Flames rose and died in Poppy's cold blue eyes. "I'm my own person. I mean, I'm not entirely, but I'm working on it." Reno paused. Gave it her best shot. "Everyone's for sale. But not me." Reno appealed to Poppy's finer sentiments. "I mean, I just took myself off the market." She looked hard at Poppy. The woman didn't follow her meaning. "They be some real bastards around here, you know?"

"An extra two hundred if you deliver the information to me before breakfast." All business. "I'll be at the usual place."

"I don't think I can do that." Distancing herself from those eyes. "Sorry if I seem difficult."

"Okay. Just get it to me by noon then."

"What if the hard disk is locked?" Reno had checked out the pocket computer, access codes, step-by-step instructions, curious phone numbers, bank numbers—she wasn't at all interested in giving the precious gadget back to Hunt. She only hoped Poppy didn't realize how easy it could be to get into Hunt's main computer. Soon as Su'ad started dancing and hypnotized everyone Reno would go to work. "And what about that Gold Card? I never tole you what name I want it in."

"We'll work everything out to your satisfaction."

"I heard that before." Reno shook her head. Breathed. In. Out. "Anyway, I don't remember where the usual place is."

Poppy laughed as she walked away. "Oh you'll find it. Ask Slow to show you."

"Twenty-five hundred. An' a Gold Card. And . . . well, I'll see you tomorrow night." To Poppy's slim back. "You know you're getting a deal."

Poppy's back shimmied. "Certainly. Certainly." She looked back over her shoulder, ran her tongue along her bright upper lip. "There'll even be a personal bonus for you."

"Terrific." Reno mumbled. "Terrific." She couldn't find Sinclair anywhere. "Shit." She opened the door at the far end of the hall onto a tiny half-bathroom. Sinclair wasn't in there, but Eva was.

Eva had her back to the door, pulling an oyster-white satin skirt over her ample hips. There was a pearl belt, a pearl-covered hugely padded bra on the narrow sink counter. Su'ad's costume spilled from a paper sack shoved in the corner.

Reno's thoughts bumped into each other, making a mess when she needed clarity. Time and silence. As Reno peeked through the crack of the door Eva leaned over to chop a line of coke.

Reno reached to her back belt loop, unhooked her key chain, took the small quarter-inch screw driver that always hung there: three quick turns and the door handle slid off the tang. She stuffed it in her pocket.

Eva finished chopping, started to draw the coke out into lines; intent on her work, she didn't notice a thing.

Holding her breath, Reno stuck a wooden match into the bolt mechanism of the door, closed it and turned the handle carefully to let the bolt slide into the door jamb. The work of only twenty seconds. She loosened the rose around the outside knob, took the handle off, slid another match into the core. Slid the handle back home. Thirty seconds more. Whole thing under a minute's work. See, you don't forget everything in prison. That was one door that wouldn't open easily.

Reno went looking for Su'ad. Found her posing by the band, soda in her hand, looking sweet. "Hey, Su'ad, I know who took your costume."

"Me too: Farouk. But it doesn't matter now."

"Like I said, it wouldn't fit him. 'Course it won't fit Eva either, maybe that's why she ain't wearin' it. Nah. That little slut think she dancing in pearls tonight."

"You crazy." Su'ad took a breath, the color rising and falling in her cheeks. "You shittin' me."

"Am I? What you gonna do if I'm not?" Reno stared at the other woman.

"Make her eat it." Brief and to the point. "But why she take it? Doesn't make sense."

"Sure it does." If Su'ad wanted to be thick as all hell there was no point in explaining. "Think about it." Reno ducked into the crowd as Poppy approached.

Su'ad greeted Poppy with a toothy insincere grin.

Poppy lifted a lip, showed her fang. "Your friend is avoiding me."

Su'ad muttered. "What she does is her own business."

"That's not entirely true." Poppy smoothed her long hair back out of her face. Smiled. Small perfectly even white teeth. Pearls. "Ah well. When you going to dance?"

"In about ten. 'Scuse me." Su'ad went into Hunt's bedroom. Had a lot to think about.

The band started up again. "A short tribute to Farid El Atrache." Lush romantic chords from the oud filled the room.

A faint rattling came from the locked door down the hall, but no one noticed. Except Reno. She moved closer; she tackle the bitch if she managed to get out before Su'ad danced.

chapter twenty-one

Fragments.

"But he never does. Not directly. That's what makes him so delicious."

"If you already have an idea, he'll clarify it."

"If you don't he'll rent you one of his for a day."

Hunt was clarifying his position to Farouk. "Don't be so petty. It's a party for you, not for me. Really. I could care less about having these people running all over my house." Injured dignity.

Farouk took his time, groping for control. "The show went rather well tonight, don't you agree?"

"Yes. And about time." Hunt smiled. Once. Sharp. "Let's step into the study for a moment, have a drink, just you and I? We were once, after all, brothers-in-law. Perhaps we could salvage something from that?"

"Certainly." Farouk's posture stiffened.

Two gentlemen, one rather older and thinner than the other, arms linked, they retired for a moment to the study. Hunt and Farouk sat across from each other in pearl gray leather arm chairs. The noise of the party swirled outside the room, not reaching them. They were, for the moment, isolated. The atmosphere between them thickened, light banter turned sly, words darted around like lasers, like razors. There was a façade of cordial relations but their interchange never acquired that roundness, that special masculine rhythm necessary to the proper appreciation of fine unblended scotch, Jamaican cigars.

They carefully avoided shifting to the bludgeons in their hearts, they stuck to the sophisticated rapier. Feint and thrust, parry. Again. Both were seasoned in that kind of combat, yet neither managed to draw first blood.

Huntington allowed himself another scotch-filled moment to remember Farouk's older, rather more intelligent sister. "I was mad about her, you know." He worked on a mellow tone. Confronted with the brother he found it hard to believe that slim silvery woman had been a close relation, a sister—there seemed no echoes of her in her brother at all.

"Aisha embroidered my shirts, my life, with a rococo detailing, smaller more intricate patterns than I ever dreamed of. She made life worth living." He realized the intervening years hadn't actually dulled the bewilderment with which he confronted her memory. He didn't say the deeper truth: that he had tired of forcibly pulling her out of her wild fantasies, her plottings. "Here's to my wife, your dear departed sister." He raised his glass in a gesture of a friend. A brother-in-law. A father.

Farouk ignored the toast. "Everybody just wants to get sucked off, don't they Hunt?" Farouk was moving in for a killer blow. "Sex is the bottom line down among the basic pubes, it's the real public currency, nothing else matters, hey Hunt? The life, the blood, the egg and sperm of existence, hey Hunt, what you say?"

Hunt leaned back in his chair, sipped with his eyes hooded, watching. Waiting. His smooth conscience wasn't disturbed by Farouk's boorish performance.

Farouk put down his glass. "I've never been reduced to fucking a dead woman." He stood up flame-faced, his mouth quivering.

Hunt may have been surprised by that accusation, but he didn't change his expression from that of a slightly fatuous uncle. "Don't be silly. Sit down. Necrophilia was never one of my things."

"Death is your only thing, Hunt. You may fool them." Dramatic arm rounding on the door to the living room. "But I know you in the foul pit of your soul."

Hunt was glad of the dim lights. He suddenly wanted to kill Farouk, pluck that one's own squirming soul out, hold it up bloody and stinking for Farouk himself to confront. Mercy? Hunt didn't know the concept. "I haven't the slightest idea what you're talking about. I'll forgive your rudeness since it's obvious things are not well with you." Placating gesture, paternal. "I assume that's the reason behind your accusations. No matter." Generous. "I forgive you. Please. Sit down."

Farouk did not sit; he prowled the room picking things up, putting them back somewhere else. "It's not for you to forgive." His back to Hunt. "This has been bothering me for years." He turned to face him.

Hunt waited, Aisha hung in the air between them, a ghost neither one could exorcise. "Aisha." Hunt paused, sipping, watching. "Aisha always got exactly what she wanted, you know. She wanted me, she got me, she wanted death, she courted it, one day she died. Things are not necessarily connected. You've always blamed me for your sister's death, but you're wrong. She always got what she wanted. Remember? What she wanted, finally, was heroin. Enough to kill an elephant." Hunt's voice was flat, didactic. "I'm sorry to be so blunt. It seemed best left unsaid. Now that it's spoken I want you to know how sorry I am that your sister was a junkie. And I hope you will understand that's my final word on the subject."

Aisha had been a fey creature with no discernible morals, or if she had some, Hunt never cared enough to look for them. Sharp little teeth and claws, fine-spun silver black hair, silver black eyes. "She was like a whippet, racing through her life until her breath stopped, her heart stopped." In her gauzy shawls, her narrow silver bracelets. "Heroin gave her the release nothing else could, thickened and slowed the quicksilver in her veins."

Hunt had bent the knee at the demon shrine. He remembered how he had loved her then as she lay stoned, languid and lovely on his couch, smiling a little at him. "Oh, this is good Hunt. This is good."

She had been there, beautiful and mindless one afternoon when he'd brought a senior law partner back to the flat. It was to have been a masculine afternoon of scotch and politics, it had been one long apology instead. When he confronted Aisha she looked at him out of large clear eyes, not a vestige of sense in them. She caressed her bruises, hissing. He decided then that she would have to go.

A man is born, discovers trees or mountains, climbs them; horses, he rides them; women, too: when he discovers women he conquers them, they were born to be subdued. Hunt believed this.

He also knew that women were entirely creatures of their own creation, each one a mistress of illusion, but also a victim of private perversion. Every time he'd climb, think he was at the peak, Aisha would show him future heights, further spaces to conquer. She exposed to him the very short way that he had come, the great distances left for him to travel. A man is born, he hunts, he dies. A woman goes on and on, appearing always just over the next ridge. "You must understand. I loved her."

"You didn't love her—you loved being loved by her, and when she found something she loved more . . ." Farouk paused, the grand gesture, he wished he had a gun but his hand only closed on the old photo. "You killed her." Move over old man move over you piddled your last pair of underwear diddled your last vanity you desiccated old bastard make way move over make way for someone who knows how to do things it's time all you self-righteous farts were killed old men need to die make room for what's comin' up.

Hunt didn't move, didn't deny, didn't grimace; his eyelids dropped to cover his glance. Nothing more.

This one, Farouk thought, keeps a tight grip, this old man, doesn't he. But he can't take it with him, oh no. He can't even hang on to what he's got. Try as he might. "Loneliness and decay is all you have left." Move over old man. Farouk sat back on the silver leather chair. Drank deep. "Your time is up, you know that."

They sat there, two mature men, bent by the wraith of a skinny quicksilver woman many years dead. The silence stretched as they plotted.

Farouk spoke again. "We have been mistaken, each about the other. You're right, it's time to clear the air." Farouk began to pull his hand out of the pocket of his embroidered vest, with the gun that was not there and the photograph that was.

There was an impatient indiscreet tap at the study door.

Sinclair stuck his head in. "Su'ad's about to dance. Come on."

"Of course, Sinclair." Hunt kept his face bland, motioned for Farouk to precede him through the door. "Wouldn't want to miss that."

Smiles plastered on their faces, the two gentlemen strolled out of the study—debonair, gracious, filled to the teeth with unspent venom.

Reno was delighted to see them emerge. The study was the one place left for her to explore. She'd been over the rest of the apartment, checking on the quality of the goods, placement of the exits, all the usual things a clever guest investigates. She hoped she could knock the computer off right then; if not, she'd return later that night. She thought she might just forget Poppy's elaborate downloading-to-disk ritual; instead she'd pop the computer and all the miscellaneous disks into the dumbwaiter in Hunt's kitchen, pick it up in the basement, sort out the take later. Sell the information as well as the machines—maybe she'd hang on to the laptop. More fun than a Rolex.

Hope springs eternally in the most confused brains; traveling money and a laptop—look out, "Life will get good, etcetera."

Reno leaned her back against the study door, scanning the crowd, her hand testing the knob, the door was locked but she could feel the cheapness of the mechanism. No problem. She fished Poppy's business card out of her pocket.

"Here, put this basket of grapes out, on that table over there." Eddie smiled at her with great innocence. "Don't eat any, they from South Africa, been sprayed with malathion."

Reno's mouth turned down, she tried to duck away from the grape basket.

He took her hand, curled her fingers around the handle. "They *much* cheaper than the unsprayed ones."

"You're shittin' me—we don't import food from there. Anyway, malathion's poison!"

"Right. So don't eat any. It's all for display anyway."

"Illusion?"

"Right, Reno of my heart. You're catching on."

"Don't want to." She shoved the basket back at him. "You do it."

She watched as he hurried to the table, her nimble fingers diddling the lock, the card pressing the bolt. The flushed arrogant faces were self-absorbed as the lock gave under her manipulation. The door slid open. "Get sick then all you rich bastards, be a nice diversion, y'all got money to keep the croaker in business."

Invisibility is a learned skill. An important skill. Reno could, when she was in top form, disappear not only from people's view but from their consciousness. She slipped back toward the study with an invisible step.

Eddie looked for her, but she had become the proverbial shadow on glass.

chapter twenty-two

S lowmotion dimmed all the lights in the living room, her portable amber strobe centered on the bedroom door as Su'ad came twirling into the room.

The wildest Hollywood fantasies paled to insignificance next to Su'ad. She wore the silver baladi dress, flashed two imperious Saracen swords above her head. There was a gasp, the sound children make on Christmas morning. The Sūfis finished their introductory flourish, moved into a frenzy of nine-eight split rhythm pounding like a huge heart.

Su'ad continued to whirl rapidly as she held the swords above her head. Then with a slow cross-step, she spiraled down until she was almost kneeling on the floor; she dropped into a smooth backbend, swords crossed, one above her chest, the other behind her head, inches from the floor. Her stomach rippled and fluttered. One of her slicker moves.

In the study Reno pushed back the lid on the portable, touched the space bar. The machine came to life. Pulling out Hunt's pocket gadget she tapped in the access code. The directory for the "C:" drive filled the screen. Names dates places numbers. Just the facts ma'am. Reno began to sweat.

As the applause built, Su'ad rose again, a rapid lifting blur, spinning with her arms outstretched, carving an actual space for herself within the confines of the room. She seemed to spin for a long, long time.

On the beat, exact, not a breath wrong, both she and the musicians, as if tranced together, came to a complete stop.

She handed the swords to Sinclair.

The clapping, in synchronization, continued. "She's good, huh?" Spines straightened, eyes brightened, people banged their hands, poked each other. Expectant.

The band kicked out all the stops, headed into the musical ozone.

Su'ad undulated. An absolute master.

"Lovely."

"One of the best I've seen."

"Is she a native you suppose?"

"Lebanese perhaps?"

"Oh, Egyptian I'd say."

"Always can tell a woman who grows up with the music: the motion, the posture."

"Yasss."

"Arabs are all left-hipped, that's the way you can tell."

"Say what?"

Condescending to an obvious cultural boob. "American dancers always begin to the right. It's a fact. Natives begin the movement to the left. See?" Pointing to the leftward-wiggling Su'ad.

The computer resumed the work exactly where Hunt had left off, in a communications program, searching the hard drive. Reno had very little time to figure it out, she racked her brains for every bit of old modem wisdom she'd ever heard. At one time she was very good at this sort of thing—in a flash of perhaps misplaced brilliance she decided to take advantage of the situation, just drop all the files on the hard drive into the program file and send the whole sucker off to Poppy's modem number.

"SEND C:\DOCS*.*. PCrypto."

Wheeeeeee.

The machine buzzed hummed burped. Reno smiled.

The Sufis stopped for half a breath then opened up with the heavy chords of a modern piece, "Aisha Kandisha" by the popular Palestinian group Sabreen; they formed a semicircle around Su'ad. She assumed the half-mad inward-turning gaze appropriate for a dance dedicated to a demon. She began slowly, half steps side to side, leading the sway of her body with her head, as if she were unaware of the audience, wrapped in her own allegory. Aisha Kandisha was, for Su'ad as well as many others, the shadowy old crone lurking in the back alley, whispering the world's darkest secrets, promising eternal youth.

The music moved faster, her long hair whipped the air, a frenzy of desire strong enough to taste, the perfect balance between control and abandonment. Release.

The contents of the hard disk fell sweetly into the mystical computer ether, apparently going on its way smoothly to PCrypto. Reno looked around the study. An early nineteenth-century celadon platter caught her eye. She tried to estimate its value, who she could sell it to. Didn't know. So much she didn't know.

Hunt's computer had true multitasking ability; on a whim she dropped back into the operating system, instructed the computer to reformat the hard disk when it was through sending. The computer asked "Are you sure?" She tapped Y. The computer asked "All?" She tapped Y. The computer, in perfect humility responded: "All. OK." She patted the soon-to-be-annihilated beast on its plastic head. She hoped Hunt would choke when he discovered his hard disk empty.

*   *   *

Farouk worked his way toward the front of the crowd; the hypnotic chords of the song ripped at his mind. Aisha Kandisha. Panting, he stopped a few feet from Su'ad, his eyes rounder, redder, madder than before; he made inarticulate noises. The toothy matron standing in front of him was pushed out of the way in his effort to get closer to the dancing she-demon.

Su'ad was oblivious to anything but the power of the music.

Just as no one had noticed Reno's absence, no one paid any attention to her presence. She stood at the edge of the crowd and listened to the loud bangs on the door at the end of the hall. No one else seemed to hear them.

Farouk swung his arm well back, then forward in a strong arc until the flat of his hand struck Su'ad with all the force he could muster.

Su'ad flipped four feet to the left, dropped like a dead weight to the floor.

The sound of the blow echoed in the suddenly quiet room. Su'ad looked up through her hair, whimpering; a red smear marred the silver dress, flowing from the cut Farouk's ring had put below her eye. She dabbed at it. Ineffectual. Shaking.

Farouk seemed to have suddenly sobered up. He didn't look at Su'ad. "There's a lot Hunt needs to explain." He gathered his shredded dignity around him, didn't look at anyone, addressed the crowd in a flat well-modulated voice. "I'll make sure Hunt explains." The tone started rising. "If to no one else, then to his God." Farouk backed out of the room. No one followed.

Eva crashed out of her makeshift prison, an apparition in full pearl belly-dance costume, outrage and cocaine dust on her face. "What's happening? Where's Hunt?" She snarled, searching the crowd. "Where's Hunt?" Hands on hips. "He planned this little fiasco. Where the hell is he?"

Sinclair tried to take Eva's hand. She spit at him.

There was obvious potential for hysteria. Eddie muttered, "Oh boy." Leaning against the wall, arms folded across his chest, small smile curling the corners of his lips up, Eddie looked very old, very wise. One eyelid drooped slowly, a wink to Reno.

Su'ad spoke with great heaving breaths, stumbled over her words, asking, "Why he do that?"

Reno knelt down next to her. "Have to ask Hunt, but I bet it has something to do with the music they played, the dress you got on."

Farouk's voice shrilled from the outer hall. "What could you have been thinking of?"

Hunt, apparently just arriving back at his party, mumbled something about an errand. He sounded genuinely confused.

The hungry crowd surged toward the sound of their voices.

Farouk grabbed Hunt's shirtfront, pulled him forward like a trophy. "Aisha's dress. No other woman is worthy to even touch it. How did that—that—person get hold of it?" He didn't let go of Hunt's shirt. "And why did you tell my band to play that song? Why Hunt? Explain yourself."

Hunt kept his voice deep with pity. Except for a small happy twitch at the corner of his lips, he was a vision of concerned puzzlement. "I thought you'd enjoy it. I really did. A resurrection of sorts." Evil. He brushed with calculated ineffectuality at Farouk's hands. "I remember how fond both you and your sister were of everything dealing with Middle Eastern folklore."

"You're mad. You're a vicious mad old man." Farouk fumbled at his shirt pocket, searching for the damning photograph of Aisha. Dying.

Hunt put an arm around Farouk, pinned his hand to his chest. He turned to the gaping crowd. "Please. Please, everyone, this is a small matter. Please. Trance affects people this way sometimes. Someone help Su'ad." He pushed Farouk toward the exit. "Please continue with the music." He waved at the Sufis, who obeyed the command with some confusion. To no one in particular, but everyone in general, he remarked,

"The whole damn race sees demons everywhere." Shrug. "What's a civilized man to do?"

The music sparked and sputtered, unsure.

Farouk safely removed to the outer hall, Hunt steered Su'ad into the bedroom. The "Syrian connection" followed, rubbing his hands.

The eyes of the crowd were bright. Moist.

"Oh my. Isn't this somethin'."

"Haven't had such an *in*teresting time in recent memory, dear."

"Should we go home?"

"Oh, that seems the proper thing to do doesn't it?"

"Well, yusss, of course."

Then again perhaps not. No one left.

chapter twenty-three

Eddie draped his arm across Reno's shoulders. Pulled her close. Whispered, "Hunt pull a fast one this time or what?"

The last of Hunt's guests lingered in front of the club, huddled close together, reluctant to leave the vicinity of interesting occurrences; talking about booze, broads, blood. Their teeth gleamed lavender in the neon.

"Or what. I'm history, Eddie." She let her tired eyes wander over the crowd in the street, forced a smile. "You check up on Su'ad?"

"She told me she needed to talk to you—we best find her."

"Shit. I gotta go." Her lips pulled tight and prim. "I'll never understand that woman."

"Ought to make sure she's okay."

"She's okay. Believe me, she's okay." Reno's leg muscles made little running motions. Away away. "Good-bye, Eddie." Finality in her tone. The fellow wasn't making it any easier.

Eddie didn't reply, marched doggedly after her into the showroom, watching her as she collected her stuff.

She pretended he wasn't there. Ploddy ploddy forward.

Slowmotion's guttural voice ritual-chanted—eerie, bodiless,

cheerful—coming from everywhere at once: "Half as much baking soda as cocaine, do-dah, only enough water to cover." In more normal, irritated, tones: "Quit breathin' on the damn candle flame."

No one was visible in the dim light.

"Acid and alkaline are unstable in solution, so they precipitate out a salt free of impurities, which is crystalline, smokable. Got that?"

Reno peered over the edge of the bar.

"Science." Slowmotion crouched over a flickering candle on the duckboards, she put a test tube closer to the flame. "Efficiency." Small bubbles rose up through the solution, the white gunk on the bottom got sort of amorphous, portions began to peel off, rise through the cloudy solution, then a cumulus cloud formation appeared. "Magic."

"Foolishness." Su'ad was stretched out in the bar-back gloom. "You been dickin' with that thing for twenty minutes." Mocking. "Booze. The only key to total. Satis. Faction."

"Patience is the seed to success, Su'ad. You know that."

Eddie joined in: "Confidence is the road to excess. Let me try."

Sighing, Reno walked behind the bar. "What you think you doin' here all in the dark?"

"Waitin' for Hunt to finish up his negotiations for my triumphal tour of Egypt." Cynicism in her voice.

"That might take a while. You hear what I'm sayin'?"

No answer.

"Hey. I got to cool this here down. Bring me that tray of ice you're hoarding." Slowmotion waved at them through the gloom.

"Stick it under the faucet. Shit." Su'ad was treating her face to a large bar rag wrapped around chunks of ice. She had her hand on a tray of ice next to her, possessive. "This my own private ice. Don't want none your crap in it." Sipping a large icy glass of something gold, no ice.

"But I need to make this co-old." Slowmotion held the tube as if it were an embryo.

Eddie scooped up two handfuls of ice from Su'ad's tray. Dumped them on the bar.

Slowmotion put the tube in the middle, then pulled it away. Tap tap. Into the ice. Cooling. Away. Tap. Again. When she was done there was a small chunk of something curved in the bottom of the tube.

"Crunch. Not crack." Eddie's voice was proud, sly. "I can do it much better."

Slowmotion laughed at him.

"No shit. I am a champeen crack maker."

"You're a champeen idiot."

Eddie held out his hand for the test tube. "Gimme."

Poppy appeared outlined in the rectangle of neon light as the front door opened. "Hey Su'ad. Sorry about your face." She disappeared into the gloom as the door closed behind her. The only sound was the click of her heels as she crossed to the bar. The woman had the eyes of a cat.

Su'ad raised her glass. No comment. Long drink.

"Hey, Poppy." Reno tried to be casual. "Check your mail yet tonight?"

Su'ad muttered. "Oh Reno. You make me sick."

Reno clenched, unclenched her fists. "You ain't suppose to drink, Su'ad."

Poppy's red lips parted in a sharp smile. She lifted her chin a quarter of an inch in the direction of someplace private. Where they could talk.

Su'ad stood up, shaky, leaning on the bar. "Don't talk to me about drinking. You not suppose to be crimin' neither but you is. Hunt supposed to be a friend of mine—but he set me up." She put some more ice cubes in the rag, pressed it back on her eye, took a big drink. "I'd like to kill him."

"Which one? Not your style, Su'ad." Reno's sarcasm didn't make a dent. "Farouk's just a pawn."

"Hell, even I can see that." Bitter. Speaking into her glass. "We all little pieces, manipulated by an uncaring fate."

"So much for free will, huh?" Poppy's voice was velvet to Su'ad's growl. She pulled Reno aside. "I checked my mail. The transmission was cut off."

Reno was suspicious.

Su'ad belched. "Assholes. All of them."

Eddie stood awkwardly, weight on one foot then the other. "Aw, don't talk like that."

"Okay, Eddie. You're right. Sinatra's God. But he ain't done shit for me yet. Get my drift?" Su'ad waved her glass, drained it. "Life sucks, Eddie. You bend over, someone's gone drive right up your ass." Sepulchral tones. "It's the way of the world."

Eddie waved his hand, small loop, picked up a bar rag as if he was wiping down the bar, snapped it at nothing, just to hear the sound. "Hunt musta hadda reason."

Su'ad leaned forward to grab a bottle. "So. A reason. Now I know."

"You gonna be okay, Su'ad?"

"Never better, Reno. Never better. I have big plans." Su'ad waved the bottle, moved Poppy to one side. Made the grand exit. Must have been something in the air at the Club Istanbul that night.

Poppy spoke into Reno's ear. Hissing. "It ain't all there Reno. You holding back on me?"

Reno looked Poppy up-and-down, "Horse shit." She knew better than to hold out on anyone like Poppy. "You got something to cover me for what you got so far? I'll see what I can do, okay?" She pocketed the bills Poppy offered her without even counting them, followed Su'ad out, closed the door behind them; a cab pulled up, Reno gave the driver Su'ad's address, ten dollars. "Make sure she makes it inside her house all right."

Reno watched the cab drive away; Su'ad, in silhouette, up-ended the bottle.

The club's door rattled behind her. Reno nipped around into the alley, slid behind a monster pile of Chinese sesame-oil tins, rolled up her sack, sat on it, hidden; she watched the street.

Poppy came out, looked around, shrugged, flagged a cab.

Eddie and Slowmotion staggered out onto the street a moment later, still arguing crack-cooking techniques. They parted, Slowmotion rolling up the street toward another after-hours joint; Eddie poking along, sticking his nose in every doorway, finally going into the dildo store half a block down.

Reno hoped they were gone for the night. She didn't want company. Her lips pressed into a line: She did her best. These people had no idea what it was like to be fate-crossed.

She waited. Occupied her mind with insignificant thoughts, paying attention to the itch right where she couldn't reach it at the arch of her foot. Her lower left eyelid was jumping. She was tired. She waited.

With an uneven shuffling step, a small stumble, Hunt approached the door to the club. His shoulders were slumped, he fumbled with the key, he muttered, slurring the words.

"Payback's a motherfucka, Hunt." Reno waited another ten, fifteen minutes until she was sure the whole building was empty and Hunt was comfortable at home. Mistress of darkness, Shadow Dancer, comfortable in the thick cover of the night, Reno was invisible; she worked her way back to the alley door. It opened to the gentle twist of her knife. She rummaged around in her sack, found the bottle of Glenfiddich, the stash of chloral hydrates she'd lifted out of Hunt's bathroom earlier. She bounced these small green objects in her hand. Checked that her index fingernail was sharp enough to puncture them. Her mouth stretched wide. It didn't look like a smile.

Reno knocked on Hunt's door.

He opened it a crack, smudges of white powder on his nose.

"You alone? Here." Reno held up the bottle. "Brought you

up something to take the edge off the night." Blinked her eyes, hoped she looked cute. Licked her lips and smiiiiled.

One of his thin hands reached through the crack, wrapped around the bottle. "Thanks."

She didn't let go. "Thanks? Thanks? That's it?"

"Yeah. Thanks. What more you want? A tip?" He pushed a crumpled five at her. "Here, you wanta tip? Here's five dollars for your trouble."

"No man. I want a minute of your time. You know. I don't wanna be treated like someone just out of the Southeast Asian jungles, I wanna little courtesy. You know, five minutes of your time, a little how's ya day, maybe a few moments for news sports and weather—I don't want your fuckin' money." She'd already stowed the fiver in her pocket. "Don't care what we talk about but I want you to treat me like a human bein'. Invite me in for a drink. That kind of thing. Five minutes. Come on." She liked the sound of her voice.

He stepped back, an odd look on his face, reluctant. But he let her in—already half-crocked, he figured it might be interesting, thought perhaps about getting into her pants, thought it would be more of a challenge than he was ready for, thought maybe it'd serve Su'ad right if he fucked her friend. Dykes all of them. He tossed his head, a nervous gesture, sniffling a little.

Reno suggested that he get a couple glasses to share a small drink of good scotch. "You must be sick of drinking the cheap shit." Reno slit the chloral hydrates; they drained easily into his glass. A pinch of bar sugar in case he noticed something odd about the taste. He wasn't paying a lot of attention as she handed the tumbler to him. "So. Been an exciting couple days, Hunt?"

He gulped the scotch, not tasting. "Yuh."

"Got lots of good copy for your column?" She watched with deep approval as he drank. "That's my little man."

"Yuh." He already seemed out of it.

Reno wondered if she'd needed to waste the dope on him.

Better safe than. Some people paid no attention to what they did. Got whacked back good and proper in a blink. "So. Mr. Huntington. What shall we talk about."

Dubious. He finished the glass, looked up at her as if he might be ready to come out with one of his traditional vicious witticisms; instead he went into a nod. Snapped his head back up. Faltering but making the debonair attempt. "Wuh?" Mouth open, small string of drool. His eyes rolled up toward what passed for his frontal cortex.

Reno leaned over him, close enough to smell the scotch oozing from his expensive pores. "Here's to the victims, hey, Hunt?" The anger rose up again, an anger that hadn't left her in years: cold rolled steel, a bullet ready in the chamber, as real as the ribbon wire encircling her cell, her heart, her life. "Hey, Hunt, howya doin'?"

He didn't even grunt, curled like a huge discarded fetus on the couch.

Reno stepped over to the study door, brisk. She pulled surgical gloves on—considering all the society that had been in the place that night they hardly seemed necessary, but she felt a lot more comfortable with them on. She'd already checked for alarms earlier in the evening so it was a simple matter of snapping off the master switch on the computer system.

She patted the portable computer, tiny sweet thing that it was, unhooked the umbilical cord, stowed it in her pack. She pulled the CPU and hard disk toward her to get at the multiple attachments, wrapped their cords around them and stowed the whole thing all in its own little styrofoam-lined box. Heavy and awkward. "But," she mumbled, not quite sober herself, "don't leave home without it."

Reno didn't like to be anyone's flunky. Three minutes. Four. Five. She tied the bundles up. Norton Utilities should bring the erased data back. Just take her a day of serious fiddling. Then she'd hand it over to Poppy, get lots of money, a Gold Card = Life Would Get Beautiful & Etc.

Hunt groaned in the living room.

Reno wrapped the small celadon platter, always room for more, in an embroidered cloth that had been used to cover the computer. Be some hours, maybe days, before Hunt could care enough to notice things were gone.

Hunt groaned again.

Reno returned to the living room to say good-bye like a polite guest.

Mr. Huntington still lay on his leather couch in the same position, breathing kind of ragged, the same line of drool curled from his mouth. A little thicker, longer.

Reno noticed a couple photos, an enamel box, a crystal chopping plate on the side table. She pocketed the enamel box (magpie), glanced at the pictures. Ugleee . . . The woman looked like she was dead. Looked like she died on the floor of Hunt's bathroom. Ugh. Looked like someone was into fucking a corpse. Reno stared at Hunt. Put the pictures in her pocket.

She took a very small, very red chili pepper out of her pocket, cracked it and poured the seeds into her hand.

Hunt rolled over onto his side.

She dropped the chili pepper seeds into his ear. One two threefourfivesixseveneight nine. He shook his head slightly, then settled back, sighing. She broke the crumbs of the pepper into the pearly pink shell of his ear, gave his head an extra tap to settle the bits too deep for a questing finger. He didn't move.

She poured herself a stiff drink. "Here's to the victor."

Took another swallow. "People like you are the piss of the earth." She walked around the couch where he sprawled, leaned over and peeled up an eyelid, spoke to the blank orb. "You're a disgusting piece of shit."

She wondered who in hell the dead babe was, dipped her finger in her drink, flicked the liquid at him. "Time to pay attention sucker."

He began to scratch at his ear, turn his head, frown a little.

Tried to sit up, shake his head. He muttered "Assholes!" to no one in particular. He pulled himself to a nearly upright position, a pained puzzled look on his face. His eyes still didn't focus, one up one down; he didn't even know Reno was there, he glared at creatures only he saw. "Assholes." He shook his head, tilted it to the left, shook it. The winter-sunned skin around his ear was already turning red, a pulse began to expand the veins across his forehead.

Reno thought with satisfaction that it would get worse. She whispered. Soft. "And here's to the women who couldn't stand him." She finished her drink.

It's an old dilemma. She didn't know if she solved it. Revenge, retribution, ethics. The broken chili pepper would be difficult to remove, getting more painful in a geometric progression, the pain multiplying itself by itself with each second. At first it was only a mild irritation. He'd need to call a doctor.

Reno looked around the after-party shambles of the apartment. Seeds and stems, glass vials, mirrors blades, straws. Chemical detritus, herbal remains.

Even when he went into spasms from the pain Hunt might hesitate to call a doctor.

These rich guys always had some doctor who would be discreet.

Reno found the phones, unplugged them, put them in the refrigerator.

Grunting, he clawed at his ear. His mouth was slack, his eyes still didn't both point in the same direction but a realization seemed to be growing in them that something was very wrong.

The chili pepper might not be discovered until it did some kind of irreparable damage. Reno hoped so. She noticed that his pants were unzipped, wondered briefly if the pain would give him a hard-on. Happened sometimes.

She gave Hunt an encouraging shove. "So tell me later if you have a good time, okay?"

He stood up, turning in circles. A strange *Wooh* sound was coming from his mouth.

"Well, Hunt, I won't say it's been fun. Because it hasn't. But it'll get fun in a while." She headed for the door. "Trust me."

He didn't respond, hung onto the edge of the couch muttering.

There was a soft knock on his door. A key working in the lock.

Reno stopped, thanked all the small local gods that she'd put the chain on, turned and hurried into the kitchen. She pushed the boxed computer into the dumbwaiter, opened the window above the kitchen sink, crawled out onto the window ledge, closed the window and did a wobbly long-step to the fire escape ladder, an uneasy couple feet. She blessed the city fathers that insisted all apartment buildings have fire escapes. Urban architecture has its good points.

Behind her she heard Hunt lurching toward the door. He was whining. Furniture tipped over.

She scrambled down the couple steps of the escape, hung from her hands and dropped; she took the drop smoothly. First Eddie's place, now Hunt's; might make a TV series: Escape from the Rich and Famous. Or, she thought in a giddy half-assed way: Alleys I've Landed In. She squatted in the alley, catching her breath; nudged the alley door open once more, tiptoed in the dark down the stairs to the basement. Her face pushed into a spider web. Maybe she ought to rethink the life she was leading. As she picked up the computer, a smile appeared on her face: hell, so long as we're all having a goooood time.

Back in the alley she listened to the howling from Hunt's apartment: a high keening wail, another, muddled.

Crouching in the shadows she inhaled diesel fumes, old garbage. The smell of freedom. Yum. She patted her pocket: even copped some dope. And those really creepy snapshots. Oh, how trendy. Things were definitely improving.

Smashing noises came from Hunt's apartment. Excellent.

A window was flung wide open.

Reno heard rather than saw a body drop smooth as a stone, felt rather than heard it hitting the cement, fifteen feet from where she stood. Splat.

"Splat?" Her face went slack with shock. "Wuh." There was a figure framed for a moment in the open window of Hunt's room, then it was gone.

Not a sound from the body, not a breath, not a twitch or a moan.

Reno felt it crunching inch by inch closer to her, skeleton hand over skeleton hand clawing its way across the pavement, angry mouth open ready to sink its yellowed fangs in her leg. She smothered a cry, fumbled along the wall behind her, sweat ran down her sides. Gibbering like a child, she peered back at the thing.

It hadn't moved.

She stood panting, looking at it. Finally she edged closer, looking, not looking, her stomach rippling behind her belly button. The body was partly in the light, didn't appear to be breathing. The head was at an awful angle. A passing headlight lit the alley for a quick flash. An unbearable sprawl.

One moment she was shivering, nauseated at the final splat of death, the next she wavered, undecided: should I check his pockets for money . . .

Take the Rolex at least.

She ought to be, she wanted to be practical; her hands clenched, curling by her sides. She forced one hand out to touch him. Her hand refused to move closer than six inches, stopped there, shaking.

Understanding failed. There was no sweetness in this death, only a great absence. Dead meat. A little blood was shining on his cheek in the half-light.

Reno slid crablike toward the alley entrance, began a mad staggering walk up the streets. She couldn't rob a corpse. Even such a recent unloved one. Cop cars radiated by her at the speed of light. Toothless headless bodiless. The bitter wind pried at her clothing. Grit under her eyelids scratched her eyeballs. Unclean Unclean.

Say you're sorry, Reno. Write "crime doesn't pay" a thousand times, Reno, spend a week, spend a month, write it again, spend all the time they promised you at birth, Reno, it's your life. Apologize to the people now, Reno, say you're sorry.

Burglar cokefiend bunco artist whore. Mayhem robbery perjury dope, Reno's the dancer at the end of the rope. She shows no sign of remorse. Lock her up. Of course of course.

"Nothing ever works out right for me." She hollered it into the wind. "Nothing." As her voice faded the thought she'd been avoiding crawled to the top of her mind: Robbery/Homicide. The things she carried tied her to that dead body in the alley the way a simple fingerprint never could. *"Shit!"*

She arranged her face: nose in the middle, one eye on each side, eyebrows level above them, and between nose and chin she put her mouth: closed, calm, not twitching, smiling a little perhaps.

Nowhere to go.

Nowhere safe.

No way to get off what she'd stolen.

Blind. She'd been blind and stupid. No matter she didn't do it. No matter anything, she'd be the one they'd blame. Her mouth opened in an unconscious O.

chapter twenty-four

It was fog striped five o'clock in the morning slick pavement time on sleaze street. A toothless drunk poked through the alley garbage cans with the same thoroughness a person of means inspected imported fruit; the old man had put together a nice little mound of fried chicken parts. For gravey there was some unidentifiable gray slurry wrapped in bits of paper. He searched further for some discarded vegetables, greens for roughage: he was conscientious about colon health when he could be.

He shambled into the alley behind the Istanbul, peering into the gloom, hoping for a bottle with something tasty left in it.

There's a feeling about a dead body, as opposed to a sleeping one. Nobody's home. He touched the shoe with his bare foot—he knew the foot in that shoe wasn't a foot anymore. The shoe wasn't quite a shoe either: filled but uninhabited.

Very little is allowed to come between a hungry bum and his dinner; he does not, in the general course of things, have reason to dwell on the amenities, those common courtesies that grease the wheels of human interaction, he merely hunts and gathers his food in the time honored bum culture fashion, goes somewhere to be alone, then he eats.

The gift of a good appetite, even when faced with gray slurry, was one of his treasures, but he felt it slipping away. Sentimentality had always been his weak point. He bent over, a quick bulging motion, fingers around the wrist. He straightened up with something that glittered gold; he folded forward again to feel for a wallet. Nothing. His disappointed fingers continued. A sweet goldish pen. Very classy.

He admired it, set his jaw, bent again to the task. The dead man was not entirely stiff but still didn't help much in the removal of his jacket. Good Harris Tweed. The bum's fingers fumbled with the knot of the tie. Silk. You never knew, he mumbled, may have a date one evening soon. Hee hee. He stowed these items in his sack. The pants, well, the pants were all around too small. Someone else might find them to their fancy, maybe when the stiff was actually stiff they'd be easier to remove. The shoes were the problem though, as if the fellow's fat dead toes gripped the soft Italian leather—like grim death, he thought, like grim death. A short violent tug. He glanced over his shoulder, the flannel-gray morning light was ten-fifteen minutes away. Thin gray silk socks. What fun. Something about the stiff's lack of expression made the bum decide not to put the shoes and socks on his own feet right there in the alley.

He scuttled out of the alley, the streetlights reflecting nothing but a shadow. He hurried down the street, a furtive old bum illuminated fitfully, looking for a safe burrow to hide in.

chapter twenty-five

B ig funeral. No one cried.
Mahogany casket, brass handles, stinky flowers.
No real mourners, just a lot of people eyeballing each
other, seeing who showed up, who didn't. A proper
ritual.

The story ran that Mr. Huntington was loaded, fell out the
window. An accident.

Some people didn't think that accidents happened with
quite the frequency other people said they did.

Some people thought he committed suicide. And about time
too.

Most people were at the church because they figured it to
be the social event of the month. Hunt always gave such lovely
parties. Of course, this one would be the last. Unless he came
back from the dead. Speculation was feverish.

A Catholic mass.

The mourners leaned their heads together murmuring like
hungry pigeons. Nice to see you. Nice to see you. Good of
you to come. To be here. Old friends and all. Practically family. Formal wear.

"Prostrate with grief?"

"Were they lovers?"

"Well, I heard . . ."

There's sometimes an advantage to knowing the truth of a matter, but not always.

Bones in a hole. That's all life is at the bottom, just bones in a frigging hole.

Of course it's nice if there's a stack of pleasant memories to amuse oneself with if the funeral oratory drones on with a litany of tearful dirgy (meaningless) words. Cardboard grief.

"Suicides can't get into heaven."

"Hunt will be lonely there in his expensive coffin. Bones in a hole."

As for the bad memories, well, burial should put an end to them. But it doesn't. Reno kept her head covered, her mouth shut; spent the time figuring out how to steal a couple of the purple satin choir robes. Better than remembering Hunt's body splat in the alley, wondering when the po-lice would come for her.

Did suicide count if it was unintentional—for that matter could it still be suicide even if the bastard was pushed? Damn. The ability to make fine distinctions is never part of any cop's equipment. Reno didn't know whether she'd let them take her, or make a dramatic stand—behind the organ maybe. Behind the altar. They'd hesitate to shoot, afraid they'd hit the crucified Christ, miss out on heaven themselves. She'd kill them with the funeral candles. Blllatt.

It might be a relief to get back to the safety and sanity of jail. She glanced over her shoulder. Nothing.

The last hallelujahs faded away, the priest waved the incense around the coffin one more time, the doleful choir slow-stepped down the center aisle while everyone else rustled around trying not to seem too eager to get out of the place. The pall bearers let the machinery of the mortuary trolley hoist the corpse up to hip height, then they trotted in a solemn procession out the side door of the church, their fingers loose on the brass handles of the coffin.

A woman's voice cooed at Reno. "Hello again. Did you know him well?"

Reno couldn't place the voice, the cloying perfume was equally unfamiliar; she turned, apprehensive, to inspect the woman. Toothy, manicured, wearing something furred or feathered around her shoulders. "No. No I didn't." She edged toward the exit.

"But I'm sure I saw you at the party the other . . . well, the night that . . . you know?"

"No. No I don't." The old crone hemmed her in.

"You weren't dancing were you? No. No, you were serving, cleaning up, weren't you. Yes that was it. And that dark woman, the tall one over there, she's the dancer. Lovely, isn't she. Was she close to him? Well, yes, of course she was, just look how awful her face looks. Ravaged. Ravaged with grief."

Reno backed up, whacking her calf against a pew. Impossible to get around the smiling old harridan. Unmournful bodies pressed in on every side. "No. No. I don't think so."

"But of course, dear. Of course. I'm quite sure." She nodded, eyes shrewd. "In fact he struck her—some lover's quarrel or something?"

"He didn't hit her." Reno had to be polite, forgotten why, but she had to be polite. She smiled a polite smile. "No no." Her face cracked, she'd forgotten how to smile, her lips stretched unequally toward her ears. "That was another guy."

The perfumy little woman put a gloved hand on her arm. "Come, talk with me. You see, I didn't know him well, but I'd always admired him. There must be all kinds of things you can tell me." She leered. "Funny that he killed himself that way."

"Don' putcher claws on me. I hardly knew the old geezer."

The ghoul showed her teeth again, predatory. "Hardly an old geezer, my dear. Well, if it's too painful, we needn't talk about him just yet. Tell me about the dark girl, the dancer. Doesn't she look good in black?"

Reno scrambled over the wooden pew. One foot on the

seat, the other swinging over, she just missed connecting with the old woman's nose by a fraction of an inch.

The shocked woman made whuffing noises. Reno slipped out the side door of the church, burrowed her way through the chattering crowd. Didn't look back.

"Hey Reno."

Reno hissed a warning as she tried to get away from Eddie. "I got to get outta here. Place crawling with police."

Eddie's voice had its usual mellow Southern timber. "Why? Just another rich man committing suicide." He put his arm around her. "Saved someone the trouble of killing him." Eddie began to laugh, couldn't help himself.

"Not now. Shit." Reno poked him in the belly. "Not at this funeral, you fool."

"Especially at this funeral." Giggles.

Reno wrapped both her hands around his arm, squeezed until her fingers turned blue, she moved him along, he stumbling, she threatening. "I'm gonna tear your arm off, feed it to you finger by finger."

"What's the problem, girl?"

"Tell me somethin' Eddie. Where'd you go that night?"

"I hung around the street." Sly. "Saw you leave out the alley about an hour after you leave the club the first time." Flat. Matter of fact. Not threatening but not particularly kind either.

"You tell that to the po-lice?"

"You kiddin'." Righteous indignation. "I dint talk to those pricks at all. Listen, that was a busy night after everybody supposed to be gone. What you do all that time back there anyway?"

Reno had given it a lot of thought. The figure in the window couldn't have been Eddie. "He was pushed, Eddie. I'm sure of it."

Eddie stopped. "No shit." He fumbled in his pocket, pulled out a joint. "You were there? Tell me." Matches. "Oh, tell me evvvvvvverything."

Reno palmed the joint, kept walking. "We ain't far enough away." She wasn't so sure. The figure in the window had grown indistinct, become only a faint wishful rattle, like dead leaves, in her ritual memory gourd. "I wasn't exactly there." That silhouette was all that stood between her and Murder One.

They paused under a tree halfway up the block. Lit up. "To Hunt."

"Don't make me gag."

In the distance they could see Eva trotting by Sinclair's side. Eva was talking to him, steady, hypnotic, the power of her body poured into her voice, hardly space for breath.

Sinclair shook his head no. Then maybe.

In her typical scattered way, Reno noticed how handsome Sinclair was, then refused to acknowledge the thought. Perhaps it was the wisest course.

Eva waved her hands imperiously. They could see her shaking her head and pointing at Farouk, surrounded by his band of ragtag musicians and females, including the perfectly square little bodyguard and the always funereal chauffeur. Reno supposed no one had told them there wouldn't be any booze or food.

Eva pointed at Su'ad, looked around for others to accuse.

A corner of Reno's mouth puckered. She hollered. "You phony Eva, you ain't shit."

Eddie jerked her behind the tree, took the bone from Reno's limp fingers, sucked. Sly. "I didn't go very far away that night. Lotta people in and out." Waited for a reaction. Didn't get one.

Reno's temperature actually rose a bit, but her body felt very cold. Had been happening like that, in waves for a couple days. Eddie? No way. The shadow in the window hadn't resembled Eddie. Hadn't looked like anyone. That's the thing about shadows, nothing distinctive about them unless they have antlers.

"Su'ad was there. Farouk too."

"That musta been cosy." Maybe they tossed a coin to see who tossed Hunt. Nice image. She smiled. Small.

"Surprised you didn't meet 'em."

No response. Reno was beyond responding, locked into bizarre scenes from the horror corners of her mind. Reno's eyes moved sideways, her mouth made that O. She kept her back to Eddie until she controlled it. "What you mean?"

"You don't look none too steady, girl." Intense. He paused for a long time. Reno didn't say a thing. He handed her the bone. It was out. "I knew you wasn't with 'em—poked m'head in the showroom. They had a couple bottles on the bar; Farouk was apologizing. Explaining about his sister and what it was like when she was married to Hunt, saying that Hunt killed her, he believed he had proof, how seeing Su'ad in the dress was like a ghost." Eddie hadn't expected to see the look of slow horror on Reno's face; he stopped.

"Farouk's sis-ter is the dead woman?"

"What you know about a dead woman?"

"Never mind that now. Go on."

"Farouk said the song was a special song, his sister's song." He looked pleased with himself. "Su'ad was gracious. Let him think he offered to have Su'ad open his shows, all as his own idea." Pause.

"Go on."

"No you go on. Tell me what you know about the dead woman?"

"I don't know what you're talking about."

"I think you're full of shit. I saw you slidin' out the alley a minute later—didn't tell nobody either." Eddie scowled at his shoes. "You oughta tell me."

Reno coughed, her lip stuck up on her gums, her mouth was so dry. The photos were the stuff of nightmares.

He watched as Reno mutilated the joint he'd just handed her. "Thought we be partners."

"What you gettin' at Eddie?" She looked up the street.

Wondered if the shadow in Hunt's window was Eddie after all.

"Eva's gone to the police." He pouted at her. "I suppose you already know that."

Reno saw Sinclair take Eva by the hand, attempt to link her arm through his.

Eddie folded his arms. "Listen to me. You so messed up, you can't see anything but your own self."

"Maybe that's true."

Eddie shoved his hands in his pockets, tipped his head one way, then the other. "Eva told the police about you. Told Sinclair you ripped off the bar."

"Oh. Well. I guess I gotta go. 'Bye Eddie."

"You think you walk away from me. You best think again." Stony. "Who you think you are? FBI's most wanted?" He snorted.

"Me. I'm me."

"Big fucking deal. You didn't do shit but you're going to take the fall like some dumb shit."

"You talkin' out the side your neck." Fists clenched.

"You been takin' the fall for Su'ad the whole of yer life. Ain't it about time you let her handle her own affairs?"

"Su'ad? Fuck you Eddie. You don't know what you're talking about." It wasn't Su'ad who was guilty. Never Su'ad.

Neither one of them had the smallest vestige of good sense left. They circled each other glaring, the point of the discussion forgotten.

"You're a fucking hypocrite."

Reno popped him one. He smacked her back. She ducked her head to butt him in the stomach, he grabbed her.

She wiggled, howling. "Don't grab me." Tears in her eyes. "I hate to be grabbed."

"You through?"

She nodded. He let go. She popped him. He backhanded her. Not hard.

"Don't backhand me." Jumping up and down in fury. "I hate that. You don't fight fair."

Eddie stepped back out of the reach of her kick. "You the one to talk about what's fair?"

"Yeah." Breathing hard, the corners of her mouth beginning to twitch up. "You got a problem with that?"

"Nope." Fighting not to laugh. "Well, yeah I do."

"Sounds like a personal problem to me."

"Listen, you could come to my place." Panting. "We could, er, talk."

Reno let her breath out. The boy was so damn hard to deal with. "You think the cops won't look for me there?"

"Lightning doesn't strike twice."

"Not talkin' lightning, talkin' cops." She smiled at him.

"Come on." He took her hand. "Come on, Reno."

Reno needed to think. Tried to light the roach, focused only on the match in the wind, the roach, not burning the tip of her nose.

Farouk and his band approached Su'ad. Dignified.

Su'ad let him kiss her on each cheek. Smiled, regal as a real Egyptian queen.

Eva, dragging Sinclair behind her, lurched up to them, her shell-pink talons raking at Su'ad's eyes.

Su'ad didn't even flinch. Farouk's bodyguard grabbed Eva's hands, crushed them into a nasty pinkish dust.

Eddie spoke quietly, his eyes never moving away from the scene in front of them. "Guess who came slidin' out the alley 'bout ten minutes after you left."

Reno gave him her full attention. Whoever it was had to step over Hunt's body. "Give it up Eddie."

Eddie tried to be coy.

Reno grabbed him by the front of his shirt. "Who did you see?"

"Hey. Don't wrinkle the silk, babe." She let go. He smoothed his shirt. "Eva."

"You swear?"

"Yeah. She came slithering out the alley, smug little grin on that face of hers."

"You see what time she went in?"

"Nope. She musta bin in there somewhere all the time."

"Thought Sinclair took her home?"

"Wouldn't be the first time Sinclair dumped her out on the street because of her nasty mouth."

Reno heaved a big sigh. She was fucked coming and going. If Eva ignored the body then she wasn't surprised to find it there—so she knew Hunt took a dive.

"Tell me what you're thinking."

"Not thinking. Not thinking." Reno got the roach going at last, inhaled, deep. "Don't hafta think, man. I know."

"What?" He grabbed the last of the roach, sucked it to infinity, never taking his eyes off her face.

She shivered. "Never mind, Eddie. This one a those times where knowledge isn't a hell of a lot of help."

chapter twenty-six

The first crew were the easiest: heavy boots, black uniforms, jowly faces not quite in focus, rude and pushy. Asking everyone in the whole neighborhood if they'd seen anything suspicious the night of Mr. Huntington's death.

"Suspicous? Suspicious? You kiddin'. Not me."

The next set of police wore cheap suits. Double-vent jackets, flared pants. Sensible shoes. Leather belts. They had runny noses. From the cold. From the coke they busted. They asked the same questions as the first lot, but meaner.

Got the same answers. The people in that neighborhood weren't stupid.

Sinclair was gracious. Unctuous. He just wanted them to go away. Leave it at suicide. He had problems of his own. His workers were nervous, his bank account wouldn't balance, his girlfriend was as vicious as a starving possum. These were important things.

The police were everywhere. Sinclair gritted his teeth. There wasn't a customer in the place wasn't secretly working for the Man. Wanting to drink for free.

Reno was equally tense. She knew they were just waiting

for her to make a wrong move. They said things like, "A draft beer please." And "Can you think of anyone, anyone at all that might have a grudge against Mr. Huntington."

"Talk to Sinclair."

To Sinclair they said, "We need a list of everyone who was here the night Hunt died."

"That might be difficult."

"Oh? Wull, you can lose your license easy, underage kids, back taxes. The health department might have somethin' to say."

Sinclair, smooth as puke, said, "Of course, officer. If anything comes to mind I'll get in touch right away."

They exchanged cards. Sinclair went upstairs.

Eva flounced in, pink ruffles under a fox jacket. "You seen Sinclair?" Didn't look at them, her nose stuck up so high she looked likely to trip over her own pointy shoes. The cop with the shelled-clam eyes followed along behind, supposed to be searching the crowd but he couldn't stop looking at Eva.

Reno sputtered, "Shit. Go find him yourself." Turned to Slowmotion. "That pet cop of hers gonna come right in his pants."

Slowmotion spoke over her shoulder to Reno. "A match made in heaven." She smiled, slow and evil, as Eva walked away. "You talk to Poppy?"

Exasperated. "When I have time to see Poppy? What with dead people and po-lice popping up everywhere, I'm damn lucky I can get to work. Shit. Too many things goin' on." Sullen. "Ain't nothin' made sense since I got out." Huffy. "Don't see how it's your affair."

"Ooh." Slowmotion didn't look offended at all. "Everything's my affair, girl. Poppy said she'd be here later. Got to talk wichyou."

"I wanta die." Reno stopped herself. "I mean I don't wanta die. I wanta live forever." Why must the show go on? When did mindless entertainment become so important? How come she was still there?

Couldn't think of what else to do. That's why.

All freedom is, she figured, is dealing with a lot of more complicated options. None of which fit her needs. She didn't look forward to much—looked to be something less than a lifetime of freedom. Maybe she'd get a decent night's sleep once she was back in jail. Shit. She moved to the far end of the bar muttering how she couldn't believe her whole life was such a total washout.

Eva slithered up. Smug. Her voice was thin, dangerous. Slimy. "You don't seem to exactly miss Hunt." Look left and right. "Certainly has done wonders for Su'ad's career though."

In the mirror behind the bar Reno could see that Eva's cop was too far away to hear what was being said.

"I know how glad you were when he died. You and Su'ad set the whole scene up. I know." Eva leaned forward, tits on the bar, to whisper. "What's my silence worth to you?"

Reno couldn't decide whether to push the woman's face in, ignore her, break both her kneecaps. "You don't seem to be exactly in mourning yourself." Reno's hands were sweaty, strangling Eva would be a pleasure.

Eva recognized the maniac gleam, moved away, a step-by-step retreat, "I'm not a phony like the rest of you. I don't hafta pretend sorrow when I don't feel it." Tossing her blond ponytail she searched the room for her missing cop. "But it's just like they say: cui bono. Who does it benefit." Her backup man was fully occupied. He leaned, one arm on the wall behind Su'ad, the other toying with her hair. He panted into her eyes.

Her full mouth curled up at the corners.

Reno replied, "You don't have to translate it for me. I got a better one for you: *cherchez la femme*."

Eva was aloof. "I don't speak Italian." Her voice grew louder, strident. "After all I didn't know the man like Su'ad did." Old clam-eyes lifted his gaze, not very interested.

"Hell, Eva." Loud, jovial, "Ya knew Hunt well enough to have a key to his flat." Reno had put a copy of Hunt's key in the purse Eva carried. Just in case she'd gotten rid of her own key.

Eva opened her mouth, closed it, opened. Didn't deny it.

"You look like a fish. It won't work Eva." Reno spoke softly. For Eva's ears only. "Didn't you realize that giving someone a hand out the window might not be universally applauded? Maybe you oughta look for work in some other city."

Eva seemed confused, her breath came in short, ragged patches. A small frown appeared. Her fear seemed very great.

Reno pushed. "Everyone knows what you're doing. Might want to put yourself out of harm's way." Reno ricked her mouth into a mean grin; she grabbed the bar knife, cleaned her fingernails. "If you know what I mean."

"I'll make you sorry you were born." Eva spoke through her teeth, her feral, heart-shaped face warping and twisting in the strobe lights. "You'll wish you were never born."

Smooth, as if she didn't put much weight on anything the other woman might say. "Nothin' new 'bout that." Reno laughed without amusement. "But you best think about what I said." She cleaned the blade on her jeans, never took her eyes off Eva's face. Thumb at the clam-eyed fellow. "Bet the man over there be interested to know you were high-steppin' over a dead body the other night, never even gave him a call."

The band started to play again. The audience clapped and hollered for Aisha.

Eva was startled. "Aisha? Aisha? Are they nuts?"

Slowmotion nodded solemnly at the stage. "Su'ad changed her name." Goofy smile. "Seemed appropriate."

Reno hadn't realized Su'ad would go to such extremes—didn't even quite know to which extremes she'd gone—but the appropriate move was to jam Eva some more. "Bet that cop would love to hear the stories Hunt told you about his wife. Aisha. Are you into fucking dead ones too?"

The reaction was all she could have hoped for and more. "Did you maybe give him a tumble there in the alley?" Reno nearly stood on the bar, hollering. "Was it finally hard enough for you when he was dead, Eva?"

Eva's face coagulated, her eyes clouded over. She darted into the crowd, the clam-eyed fellow following close on her wiggling ass.

"What? What you mean by that?" Slowmotion didn't sound real concerned. That's how Reno knew she was.

Reno was shaking. Breathe in. Out. Calm? Her voice wobbled. "You have to ask Eva." Backing away. "She knows more'n I do." Reno waved her hand at the stage. "Hey, get back to your soundboard, girl. The fans are waitin'."

Slowmotion looked at her, a small smile puckered in the dimples of her broad cheeks.

Su'ad danced like she hadn't a care in the world. Club Istanbul had been on the eleven o'clock news two nights running with a thirty-second clip of Su'ad/Aisha dancing—very hot.

"Belly-dance Melee. Columnist dives to his death after wild party."

The Istanbul was mobbed.

"Coroner's report says probable suicide. Police unsatisfied."

Reno shivered. "Being in the news ain't always such a good thing." She wondered what would happen to her; no one would believe her against Eva.

The chili pepper in Hunt's ear—now if only Eva had stuck a cucumber up his ass, maybe the papers could make it out to be some weird vegetarian suicide ritual.

Su'ad, finished with her set, came over, hugged Reno hard. "Hey. Don't worry. Everything's gonna work out fine." Reno would be a fool to think anything ever work out: check it out, she was being squeezed to death.

Slowmotion hissed. "Don't look now, Reno, but there's someone here to see you." Reno looked around, wildly. "She's over there—" Pointing to a woman in a tight woolen business suit frowning at the half-naked dancer on the small stage, her mouth buckled firmly over her teeth. The woman seemed trapped inside a body that hadn't had a moment's honest pleasure in years. Sensible shoes. Briefcase. Handcuffs.

So much for "Life As It Oughta Be." So much for great riotous sex. With Sinclair. With Poppy. With anyone at all. "Shit." Reno mumbled. "Didn't even have a chance to have a decent dinner." She looked at Su'ad. "You know, candlelight and wine? Ice cream for dessert?"

Slowmotion said, "I told 'er I hadn't seen you. Whyn't you quit moonin' and get your ass outta here."

Reno got.

At the end of the night Sinclair mentioned to Slowmotion that the bank desposit the night of the party was a hundred short. And, he remarked casually, it was a funny thing how Hunt was a writer but he didn't seem to have any writing tools. . . . He hastened to assure her that these were just idle musings—it seemed there had perhaps been some professional thief on the premises. Speculation, nothing serious.

"Good." Slowmotion grunted, peeled off five twenties. "Don't worry about it, Sinclair." She shoved the twenties in his pocket, hit the lights. "Forget your idle speculations and pay attention to what's right in your lap." She left.

Sinclair thought it was a funny thing that no one except Eva wanted to talk to him about his suspicions. Funny thing how there were so many funny things about Hunt's death.

There was a lesson in there somewhere but he be damned if he wanted to find it.

chapter twenty-seven

Reno sweated over the computer in Eddie's sloppy digs, tried not to panic. She paced from one side of the room to the other—three steps, five steps. The place didn't hold much charm for her. She went back to battling the computer.

The door rattled. Followed by one of those pregnant silences that only real perverts love.

Reno didn't look up. Life was over. Why make it more painful by acknowledging that fact.

"Hunt was a blister-souled old pervert." Eddie poked his head in the room, taking the whole situation as a joke.

Reno answered, flat-voiced. "We know that. But we need to be able to prove it—the information we need is buried in this damn machine. And I can't bring up the tiniest blip from the hard drive." She scratched her face. "Thought I was so smart." Half of her was in the room, half back in prison, half at the beach. Too many halves but she didn't care. She ran her fingers through her hair, mumbled. "Didn't even get to the goddamn beach this time out." Piss. "Wonder if the rest of the files were sent somewhere else—" A scientist in Switzerland was reading about the bizarre sexual adventures of a local arts columnist?

"Poppy says she'll pay you three hundred for the machine."

"Wellll. It's not exactly what I had in mind."

"Never is. Never is. How about five hundred for the whole machine. Monitor, cords, CPU, and all. Deal?"

"What you know that I don't know?"

Eddie grinned. "Actually not all that much. Just saw Poppy. She said if you bring the machine down to the club, she'll stand by her original offer."

Reno folded her hands in her lap. Looked at him. "You must think I'm stupid."

"Hey—don't worry about it." Eddie prowled the messy little room like a cat in heat. "She wanted me to ask you if you didn't pick up anything else while you were there. Did you?"

"Yeah. Some dope but it's long gone."

"And?"

"And what?" Reno couldn't believe Poppy wanted the Chinese platter or the embroidered cloth. She didn't even consider the nasty photos. It was one of those things she preferred to forget.

"You pick up any snapshots?" Casual—pleading.

Reno got up, convinced at last to play the hand she was dealt. "Almost left them behind." She didn't look at them as she handed them over. "Poor girl. Take someone real cold to stand there and document what he did."

Eddie clutched the photographs. "How would you like to marry me?"

Reno looked out the window. Her back was very straight. "Whyn't you just take this shit to Poppy, let me know how it goes. Long distance. You know?"

Eddie's sharp eyes were dancing. "Seems to me that Hunt might have documented a lot of things. What you think, Reno?"

"Put a bag on it."

Eddie grinned. "The good part's still to come. Look. Here's five hundred. Good faith. Poppy wants us to bring all this shit to the club to show Farouk—he seemed real impressed with some of the stuff we were telling him."

"Show Farouk?" Shit. Tell the whole world what a stupid thief I am. Shit.

"He had a couple snapshots he'd picked up at Hunt's all on his own. Taken a little later in the proceedings. Altogether they make it pretty clear that Hunt murdered Aisha." Eddie was unsure if it was all right to be pleased with himself. "Hunt was a bastard. My dad always said so."

"I ain't going to the club. Gimme the five hundred and I'm outta here."

He didn't hear her. "Poppy says the DA can't prosecute a dead man for an old-maybe murder. But these shots would further the claims on his property by people who wouldn't otherwise have a right to inherit." Quietly. "That is, Farouk as the brother of Aisha." Bright-eyed pause. "And me, his nephew."

"Say what?"

"My dad was his younger brother." Quietly. "I am not eager to claim kinship. Believe me." He laughed, low and mean. "But the incentive is strong. Hunt owned that building. Didn't leave a will. Everything would go to the state." Eyebrow lifted. "We couldn't have that. The irony would be too great."

Reno pulled back, screwed up her face. She looked confused. "You fuckin' pushed him?" An edge to her voice. "You?"

Eddie looked shocked. " 'Course not. Sure I'm glad he's dead but I didn't do it. Su'ad and Farouk will back me on that." Serious. Meaning-filled. "It's pretty obvious who did it."

Reno shook her hair into her face. "Don't look at me. How should I know?" Suspicion. Confusion. She didn't want to ask if he suspected her—it was okay for her to suspect everyone else, that was only natural. But if Eddie thought she pushed Hunt out the window, it might be a bit too much. Better she didn't ask. She asked. "Come on, Eddie. Who you think tossed him out the window—and what's your supporting evidence?" Supporting evidence. No sense of security in the words.

"We're filing a petition to transfer the ownership of the building to Sinclair, as my agent, because I'm underage, and Slowmotion, as Farouk's agent, since he's not a citizen."

Reno grimaced. "Who."

He still didn't answer. "Shake the hand of a very rich man." He held his hand out. "Now will you marry me?"

"Not on your life."

Eddie looked crestfallen. "Okay. Will you marry me if I tell you I'm sure it was Eva."

"Nope. You would tell me it was Eva because that suits me just fine." Pause. "Um. Does Sinclair know?"

A whiskey voice from the doorway: "I hope you learn subtlety one day, Reno, you'll be a far more interesting woman."

Reno jumped out of her skin.

Slowmotion laughed and laughed. "Subtle. Right. Come on, Reno. It's not a setup, it's a celebration. Bring the damn computer or leave it here, no matter. Poppy can pick it up later. Just come *on*. Sinclair and everyone's already at the club."

What ya gonna do. "Oh hell. Fuck subtlety. Let's go to the club. Beats sitting here waiting for those turds to come get me."

chapter twenty-eight

"**H**ey, Reno. What's happ'nin." The tall elegant black lady pushed the mop bucket up to the bars of the cell. "You weren't go-one but a hot minute."

"Hey, Queenie. Ain't no news but bad news on the streets, know what I mean?" Reno didn't get up off the plastic mattress.

"What you doin' here in county?"

Reno sat up, smiling. "I failed me a piss test. Failed it good. The dope residue so strong I bet they distilled it, sold it for special golden showers." Wicked.

"Yo. That be my downfall: pissin' in someone else's dirty cup." Queenie knew Reno appreciated the humor. "But then again"—Sly—"I wasn't lookin' at no murder one."

"I wasn't lookin' neither, girl, it was just a quick glance, then it faded." Reno sashayed over to the bars. "It faded. Alls I've got is the tail of my original sentence."

Handy to have a distant connection to the DA's office after all. She looked around the dingy little cell. Safe at last. Home: three hots and a cot. Shabby but not too bad. She wondered what else Poppy and Slow were up to. Whatever it was, Reno was grateful. "Coulda bin a whole lot worse, you know?"

Poppy would be mayor some day. No question.

And Slowmotion would be the power behind the throne.

"Ten months to finish out on a little burglary look good after what I bin through. Least now I might get some rest."

"It can be rough, havin' a good time." Queenie nodded. Slipped Reno half a pack of Camel filters. "This hold you till you get outta quarantine."

"Thanks, Queenie. You're the best."

"You can say that again." Queenie pushed off. Rolling her narrow hips in a way no ordinary queen could hope to match.

Reno kicked back on the plastic mattress, they hadn't let her have any sheets yet but she didn't care. She sucked the smoke deep into her lungs, content.

Eva pranced across the top of the narrow wooden bar with bright, deliberate steps; even in the Arizona heat her bouncy false cheer didn't desert her. Her Wednesday show at the Bush Pussy Bar was always a little slow. They promised to get a band in from Tucson for the weekend near the end of the summer.

"It don't matter, gal, they don't come for the music." The bartender rubbed his greasy hand on her ass. "This what they like." He grunted. "I like it too so don't be shy."

Arizona: sunny days every day, great sex, good money every night. Life. The way it supposed to be.

Eva wasn't sure but it didn't seem to be working out that way. Nothing seemed to go the way she planned. She could call someone, tell them, they might be worried about her. She didn't want to admit she didn't seem to be able to make it alone; some company would be nice.

She never was actually charged with Hunt's murder, but she didn't get let out of Langley Porter Mental Health Clinic for almost six months; when she did she was Thorazine fat with half-a-dozen sequined costumes she worked on constantly. And lists, lots of lists, she was always making lists:

important things to do, places to go, appointments to keep. She had a busy schedule.

She wondered if Sinclair moved into the flat above the Istanbul. She didn't care about the rest of them. Sinclair was the only one—he always was weak for her. She thought perhaps she could call him. He'd set her up somewhere better, somewhere more her style. She didn't seem to be able to find his number.

Or she could call the hospital, it was one of the orderlies at the hospital who fixed her up in Arizona. She'd called him when the first job, at the massage parlor, hadn't worked out. This job wasn't much better. The man said to stick it out, the alternatives were far less pleasant. She wasn't certain that the orderly was such a good friend either.

That's all she was looking for she decided, a good friend. She simpered at the acne-scarred teenager in the first row, climbed down off the bar, flexed herself all over for him. He put his thick hand between her legs. Friendly.

Eddie promised to wait for Reno.

Reno said, "Oh no, please don't."

He scowled, "Ingrate." Kissed her hard on the mouth before they took her away.

She smoked, remembering. Rattled the souls in her ritual gourd. Some of them seemed to have a little light left. Things maybe work out all right. Life would get good and all the rest of it.

Dear Sinclair.

I will be out in two months. I was thinking maybe I could learn to dance now that Su'ad's traveling so much with Farouk (is her name still Aisha?) and Eva is gone. Or I could tend bar since Eddie's back in school. Please let me know. I'll be at this address, I ain't going nowhere.

                                    Your friend. Reno.